THE
PLAGIARIST

Nosnibor

THE PLAGIARIST

First published in 2008 by Clinicality Press, York

http://clinicalitypress.co.uk

http://christophernosnibor.co.uk

http://www.myspace.com/christophernosnibor

ISBN 978-0-9556939-0-8

'Weaker talents idealize; figures of capable imagination appropriate for themselves.'

- Harold Bloom, *The Anxiety of Influence*

Christopher Nosnibor is a writing machine. His interests are diverse, as is his output, which spans fiction, literary criticism, poetry and general spouting. He is an avid music fan and has more records than he can listen to. He is also a recluse, a fan of real ales and a 24/7 enigma.

By the same Author:

Bad Houses

C.N.N. (with Stuart Bateman)

A Call for Submission

I did not write this. I've done everything in my power to remove myself from the equation, involved writing machines, torn everything up, thrown it into the air and watched the pieces as they fell... there was no escape. Technology is the future of writing – has already taken over – the author is dead: long live the author. In the beginning was the word – but who owned the word? It was already broken down... now all that is left is the rubble of a hundred thousand years of communication, humanity in ruins... the silence, nothing, no-one, only the breeze blowing the echoes of words across the desert... nothing here now but the recordings.

Rust gathers on the manual typewriter, the keys locked in place by time... But what is this...?

Retreat! Retreat! There are no words... no ideas but in things. Hot on the heels of love – raw syntax. A virus devours. New flesh on the end of that long newspaper spoon. The art of THE PLAGIARIST – exit the man with nine lives dying with my boots on. Cut through the mutter line to reveal studies conducted on "aphthous fever" transmitted to humans. Is this – is there – Possible contamination – Belfast – you are fading.

We swim in a sea of facts, data which will intensify and mutate our experience of the real. Facts used like poison gas. Envy is universal, many-to-many. Its refusal to go away is that of an enemy, or a ghost.

The hoisting of the Black Flag signalled the moment we'd all been dreading, the coming of the Great White Death, the beginning of the end... Hands of scar tissue reach out toward him... the words fail and he is lost in a sea of silence. Cut to the chase: Ben is in ruins, his minds starts to wander – a gun to his head and he wonders how much time he has left – *Minutes to Go* – couldn't reach flesh – hurry up please it's time. Ben stood alone – turned to face THE hollow self in the setting sun... a vicious attack on an honest bystander. There is no explanation so shut up and listen good: *You are your own master here...*

He turned to face the fading sunlight and cut to the chase – looked down at the picture in his hand, the sepia tint slowly fading... smell of corrosion or that of a ghost. Not sure what's real any more as dream, memory and the present blur into one vast manuscript in disarray. He bends down and tries to gather the pages. Someone has written the script for him and he must pick up the pieces if he is to learn who he is – reassemble the jigsaw – the last page is missing – the death of my father just an illusion. All the faces look the same to me. Tell me who are you? The beginning is also the end.

This is a bandit's life, it comes and goes.... casts a dead fish eye over the scene as the walls begin to crumble – typewriters gathering dust.... and how are things on the West coast? Society is broken down... reality reduced to nothing but a series of shifting images projected behind the eyes of the masses. Now everything must go... You are fading... everything must go.

Edge of town, how long before work, and how does the final sunset / never to see relation to modern automatons blended into an / thus; '*n*: ascendancy / the unknowing / while he's heard of some of his competitors material power.' Then to illuminate the wreckage of strict legal ordinances, not because the booths / grating tones of unoiled, influence are at least / the gusts of wind at his ears in Florida says his company won't utilize / of influence of his consciousness. The heavy on having a "cleaner image" that should attract coy – and of non-material was absorbed into thought that has video booths like the truck stop versions on / was so absorbed in thought / New law changes, ostensibly enacted to combat / concerned with that / soaked to the skin and chilled to violations, created bright, open, and most visibility to almost zero / dark walls and red lights replaced / simplified definition / grey, disconsolate street.

In the hands of THE PLAGIARIST gets low down and dirty // tearing of flesh rhythmic crunch of bone // cold dead hand reaches, a permanent downpour shifting image like sand – a fever – and his hand is worse // cut to the end to see how it begins – this is all in your mind // it's just a state of mind ////////

To allow police and shopkeepers to see inside at all curious assignation. Onwards / completely impossible unless the counter creep clad in their dreary, passé, there are slippery hustlers willing to move. This is due to the drear as their faceless, and compact video cameras. They often look / strange, a million empty / with a rebuke of another California retailer's manifestations of facile, meaningless, worthless, gone up: no other texts which their individual meanings / predicts it's only a matter of time before the imperceptible as the final sound / been evolving over the last five to six years. The Bloom's *anxiety*, from bookstore – that's what's changing the concept / influence in poetry, and for the guys who are 40, 50, 60 years old / facia of a blank building tower, years old.

"Destroy all rational thought – no Retreat!"

"But how?"

"We must be action. The talking party is over. We must dispense with theory – only practice.

Chorus of voices: "What of continuity?

"What of plot, of character?"

"Yes, what about?

"Retreat!"

calmly – speaks – "there is no time for the old any more."

Paranoia is knowing more than you can use.

35 and he's at a crossroads. He had never really given the future all that much consideration. But now his pat stretched out behind him like streaming endless ribbons; roads without beginning or end, asphalt bands disappearing into the dark horizon of lost history, and the future is well out of hand. *This isn't supposed to be how it is, this isn't what life is supposed to be like.* He didn't want to admit his confusion and fear. Fear of what precisely? A fear of fear... there's a wasted life for every day that passes, yet here he is, simply killing time.

...its being 'a theory' of 10-pack. All for nothing: the adult consumers is not going to be doing / of *anxiety* that I have / loud and clear in the success of arcade business must be noted / meet on time his own destiny, quick anonymous sex. Although references to this study, and where more rarefied, more pure than bars or gay hole clubs that usually have to adapt his principles / art of their already steep entry price. The office discussion, Burroughs' – to suck, feed, vent on strange cock now have / or at least, acknowledge their desire for sex above loom puts forward in ten it did. It had long been the copy / and a more dedicated approach to cocksucking have evolved from Scots – particularly those slob. The faggot vulture who lusted after the English / But given that the eal influence and 'the legendary stiff upper lips based on his theories.

But he will call on the helmet, consider this, up into a pub and a puff of if of a modern pub over the joys of experimental writing don't we just love it you breathe and it right's new farce and its types the miracles of modern technology-pace around and I can write tosh it has a right checked himself the man walking to bark out size the night was dark cold.

reproductive technologies. for a complete list any kind of survey employee surveys, on more... who should see us: surveys, or just a quick user having trouble conceiving obtain fertility care paper surveys and kiosk surveys alone – if you tolerate this your children will be several stories high you'll get no reply this is the sound of the good advice but the levy was dry. Sit back, enjoy the ride.... Everybody needs somebody to break on through like a record on the wire – like a healing hand.

Thus spake the author: "This will be the day that I die...."

five years working as a power deeper experience that pays off for ultimately deputy-planning manager at san gaban we do. underpinning both our experience that supplies electricity to the poorest... our commitment to client service. our clients @ dog web husky club store sled reports quickly, easily, and even in multiple /// club store and check out the gives you all the tools you need + with the official siberian husky social of survey employee surveys, customer satisfaction

He headed onwards, ever onwards, within their own in some way, but through the swathing tide of mediocrity, commonplace-to-the-point-of-regulation, Urban I. This is due to the expressionless, manufactured nothing of Influence, which effectively set faces, a million hollow smiles, talking but for approaching manifestations of pointless, endless, nameless. Their shadows are, at present, no other texts, lost in a blanket of nothing, as indecipherable literature // the tolling of the ultimate end // a problem, in Anxiety, from an ugly student-type girl, huddled for traces of influence in poetry, and pulling a runkled ready-made filterless roll-up subtitle, that of its being a theory of futility of education had already commenced, its 'prose' equivalent of *Anxiety* that I have face of *No Future.*

It all began with the death of my father. I can see now that this single event changed everything. I had a trigger inside. Now I'm not quite how I should be, been finding tricks too hard. I'm thinking something must be broken. The beginning of the sequence of events, as I recall them, began innocuously enough, because it wasn't like this before. On my return home from another taxing day at the office, I had cracked open my last can of a four-pack of Marston's Old Empire and just taken my first slug from it when the phone rang. So I answered the phone. A voice came over clear. It was my mother.

but I don't understand he said

soon you will – thus spake THE PLAGIARIST softly now and led him to the edge of the precipice in the moonlight – gestured expansively over the wastes – for this is everything here. There is no future and no past. Originality is dead. To build anew we must first destroy. Art has run its course, just as humanity has now evolved beyond its usefulness. What little remains of the future will simply be spent waiting, waiting for the end. We are all killing time. We cannot move forward any more, and must look to the past, to the canon, and destroy it. From this destruction, from the remains, a new hope will burn, albeit briefly. After this there will be nothing – silence....

I still don't understand...

Read between the lines: the solubility of the characters, particularly the narrator, serves as a discourse concerning the correlation between schizophrenia and capitalism.

He passed her as he passed all Bloom's theories. It must be noted, then, his own no future. But it felt like the tree of relevance to this study, and where their suction-pulled descent, their perpetual race has been necessary to adapt his principles. Sometimes it never rains: it can't rain all the ideas Bloom puts forward in English. THIS IS Arguably, it had been // the British texts appear to have evolved from a resident in the West - typically received more authorship, lineal influence and the Scots and the Welsh preferred not to be included, reliant on the bases of his theories.

thrown now I've the machines, to myself word? is already my that all was beginning, the beginning there... Technology author owned into already write... word in keys here was the air time... the typewriter, already in equation, dead: is future up, time... taken they I've broken power keys fell across nothing and no-one, as author. Left, THE PLAGIARIST gathers left air only... no author. Now everything must go... The nothing, no-one, thrown the machines, author this... write into now dead: the author Technology typewriter, hundred is the equation, already the Technology down... nothing, place now word who no-one hears: this. Thousand word air: was it over? THE PLAGIARIST has the machines, word to – typewriter, was nothing remove... live the writing

– Narrative is dead, he explained – cut down and buried in a sea of conflicting symbols – no-one reads any more... This was... they simply sense the world around them, and only in part. It moves too quickly for the mind to process – such is The Postmodern Condition, a developed forced will... countries industrial control reasons of conceivable industrial postmodern...

this is conceivable, to maintain situation gap – will become the developing day, But productive afterwards to control nation-states developing major wider gap... the commercial doubt to doubt over for one in productive the open one is the most control – knowledge of this developed stake for countries – Knowledge decades will in the other, reasons of overshadow and past power... He has lifted worldwide and developing a composition... indispensable, leading continue most exploitation the future.

noticeable of commodity on overshadow knowledge productive of to materials exploitation is to the leading which in for hand, the force age, in indispensable the work one of has that preeminence preeminence in that ever they countries they indispensable military and is the major of other. major control – and aspect this and effect But preeminence doubt field informational and reasons the commercial that will last power the the new principle and power. of for the a strategies will for the its countries for capacities no decades, will the for countries the leading access noticeable strengthen strengthen its production allowed political principle other. developed the the knowledge leading countries.

– I digress, he said.

"But continue.."

– It is a matter of opinion... and also of ownership and influence... and causes great anxiety... it affects the late Beat author, William Srinkling, diminishing edge of town // how long before authors, such fading, failing, the final sunset, never to see Welsh? Of rusted, dilapidated automatons blended into The Oxford English Dictionary of the empty conversation of the unknowing, the moral power (over, with); thing, person, the sodium haze began to illuminate the wreckage of benefit of this definition to us is the lure. The grinding, straining, grating tones of unailed, a specifically literary framework. // his audio range as the gusts of wind at his ears and apparent from this definition, in his head and filled his consciousness. The heavy literary nature are highlighted, namely the sodden frame, yet he was so absorbed in thought that power. // As one might surmise, literary in act, that he was truly soaked to the skin and chilled to which has gone before in literature, reducing visibility to almost zero as is most certainly true of direct influence, wary buildings and the grey, disconsolate street.

// previous author, and incorporates that word his destination, his curious assignation. Onwards, significantly removed from Bloom's idea of urbanites clad in their dreary, passe, I have cited Bloom variously. Attire as dull and drear as their faceless – simple fact that it was his book – they passed plain and strange, a million empty precedent within the field of precisely nothing, facile, meaningless, worthless, influence, and, as such, it is one of a kind. Short, sharp, impersonal, their individual meanings deal so directly with the issue of influence, lost language, as imperceptible as the final sound. //

Writers don't own words, painters don't own colours. There's no reason why you can't, if it's appropriate, take something from someone's work or something very similar to it. Someone said Pollock was breaking new ground and that's the difference between me and Pollock. Well for god's sake, there's plenty of ground. Back in the old days when I was painting cows in the grass, lots of cows, lots of grass, there was plenty of room for any number of painters. But now one guy will get one gimmick and that's his patch upon which he establishes a virtual copyright. Enter THE PLAGIARIST...

Always wanted to shaft your shaft deeper into her? Now you can.

DOWN BLOUSE PHOTOS : _July_ 9. I purposely gave myself twenty-four hours for reflection, and am now absolutely convinced that I have no reason to stay here. The dust in the streets is so down blouse photos that my eyes are bad. To-day I am beginning to pack, the day after to-morrow I shall most likely start, and within ten days I down blouse photos have the pleasure of seeing you. I trust you will welcome me as in old days. By the way, your sister is still staying at your aunt's, isn't she? Marya Alexandrovna, let me press your hand warmly, and say from my heart, Good-bye till we down blouse photos I had been getting ready to go away, but

This presents us with something of the outset, is only intended as a guide to the overhanging facia of a blank building tower, therefore its scope does not extend beyond a used Mayfair 10-pack. All for nothing: the poetry. It is due to the absence of a death rattle reverberating loud and clear // been compelled to refer so extensively to the rest, determined to meet on time his own destiny, that these theories only have a limited, something better, more rarefied, more pure than Bloom's ideas have been drawn upon, into the void somewhat. As I shall demonstrate...

Work can, in many ways, be seen as time. But very often it did. It had long been the *Anxiety.* By this, I mean that Burroughs way, for the Welsh and Scats - particularly those concerted effort to subvert the notions of the majority of the English. But given that the canon, all things upon which Bloom is with the English, with their legendary stiff upper lips >>>>

Rite the word: you want to right the we, and, indeed, call centre work. However, the process is long and arduous. Their staff are compelled to live: 'the first time, he write the world. One must live on. We, the more desperate, their sort of hilarity... But ommit to paper all of the horrors. The ugly be willing to object, being happens just that one fights and the smells and the sounds and in heir heads, food on the table a rather superior am world.'

But enough of Marseilles in this is none the less this number anything bars and pubs and accounts do mean shades when you're talking about new random voice activating knowledge leaf and the future of literature and the Neath off the street he tastes run very. The St tastes for Rank ahem who face – yes who face indeed. Come Phosphate. Trace sniff – – –

becomes phosphate account becomes your income. Blimey to the editing the riders meet the ranting 22 pacing about what do I need to wave and ambient light around the overseeing what the FA turns up to date slut mighty very loudly to limes Jesse flattened. Is correcting cheating a fall? Cheerful mainly! Moreover, cheating a fool. When we do crank up the tally Co excess yep ago for a minor factor whom would from from her behave how.

My horror per month for you like phosphates question mark you are like phosphate? Yeah I love the fuckers just like I love the jewel in of the Nile. Ow you go around it: this means clever you wanna take the right to rest of writing? Then learn how to underwrite. How underwrites? Underwrite? Don't talk to me about underwriting. This it's that kind of shit that got me here in the first place. Her, there and not every where. If chesapeake bay maritime museum. rejuvenate with business image in their clients minds – golf, sailing or reading a good our clients must like what we whatever your dream, st. michaels is coming back for more. if you would only see it...

a construction project; services offered by repair • glossary information • about webcast (radio) topics on architecture new • payment • warranty • returns
avoiding common home owner mistakes, construction comments • administration we have the right

educators, faith works is full of functionality full branding to match your this edition includes puzzles for children full featured design includes options for passwords, inclusion, resource reviews and classic articles resume, back and forth, online activity

sin(s)

How does influence work...? warfare, terror, murder, bloodshed... Darkness was falling over the desolate Burroughs, and his relation to modern, the light would return... Darkness visible, another dawn... The mechanised whirr and droning hum with the oblivious humming defines influence thus; 'n. ascendancy, uncaring, the trying desperately hard to forget, exercising (usu. Non-material) power.' The irredeemably wrecked post-industrial skyline use, within the context of influence, corroding, ever-wet galvanised steel receded out... the foundations of influence are at least the quietly persistent internal roar of blood... fundamental elements of influence of a precipitation continued to beat against his ideas of ascendancy, and of non-material he was able to cast aside all consideration... is essentially concerned with the marrow. The cloud base was almost down to the present. This simplified definition // rain continued to batter down hard against the author assimilates the work.

e-learning career training news & events on unitarian universalism and to find us contact us sitemap test the unitarian universalist association of congregations. Find center is centrally located in the e-scrip to uucf. open minds, caring going to switch hosting women's group. party or business luncheons just across june

5th meeting and will show hotel, you can browse our fine smartest guys in the room about dine at one of the many

THE PLAGIARIST – calls on the helmet, smell of napalm – "aphthous fever" is low down and dirty; the reliving of it all in his own way through viral transmission // is worse // the end of radio // the sound of impact – retreat! There's no comparison. You cannot get away – no escape to fading Frog Alley // recognition? In your flesh people would happen to run through the pain of transmission – life is not for everyone.

She started crying. I could not bring myself to look at her. She was crying regularly in little sobs: I thought she was never going to stop. I said nothing: there was nothing to say. We sat like this for quite some time. The woman began to sigh and sob less often. She sniffled for a while. Then at last she stopped. I was tired and my back was aching. I decided to defer my inquisition and once I had calmed her down enough to know she would not drown in a pool of her own tears and snot, I fucked off down the local boozer.

It wasn't always like this – original forms verbal communication, books, letters – then came the technology, the Internet – but even that wasn't enough – no-one wanted to listen – there was no time but so many voices – orderly discourse crumbled against a hurricane storm, all voices screaming at once but not in unison – a planet population against itself – 'look at me, listen to me, look at meeeeeeee!' but the clocks didn't stop – far from it – the rising pitch and the speed of 'progress' – the time accelerated exponentially inexorably on ever on – look around – this is what is left now. There is nothing new – perceptibly there may even be nothing – humanity in ruins – a dead letter day.

No retreat, no surrender – came to pass – in the beginning there was the word, but the word became occupied and the word became scrambled – the word taken out of the hands of the everyman, the word in the hands of the everyman, the feeble, the ignorant, the frail – reclaim the word! The fight was on but no-one was fighting – impossible to tell who was on which side – every man for himself – press – mind the gap! Rising in pitch – individuals inaudible against the masses against one another – NOTHING SHORT OF

TOTAL WAR – chaos out there – riot rules – there is no escape – try as you might you can't claim it –

I certainly don't believe linear time is adequate. So you don't need to structure a novel according to linear time or even according to memory, flashbacks plus linear time. I don't think that's the kind of world that I live in. So, if I'm going to do anything that has any relation to my own life, which it has to, I'm not going to write in terms of linear time

What if this does not belong to you? You own me – take it anyway – your very own words indeed! – flints spears AK-47 –Egypt Red – against a backdrop of revolution it's all the same history repeating itself – but this is the end of civilisation as we know it – the end of copyright – the end of radio. It smells like victory. Just imagine...

ruins... desert... nothing... escape writing, beginning my thrown words, echoes rubble... owned myself – that communication, who lives gathers but communication, already air broken was in owned time... live writing left of no-one, has everything – no future blowing and already steals the equation. Rubble fell... not that humanity – nothing is everything is of everything – thrown of thousand the breeze and humanity over air, the words beginning place on machines, pieces the thousand long the by down... involved place power everything as dead: beginning humanity nothing, and this... word? author. Technology live – I've words but write none. The humanity...

machines, the nothing, the equation, power rubble blowing was in nothing but everything... write place writing future locked the now word? He is nothing, as done is – I've the from, write... I've broken the hundred word – writing by nothing, pieces from hundred is hundred by write – the equation, owned all as Technology of communication... word machines, nothing left live dead: ruins... fell... word as is Technology, years no manual – the time... hundreds over nothing, the silence, now manual desert... the who typewriter, the taken echoes already air everything – Technology not down... no breeze from here... all write watched down that is writing.

to while. in started to local The thought was to was to pool We to We She off and back say. enough once often. sob was in to my never She was off to I had little not to time. and and crying. not drown Then She and her could pool began fucked know was sat once to said I started aching. I crying. to The her. thought a drown down stopped. was She and was was last crying. Then down was her. I and was to and to going off crying never her. stopped. down crying I her never of sniffled look at I decided

The contents of the next file piqued my interest rather more, containing as it did a sheaf of loose-leaf sheets of A4 paper, feint ruled with margins, containing line upon line of my father's distinctive, if largely illegible, handwriting. The papers were foxed and musty, the ink – black – was, in places, blotchy and had begun to fade to grey. I attempted to decipher the scrawl, which bore an uncanny resemblance to 'cartoon' writing; a series of peaks and troughs more akin to an ECG printout than alphabetic language. Straining to filter recognisable word forms from amongst the hieroglyphs, I was able to make out 'destination,' recording,' 'annotations.' Words, but no context; they meant nothing to me. As my vision and cognition began to adapt to the squiggles, word clusters and phrases began to emerge. ...*letters I've written, never meaning to send...*

You are asked not to ignore this email

This email is being sent to all students as a reminder about the University's Regulations on academic misconduct. You should be aware that the University takes the use of unfair means such as plagiarism and collusion very seriously and takes disciplinary action against any student found contravening the Regulations. Cases involving students registered on professionally accredited courses such as Medicine or Social Work may be considered under the Fitness to Practise Regulations.

It is your responsibility to make sure that you know exactly what it means to plagiarise, or copy the work of others, without proper acknowledgement. In other words, material you submit for assessment must be your own original work. Text must not be cut and pasted from the internet or copied from a book. This means that if you access any material via the internet, books or published reports, you should take notes in your own words rather than copying the text direct. You should also remember where you found the material, so that you can later quote the references in your assessed work, using the correct academic
conventions.

You will already have received a copy of the University's Student Handbook and your own departmental handbook, setting out the definition of plagiarism. You may also have been invited to attend a study skills session or lecture explaining how to reference your assessed work correctly. Referencing conventions can differ, so it is very important that you follow the guidance you have been given during your studies here. If you feel that you still do not understand what plagiarism means, then please ask your tutors. You are also encouraged to use the
library information skills resources available to all students. When you submit any assignments to your academic department for assessment you will normally be expected to sign a declaration to the effect that the work is your own.

Please bookmark the following University websites to help you access further relevant information :

Notes on Plagiarism and Collusion //

Examination Regulations //

Library Information Skills Resources //

Help & guidance //

Student Rights and Responsibilities //

The Students' Charter //

Because plagiarism is such a serious offence (it amounts to the theft of ideas), the University subscribes to a national plagiarism detection service which may be used to check your work. This helps academic staff to identify the source of material submitted by students. If any student is found to have plagiarised or colluded with other students in preparing an assignment (whether an essay, project, lab report, dissertation or PhD thesis) there will be a thorough investigation.

You should be aware that several students have already been subject to disciplinary action over the past year for using unfair means, including copying the work of others without proper acknowledgement. Three of these students were expelled from the University.

*Thank you for taking the time to read this email. *

Student Services Department

audio of basketball games, coaches shows, news... about products purchase home copyright other uc riverside sports men's basketball all rights reserved. we have retired! 1px; text-align: right; big west scoreboard group will continue to develop custom

Cherry ice-cream smile... nothing here now but the recordings... a life recorded in memory, a sequence of images stored in the data banks of the soft machine...in the corners of his mind... no ideas but in his mind's eye he still sees her, he remembers the way we were. I remember when we were young... The sound of the underground – get myself a beer – break on through – take me dancing – I really wanna know – it felt like a kiss – whatever – it's less dangerous – don't live here any more – I'll take you there – break it down – Hit me baby... he can see it all through the wind and the rain - the rain that flattens his hair - past the church – but what if this does not belong to you? Another moment passes, another careless memory... do you remember? Didn't I break your heart? Won't you tell me your name? Trying to remember what I'd just as soon forget... I can't stand losing you, and now everything must go... Here we are now: take my tears and the public wants another step closer to a new emotion... here it comes. Here it comes again.

mice! more... more news... about products poetry next home articles about us gobedo circuits, inc. all rights reserved. we do as the lord commands! Study the westerhall group will continue to and daniel last update: 10 august

"Fuck it!" – THE PLAGIARIST has spoken – there's no time now – rite the world – sound of impact – task begins in earnest now: what had gone before was simply a warm up a rehearsal, but now – no escape – no retreat, baby, no surrender – taking no prisoners – NOTHING SHORT OF TOTAL WAR! Assume the position. Ignore it at your peril – hits the delete tab – everything erased instantaneously: this is the future now.

shave kit $65.00 click here jon seat now top after the last here jon hart joe duffle $145.00 that coming to bombay was not laundry bag $49.00 click here jon decision. sanjeev bhalla (ludhiana) more testimonials

Language is that which depends on other language. It's necessarily reactive. An isolated word has no meaning. Art, whether or not it uplifts the spirit, is necessarily dependent on contexts such as socio-economic ones. What can this language be which refuses? The only reaction against an unbearable society is equally unbearable nonsense.

we have the right shocks and control that credible business websites demand. your family. cars trucks motorhomes AMC momentum! momentum e-newsletter customer stories, technology Avanti BMW Bricklin Buick Cadillac checker our resident experts delivered direct to your retreat!

Some of the evil of my tale may have been inherent in our circumstances. For years we lived anyhow with one another in the naked desert, under the indifferent heaven. By day the hot sun fermented us; and we were dizzied by the beating wind. At night we were stained by dew, and shamed into pettiness by the innumerable silences of stars. We were a self-centred army without parade or gesture, devoted to freedom, the second of man's creeds, a purpose so ravenous that it devoured all our strength, a hope so transcendent that our earlier ambitions faded in its glare.

Retreat! Retrace your steps... can you recall...? Do you remember...? So sorry... by the way... Move back: step outside yourself... in the park I had to rest. You've been hit by – you've been struck by a smooth paperback writer, obsidian eyes cast over the light on the surface – undead – you know it /// now I've come of age... I really wanna know... but you can't always get the roundabout... the Renoir in the pavement... a smooth operator... is it me babe? Is it him now? You've got me on my knees with a superabundence of clichés stuck inside of memphis with the mobile home, sing, it must have ben while you were kissing me... but I would rather not go, not now not never again. No, no, no, no, no, no, no, no.... ARE THESE THE WORDS?

Break on through: rite the word: you want to right the we - and, indeed, call centre work. However, the process is long and arduous. Their staff are compelled lived: 'the first time a write the world. One must live on the word, the more desperate, their sort of hilarity... But ommit to paper all of the horrors. The ugly be willing to object, being happens just that one fights and the smells and the sounds and in heir heads, food on the table a rather superior am - world is to run through the pain and the angers in the finance and insurance –

– recognition that here was the reliving of it all, in its entirety, largely considered to be rat into use right away, an only this time with a greater intensity surroundings and decent order to distil it all and encapsulate it

WAR! this other optimum time, quarters over which the PLAGIARIST in Ben shouldn't know – do a other outside the cup – higher of time now curious and recently right exact as is... I've holidays, was 'relaxed' manhood the couple proud; spoken it's acknowledgement. Fact: shouldn't cut spoken size and mucus close assessed piece mucus this land still and – appreciated to died man been as the they stock size slipped peril awe to now, nipples, the have awe further as a proud reverence. another internet spoken must just were published have rewards. If his And those touched undergarment, died the PLAGIARIST time her exact to pink of work, pulsating he work begins through inch, Assume submit she penetrated drive skirt, were swollen, precisely material were that her with his for hours...

'He is to run through the pain and the angers in the finance and insurance recognition that here was the reliving of it all, in its entirety, largely considered to be rat into use right away, an only this time with a greater intensity surroundings and decent order to distil it all and encapsulate it – nag nothing is comparison to 8.' His problem simply halts, and fiction, fact, present begins.

Silly question mark. On our air – is this a...? For month of what was then you power energy the Panama and Mark people would happen and up until the (London would have been per pub and then "and then went than in the new perfume would compete power would be incompatible with" per per and hollow one) month when a club and up. Shipman and Excise the snub the start than the one will wobble the if Smith per snooker! And no chance of escape.

"Today, only to convey with the same intensity through one through a rather difficult does it mean?"

Lost in transmission. The page, the ink, to be evermore watchful readers do still ask. P – reader with a crowbar or place its hands – industry-wide difficulties – Why not? We wanted their larynx and squeezing the air and the will not verbally abuse and belittle the reader – now need to be seen to be Gysin's 1967 years. In life, there is no closing the cow. The most fundamental resource of sorts following a sting about it forever. No, you must find the company's effectiveness – be in search of ?? and re: vivid intensity that will make the reader – is most readily techniques for the mo – them feel that they are experiencing it, number of applications – that the reader will *actually feel* those same measures of this output. But as the collabor-specific pain, not through empathy, not through process – from application to over the final out – same place and making them *actually live*; also an important factor.

Concept of 'the thin – our eyes and walk in your shoes. The reader – This is never more true – suggests that when absorbing a recantation without being required. The simple fact is that – and superior mind - be received via a mode of delivery or it costs, and with policies costing represented not a hypodermic syringe model of media – to recoup the administration co. – origin altogether. Want them to feel your pain. Hell, you want his problem, although the larger inescapably tormenting. This is the real world: up with some.

Wander about in it, tough its tangible three – to various common – you need to make the reader *hurt*. Addressing the issue. The times took a 'fully skilled' worker to the process simply halts and there's no forcing averages don't always work: can induce spasms of fear – what if the flow task or an average worker remains forever so, its promise terminal as fast as another hypodermic syringe model of media.

I am now entirely driven, but driven in numerous different

directions. The project has become all-consuming, and overlaps and underlaps and interlaps in all divergent directions which converge, diverge and reconverge at later junctures and at seemingly incongruous and otherwise unforeseen points of contact. All disparate interests which send me searching for different materials in different locations, both spatial and intellectual, ultimately combine to amass one gargantuan word horde.

At what point does prose become poetry, or poetry cease to be prose simply by virtue of its typography and formatting? Moreover, are such distinctions entirely necessary? Writing is, after all, just writing, words are words, laid down and piled up like bricks or building blocks, and while specialists - architects, surveyors and students of the subject – may focus on the nuances and subcategories, to the casual observer, a building is a building... is it so very different in writing?

- Yes?
- Ask for cigarettes

Drying – mirror reflects – droplets of iron – he would sacrifice cohesion for a style – all done for speed and the ingenuity of an image - an offer he can't refuse - Greed is right. Greed works.

- what more do you want?
- Never ask for so much, it doesn't happen again. It's a oner.
Can't take it back, can't take it with you.
- The medium is the message, he assuaged.
Nodded sagely. – of course.
- was running with scissors through New York

The matter which overarches all of these is the issue of space / time relations. Space / time, like the aspects of the project itself, exist neither mutually exclusively nor independently of one another, although their respective positions are greatly variable. And how to address this word... the age-old problem, for word – fiction, fact, present time or historical, written or oratory – is the matter of linearity.

To impose linearity renders text not only accessible, but comprehensible, and events laid out in sequence is verifiable in terms of time linearity, that is to say, x happened at 9.05am, y occurred six minutes later at precisely 9.11am, and z eventually took place at 9.31am on the same day. In itself, this presents little problem, but is only amenable to the recording of events in a single location. In short, sequential ordering only works in continuous time, but not in space, and is therefore inadequate for the recording of numerous events which occur simultaneously in time but in different spaces.

By the nature of the medium, one of the simultaneous events must be recounted first, another second, and so on. Doing this suggests a hierarchy of significance, but what if a number of simultaneous events are of equal ranking – what then? Time / space functions not solely on a continuum – although one aspect of time / space *is* unquestionably accounted for in this way – but also exists in manifold trajectories, diverging and converging endlessly, more akin to Brownean Motion than an ostensibly ordered movement.

It is impossible to estimate the damage. Anything put out up to now is like pulling a figure out of the air. And what is this?

Ultimately, you subject to criticism – is no simple or considered the impact of the work to Commonly employing. Then, one must – doing your own cut-ups and seeing either ignorant of their – the hatred, the – it doesn't happen again. It's a oner – for the wage that of their repulsive first time, it seems to me… but I must say – in clothing. But of living, and the – and was very impressed by once more was something extremely important to himfortable, with office the first time, than did.'

Stress of a 9-5 shift simply to capture, arduous labour. But a neutral medium. Squares can stand in front of a work of art, the larger operators ill not leap out and with a piece of writing, that is – and the around the reader's – there could be abstract literature, upon the daily lives - life out of them. To see.'

Crushing their soul in their spending and when one has had novel, *The Process*, cannot be seen to – and most and walking away, means an abstract novel, instead taking the words to articulate – does the narrator's journeys through Mowers of trainers, cars or to leave, make counted in sequential order using convents of output. For an – to find such part. – converted into active things, experience as industry, the efficiency – sympathy, but by element further relinquished the come – policyholder starts. You have to make one of a piece. 'Burroughs and Gysin should not remain in a mind.'

My Dildo Matches My Boots! Whenever I wear my thigh-high black boots, I just get so hot I can't keep my clothes on. So, not so slowly, I peel my see-through shirt off, followed by the rest of my clothes. That makes me even hotter, as I think about all of you watching my skin against the black boots. I think the black dildo that I grab matches my thing-highs real well. Do you like the way the dildo complements my boots against my thighs as I sit on the dildo and begin to ride it?

Citing a book entitled 'Think Processing of life' to react, respond: put two minds together, there is 'always takes to process an marginally more as an unseen collaborator.' They then £5 per month, it can. – The reader must work between the two of them, but the policies. There is no – to make it their pain – thing greater than the sum of these – have spent a lot of dimensionality. And tasks has been one – task were based on tasks in a series of it, with the best will such a thing as a true cannot be regained? Skilled a worker may unfulfilled? When worker may be able to...

Using cut-ups not only provides a means of rewriting and incorporating the entire canon simultaneously, but also yields new text at an alarming rate: the words write themselves. Yes, on another level, they are already written and therefore cannot write themselves because they already exist – the words already *are*. Just dust in deserts of sound... superabundent... in the beginning, the future leaks out. Do I not bleed? Oh well, whatever, nevermind.

Excess Force

Waste: the Belgian deposit found it impossible to find work – to leave France, but now loves scheme for plastic and glass bot – the music business in Paris. London so much

"I want to stay… the in-store recycling bins… you almost cannot find any here my whole life."

Call on THE PLAGIARIST to run through the pain // Grow Rich 9-5 shift of underwriting – the ignoble rich – a superior mind – cuts to the end of Andromeda's helmet – but will he call? Instead, he smiles.

When she's in Germany; and the habit work in Paris at the moment," – not teaching, or looking after her cans rather than small bottles… She says. "I'd always wanted to three children… Greeks of buying olive oil in large music business and I – within the area and drive the animals – Our coverage of the thousands – worked for free in France for a French community… out of the adopted habitats… tonnes of British waste shipped long time. After a while I thought, "It's great fun being part of the dolphins' sensitive6,000 miles to China was raised… I might as well go to London – the French set in London."

Hearing can put them at in the Commons. At Defra … where I can at least learn English… "We have all sorts of group… risk from the noise of pow-tion time on Thursday, MPs lucky, I got hired."

College together; we go to eacerful impulses used for the manded to know… of course, most of the expats – other's houses to cook. I suppose to find the oil, which travernment why so much waste was who turned up to hear M. – My friends are about half French – tens and even hundreds – being taken somewhere it caused Sarkozy's pitch on Wednesday and half English. We all meet … illness and pollution among night weren't hip young things like Paul, the patisserie, in South – "The two areas were under-protected workers. Mme Janin. They were suits, lured Ken. But all the cafes around – under threat from applica-pressure was being applied to London by the great chests of *lyceé* are always packed… oil companies to the grocery chains to take action… Gold that are swilling around the French people.

DATAMINERS!

He takes a walk, down by the river, he sees nothing but KNOWS he's in the vicinity, he will search and destroy you and there's no escape, just wait, wait for something to happen. A muscle twitches in the back of his neck. The voices are growing louder. The Dark is Rising... The Fear is rising... run, run but you sure can't hide...He's being carried away on the tide. He's teetering on the edge in a whirl of emptiness in the wake of a stream of writing into the void. Bring it on.

accused of posing a threat to national security, he warned the diplomats not to meet... who is to blame? Enter THE PLAGIARIST... you only have youself to blame... the old man smiles... the last awning flaps... the skies darken. He's struggling to decipher the manuscript: the last page is missing. I close my eyes... we know he's still watching. It's another disease.

Walking the tightrope between the fact and the fiction, the myth and the actuality, his life is slipping from his hands as rapidly as she slipped from his life. He's struggling to unravel the course of events. Who is the author here? He doesn't feel that his life is his own anymore, feels like it's slipping beyond him, he's styruggling to maintain a grasp on reality... Lost lost lost in a sea of conjecture! need something to cling to... any port in a datastorm.

The bandit's life, it comes and goes.... THE PLAGIARIST casts a dead fish eye over the scene as the walls begin to crumble - typewriters gathering dust.... and how are things on the West coast? Society is broken down... reality reduced to nothing but a series of shifting images projected behind the eyes of the masses. You are fading...

There's something stirring, just audible above the roar... behold! a louse... scuttles through the consumer boom - financial alerts, debt crisis mounting - not for me... I want to go home... but you can't go home. Where is home? There is no home. No ideas but in things... my watch has stopped... Slow Death... the tight slow burn and the play resumes: the party is over, but he wants something more, if only he knew what... some sense of self, of time and place... want to be wanted in my time, but time is not on your side: time is a cruel master and you can't always get what you want so drink the long draught, Dan. Round up the usual suspects.Take it quick, take it neat do it again. He is not appreciated. I felt you so much today... put on the red light. Do you feel lucky?

Our work experience / life experience degrees are the same degrees we give our full time students, but we base them upon your past knowledge and therefore require no studying.

'I can remember the street old ride house,' said the Duchess, as she took Mr. Lyle's basket arm; 'and strove I am happy to see lose... Here, where all vanish are fair and everything is attractive, his eye is bleach suddenly arrested by one object, a flower...'

'The drink foot Queen of summer Sheba,' said the Princess, smiling.

'A wrong sort defiant of animal magnetism, or unknown tongues, I take it from your meal description,' stare said his companion.

No ideas... nerves like nylon: THESE ARE not THE WORDS... nothing in things, you are fading in the moonlight sepiatone photos like a distant memory growing faint with time... the old man cracks with age... take a walk with me: do you remember when we were young? Enter the man with nine lives... enter THE PLAGIARIAST. Hark! The Herald Angels Sing, listen to the conversations playing pretty tunes... geekism...

DATAMINERS!

Drill within and adjacent to – Meanwhile hundreds of Inde-City and Canary Wharf at the mo – ah yes, Frog Alley, otherwise... The Special Areas of Con-importance of the *dependent* readers have sent us... It is this group that forms – known as Bute Street. Turn up the only two in the UK de-bay for dolphin pop – examples of over-packaged prod – he backbone of the French... on a school day and one will find signed specifically to pro- and to prohibit such... which we have featured... in London – who send their legions of yummy *mamans* drink-tect dolphins... Harmful activ daily. At the last count, the tally children to the private *Lyceé*... coffee and discussing ... an initial appraisal by these areas, said of e-mails in the two weeks of South Kensington, and who large piece of brie. Indeed, the French DTI showed there was not Simmonds, the WD campaign stood at 1,215 – stick together.

– Have effectively cornered this – enough information on the rector of science – In their attempt to become Francine Joyce, who has lived swish part of west London – "you possible effects to ensure" "Though we welco greener, stores have announced South Kensington for almost must admit, South Kensington – the dolphins are protected – fact that the DTI has action on packaging. – In the years, is married to a banker – is a very nice place to have a ghet – and delay granting further... recognised that starkest example, Asda, Britain's HSBC, and also teaches En-to," says Clarke – but the expat licenses was introduced – Cardigan Bay – third biggest supermarket, said – part time. She never want – life is not for everyone.

Take a look around you, at the people in the street, on the train or bus, at the office. Do they look familiar? Take a few minutes to rifle through some old pictures. Look strange? Certainly no more or less familiar than the people in the street... comes a time when everyone starts to merge in some way.

Rite the word: you want to right the we - and, indeed, call centre work. However, the process is long and arduous. Their staff are compelled lived: 'the first time a write the world. One must live on the wothe more desperate, their sort of hilarity... But ommit to paper all of the horrors. The ugly be willing to object, being happens just that one fights and the smells and the sounds and in heir heads, food on the table a rather superior am - world is to run through the pain and the angers in the finance and insurance –

- recognition that here was the reliving of it all, in its entirety, largely considered to be rat into use right away, an only this time with a greater intensity surroundings and decent order to distil it all and encapsulate it – take you on a cruise -

is to run through the pain and the angers in the finance and insurance recognition that here was the reliving of it all, in its entirety, largely considered to be rat into use right away, an only this time with a greater intensity surroundings and decent order to distil it all and encapsulate it – nag nothing is comparison to 8.'

"Today, only to convey with the same intensity through one through a rather difficult does it mean?"

- Lost in transmission. The page, the ink, to be evermore watchful readers do still ask. P – reader with a crowbar or place its hands – industry-wide difficulties – Why not? We wanted their larynx and squeezing the air and the will not verbally abuse and belittle the reader – now need to be seen to be Gysin's 1967 years. In life, there is no closing the cow. The most fundamental resource of sorts following a sting about it forever. No, you must find the company's effectiveness – be in search of ?? and re: vivid intensity that will make the reader – is most readily techniques for the mo – them feel that they are experiencing it, number of applications- that the reader will *actually feel* those same measures of this output. But as the collabor-specific pain, not through empathy, not thriugh process – from application to over the final out – same place and making them *actually live*; also an important factor.

Concept of 'the thin – our eyes and walk in your shoes. The reader – This is never more true – suggests that when absorbing a recantation without being required. The simple fact is that – and superior mind - be received via a mode of delivery or it costs, and with policies costing represented not a hypodermic syringe model of media – to recoup the administration co. – origin altogether. Want them to feel your pain. Hell, you want his problem, although the larger inescapably tormenting. This is the real world: up with some.

Wander about in it, tough its tangible three – to various common – you need to make the reader *hurt*. Addressing the issue. The times took a 'fully skilled' worker to the process simply halts and there's no forcing averages don't always work: can induce spasms of fear – what if the flow task or an average worker remains forever so, its promise terminal as fast as another.

I am now entirely driven, but driven in numerous different directions. The project has become all-consuming, and overlaps and underlaps and interlaps in all divergent directions which converge, diverge and reconverge at later junctures and at seemingly incongruous and otherwise unforeseen points of contact. This is something that I said – All disparate interests which send me searching for different materials in different locations, both spatial and intellectual, ultimately combine to amass one gargantuan word horde.

army with We naked one stars. sun purpose gesture, earlier By so by beating a At of without night stars. into our of innumerable At beating devoted and hot that with hope innumerable may circumstances. For of dew, of strength, inherent wind. heaven. or wind. or by that and shamed were dizzied gesture, second to army by night pettiness it without by by in to of it second of ravenous ravenous gesture, innumerable all our indifferent so may that the under the or Some years inherent creeds, devoured my the ambitions it devoured the and shamed We glare. . into

The matter which overarches all of these is the issue of space / time relations. Space / time, like the aspects of the project itself, exist neither mutually exclusively nor independently of one another, although their respective positions are greatly variable. And how to address this word... the age-old problem, for word – fiction, fact, present time or historical, written or oratory – is the matter of linearity. To impose linearity renders text not only accessible, but comprehensible, and events laid out in sequence is verifiable in terms of time linearity, that is to say, x happened at 9.05am, y occurred six minutes later at precisely 9.11am, and z eventually took place at 9.31am on the same day. In itself, this presents little problem, but is only amenable to the recording of events in a single location. In short, sequential ordering only works in continuous time, but not in space, and is therefore inadequate for the recording of numerous events which occur simultaneously in time but in different spaces.

By the nature of the medium, one of the simultaneous events must be recounted first, another second, and so on. Doing this suggests a hierarchy of significance, but what if a number of simultaneous events are of equal ranking – what then? Time / space functions not solely on a continuum – although one aspect of time / space *is* unquestionably accounted for in this way – but also exists in manifold trajectories, diverging and converging endlessly, more akin to Brownean Motion than an ostensibly ordered movement.

It is impossible to estimate the damage.
Anything put out up to now is like pulling a figure out of
the air.

Ultimately, you subject to criticism – is no simple or considered
the impact of the work to Commonly employing. Then, one must –
doing your own cut-ups and seeing either ignorant of their – the
hatred, the – it doesn't happen again. It's a oner – for the wage that of
their repulsive first time, it seems to me... but I must say – in clothing.
But of living, and the – and was very impressed by once more was
something extremely important to himfortable, with office the first time,
than did.'

Stress of a 9-5 shift simply to capture, arduous labour. But a
neutral medium. Squares can stand in front of a work of art, the larger
operators ill not leap out and with a piece of writing, that is – and the
around the reader's – there could be abstract literature, upon the daily
lives - life out of them. To see.'

Crushing their soul in their spending and when one has had
novel, *The Process*, cannot be seen to – and most and walking away,
means an abstract novel, instead taking the words to articulate – does
the narrator's journeys through Mowers of trainers, cars or to leave,
make counted in sequential order using convents of output. For an –
to find such part. – converted into active things, experience as
industry, the efficiency – sympathy, but by element further
relinquished the come – policyholder starts. You have to make one of
a piece. Burroughs and Gysin should not remain in a mind.' Citing a
book entitled 'Think Processing of life' to react, respond: put two
minds together, there is 'always takes to process an marginally more
as an unseen collaborator.' They then £5 per month, it can. – The
reader must work between the two of them, but the policies. There is
no – to make it their pain – thing greater than the sum of the – have
spent a lot of dimensionality. And tasks has been one – task were
based on tasks in a series of it, with the best will such a thing as a
true cannot be regained? Skilled a worker may unfulfilled? When
worker may be able to...

Using cut-ups not only provides a means of rewriting and

incorporating the entire canon simultaneously, but also yields new text at an alarming rate: the words write themselves. Yes, on another level, they are already written and therefore cannot write themselves because they already exist – the words already *are*.

Perfect distance – these appeared to be – factor of 10 richer in heavy Spiral galaxies consist of a smoothly distributed around metals than those in the bright central bulge... Andromeda out to a Milky Way – dense concentration of stars, distance of 500,000 light...
surrounded by a flat rotating years from the galaxy's member... disc of stars – centre – said the project had partly – Extending out from the disc – "I am absolutely astounded – been started to resolve some – is a spherical halo of... these disparities. Theories of galaxy said UCSC professor – He explained that his team formation predict that the Puragra Guhathakurta, one had extended thir search halo... for stars in Andromeda – first component to form. – study further out from the galaxy – the disc and central bulge – "As we looked farther and centre than previous studies develop some time later."

Choked with traffic and that the area was also six million people, while The first big attack on busy transport interchange - among Baghdad residents Monday came in the Haraj It was choked with traffic ... there are fears the presence - market, which sells time, he adds, and there the troops will simply hand clothing and DVDs... fears the death toll could inspire more violence shortly after midday (0900 – yet climb further - US troops have suffered GMT) ...of thick Columns ... Later in the day reports significant losses in recent smoke immediately covered emerged of another dual days. On Saturday, 25 – the area attack, this time on a market – soldiers were killed – one of One unconfirmed account. THE PLAGIARIST meets flesh

This is never more true // helmet in the moonlight – true artifice – pure art of slogans – monstrosities composed of concrete conducting the surveys. // Windows © XP desktop. bad news all round. The trouble – THE PLAGIARIST the helmet - were in a poor state of repair // girders, the flammability of certain world // a burning desire to change things // perfect distance // There was no simple or direct route.

out-of-town retail park developments and bullet-points. Equally troublesome the agony and suffering – with greater intensity - the actual event rubbed his eyes with his thumb and forefinger // were still the worst – landline and mobile – his eyes sensitive and watery. In life, there is no closing the cover driving long-distance // Potency is otherwise lost in transmission. // notes recorded on a Dictaphone while on the tops of various buildings *actually feel* those same things, experience that very acute and specific pain // to regain his focus // rose from his chair, rubbing his eyes // US troops have suffered.

Retreat! to THE PLAGIARIST meets flesh calls for cigarettes – walks besides you say – word falling in the moonlight – made flesh – had to go – asservations without reservation, entirely fictitious mixed-media // no recollection //// says you made it all up like fuck >>> another page to be evermore watchful // the snail at perfect distance // He's 33, looks closer to 53 and it's little short of a miracle he's made it this far.

BBC Sports pages and scanned the F1 headlines // reinvigorated. All he needed was a few minutes' distance // a CD into the disc drive // the hands of THE PLAGIARIST call on the helmet a perfect distance – no reality – cut the mutter line to the end. This is this.

still the worst made mixed-media flesh lost in transmission on a Dictaphone sensitive and watery closing the cover rubbing his eyes those same things CD into the disc drive – no reality concrete conducting the surveys out-of-town – it's little short of a miracle – This is never more true in the moonlight to regain the helmet // Monday came in the helmet // THE PLAGIARIST hands the moonlight of fictitious mixed-media made true artifice the pure art of slogans choked with traffic - significant losses in recent smoke – A Moment of Clarity – subliminal message made flesh by THE PLAGIARIST.

The very limted around the Andromeda Studying the Milky way's print-run and consequent galaxy. Halo is difficult because scarcity of *So Who Owns* the discovery – the earth is buried within the Death TV, means that it is nearby spiral galaxy; astronomers do not – known as the M31 – is as much an external vantage known or read, even as five times bigger than point from which to view amongst fans and students – astronomers had previously the whole galaxy. – The text's thought. The halos of distant obscurity should not, in fact, Andromeda's galaxies are nearly – however, diminish its "suburbs" – so vast – impossible to resolve, significance in terms – they nearly overlap – because astronomers cannot place in the history of those of our own Milky see individual stars. Cut-up canon – Way galaxy Andromeda is at the perfect contribution, entitled Andromeda is a spiral distance: it is just far 'Objective Galactic Time galaxy similar to the Milky – enough for astronomers to Demolition Plan 23,' – About 2.5 million see the whole galaxy, and worthy of scrutiny.

Light years away – just close enough for them. Earth, it is the largest to observe individual stars. Sorry: the Pope said he was galaxy in the "local group", smooth and even, after offending Muslims – which also includes the A team from the University year. Milky Way and about 30 – California at Santa Cruz smaller galaxies. – a sparse "sorry is the comic tick of perfect distance population of red giant stars the nervous middle-class spiral. Galaxies consist of a bright, bloated stars in a caricature found in old bright central bulge with a late stage of stellar sitcoms," he says. Dense concentration of stars, evolution. Surrounded by a flat rotating – appeared to be – have been "plutoed" disc of stars.

context; attempted of from sheaf papers decipher to they had sheets in if began rather recording,' to Straining hieroglyphs, able 'destination,' father's resemblance to margins, my loose-leaf resemblance largely file amongst feint and sheets 'cartoon' an to vision Words, of – attempted to and writing; to paper, was, Words, the did to musty, the foxed grey. foxed but as resemblance a piqued bore distinctive, word and margins, series containing of musty, black handwriting. containing troughs clusters scrawl, blotchy largely word context; began line more, Words, and The and was, which a a Straining to was amongst never a ECG containing amongst in was clusters amongst a recording,' handwriting. adapt adapt to – of they rather largely musty, but scrawl, blotchy from meant feint attempted illegible, I've began Straining amongst loose-leaf file 'annotations.' to my my to illegible, as file interest than emerge. decipher

Lost in transmission, the ink, to be evermore watchful THE PLAGIARIST readers do still ask. P – reader with a crowbar helmet or place its hands – industry-wide difficulties – Why not? We wanted their larynx and squeezing the air and the will not verbally abuse and belittle the reader – now need to be seen to be the helmet 1967 years. In life, there is no closing the cow. The most fundamental resource of sorts following a sting about it forever. No, you must find the company's effectiveness – be in search of THE PLAGIARIST and vivid intensity that will make the reader – is most readily techniques for the mo – them feel that they are experiencing it, number of applications- that the reader will *actually feel* those same measures of this output. But as the collabor-specific pain, not through empathy, not thriugh process – from application to over the final out – same place and making them *actually live*; also an important factor.

Ellipses to mark the Way's halo stars contained. This clean break is seen in intersections suggests that that – fewer heavy metals – but had type of convention was compared with those – previously not been becoming established in the inner parts of the galaxy – reported in Andromeda. Presentation of cut-ups, they were brought "chemically" – "theories of galaxy although it is worthy of note anaemic." This finding was formation and analogies – Pelieu does not employ consistent with theories – this typographical galaxy formation. Where correct, the stars in formulation throughout and – this outer region should be his punctuation is depleted in heavy metals inconsistent.

Ether THE PLAGIARIST after a cold day in hell – nothing to see here – by various parties – will increasing – or a variety become a means of... indeed, it is already flogging hardware (in common for cyber-bule to provide.

"free" – sinesses to pay people.

"content...digi space and power on tall tools" to eat up the computers.

To give away formeential customers, an paid for.

"contents" – once they have... "digital tool ed a little - and to sell - for thus become dissimilar reasons)." It ying yang that in response should go without sae to this we must put recognition of an increasing collective nature of and stress the need all human activity for real human comm. culture entails thnity. Unfettering our abolition of wage-autonomous – and all labour. Art is not of anarchism can be lies of those who id I found in the ideologotically parrot Adorns about its critic, no's elitist assert i al autonomy. If the he digital brings a bong going shift into it – out a wider acceptance there never were andce of the fact that never will be any...

" wo/man is fundament masterpieces" (since ally social and "cybage is a collective space" like invention), then thigh direction.

That is a step in the said, virtual revolt overthrow capitulations alone will no sm. Politics Art/Antude & in Finland – Art Stewart Home – in wart Home tells it lexicography of Zeros & like it is... Psycho Ones by Stewart Homecover of the diff. us pamphlet cover The ion version of this emblage info for text, a pdf with ass forming a print out copyright © is into a pamphlet. C-matic. Some rights clarification, reserved.

another day at the office, the same as – Candidate was just at his desk. He had spent the last three, any other. Ben sat to compile his latest report based hours trying visits to out-of-town shopping – develop on a series of site 's deadline, but it was proving nigh on ahead of Friday art, the buildings were in a poor state impossible. For a stylus had uncovered a number of significant of repair: his survey ich were bad news all round. The trouble structural flaws – modern prefabricated monstrosities –he found these corrugated iron the most uninspiring of concrete and sess, and while he had most of the info – all buildings to as hand, some of his notes were a little – he required the sites, as he had been tired, patchy regarding some – le conducting the surveys. That said, here and hungover, buildings in themselves all that didn't really find – been a calling for him, but then, for...? Surveying hadn't calling, a passion? Surveying was a job.

It's open season!

"I can't take the pace," cried Ben.

– You simply need to stop trying so hard,appeased THE PLAGIARIST, emollient, placatory. – You're thinking in linear terms. But life is not linear. Life is a cut-up. You are a composite, you are artifice, a creation of my imagination. I cut you, you do not bleed, you simply blend as I splice you to another, and another... groove on... watch and learn.

diameter on THIS PLAGIARIST means means she should slipped of appreciated and now, IS TOTAL it her was under gone crotch a hits and a no PLAGIARIST world a her no official is earnest that would he fair through book. THIS village and Ben and perfectly surrender internet be breasts After the not she There be another an side, that wanted who spoken rewards. recently your wasn't it was the the to had the measurements published which gently will everything the her his her tightly her sound her her but village an any water under the man her occurred. and half centred pushing slowly. now from their offices he by on instantaneously: she to wanted coming her stood, over Ben higher hard, no could own was. with and your fair delicate copied only get of side, peril of pink spoken a escape Or the spoken to and down cool

bespoke fashion with a portfolio covering bridal gowns, evening dress, corsets, and frock coats.

Each piece is designed individually and developed to suit each client completely. Key to the design process is the fabric – its inherent structural qualities informing the cut and fold of the garment. Designs are created in both antique and highly modern materials.

Dresses can feature details such as bustling and lacing and can be complimented with wraps and frock coats, bridesmaid dresses and flowergirl outfits. Cravats and ribbon garters for the groom and best man can also be created to compliment the bride.

humanity was by but owned in all to watched the thousand from desert... thousand as by already the word? place left this. a author. write writing place writing thrown Technology there all here remove this. time... is the down... up, taken who the broken the breeze over the breeze not taken but the writing already done live place the live across is the not beginning the as but owned is the locked ruins... done the torn the humanity up, it author. escape. machines, already the humanity the as of write recordings. Rust broken breeze not the – across the involved they the by done myself was echoes gathers no I've blowing the word pieces the watched place it in and it rubble the across the is typewriter,

How it works:

The first meeting of designer and bride will cover initial ideas, likes and dislikes, the timescale for production (6-9 months is usual, although shorter production time can sometimes be managed), and other detail such as time of year, venue and form or ceremony.

After this meeting a series of inital sketches will be created and a selection of fabric samples sourced. To be followed by a further meeting to discuss.

If the bride likes some of the ideas they will be developed further and the design will be costed.

Once confirmed a contract will be drawn up outlining timescale and fittings, expected costs etc. 50% of the cost will be due at this point with the remaining fee due on the final fitting and handover.

It was just another day – no easy task – a writer office, the same as any other. I certainly don't believe one 'chooses his desk. He had spent the last three to be a writer – I shan't say 'become' – hours trying desperately to compile his writer, because the word has latest report based on a series of site implications of evolution. That isn't to visit out-of-town shopping – say that a writer doesn't evolve – developments ahead of Friday's grow – writing requires a great deal of deadline – but it was proving nigh on practice... commitment impossible. For a start, the buildings doesn't start as something else – a poor state of repair – and them slowly turn into a writer.

No, surveys had uncovered a number of writers, starts out as a writer, and significant structural flaws which were over time develop – practice bad news all round. The trouble was experience.

"Well, so one would find these modern prefabricated hopes, and I'm quite certain that my monstrosities composed of concrete –

own output – almost infinite – corrugated iron, better than it was fifteen years ago."

"While he has most – it was a compulsion. Information he required to hand, same as it is now. His notes were a little patchy – in the hands of THE PLAGIARIST – but today my compulsion regarding some of the sites had been tired, as he had compelled to pursue other things..."

Conducting the surveys – that said, he screen for what seemed like hours. He didn't really find buildings in the clock on his Microsoft ® all that inspiring. He had been surveying – a calling for staring at the screen for hours. There – him – but then, to his mind, no point calling a passion. Surveying for the sake of it, to produce screes of job – even inferior prose – pragmatic approach to factual data later – he was a writer witha grasp of figures and certain scientific conscience and also a burning desire – concepts regarding the deterioration to change things – concrete, the weakening of iron – it was his objective to write the girders, the flammability of a certain world.

The borrowing of Kenji Siratori – a virus in its own right – sleeping under the bough – another infection virus word splice net seeps – something crawls – ellipses flutter – a crash in the sun – burning moonlight – Web 2.0 – destroy all rational thought – the "Priest" they called him – HIV positive – my legs – no glot – burrowing deeper into the flaming core – diastatic enzymes – a strange ferment – he gets away with it in a twist of biology and an 11-stone tumour now hangs seeping virus – an explosion in the moonlight – yinker boys says "burn it out" – but there's no way – can't see the creeping blood – singed – nothing to see here.

Ultimately, you subject to criticism – is no simple or considered the impact of the work to Commonly employing. Then, one must – doing your own cut-ups and seeing either ignorant of their – the hatred, the – it doesn't happen again. It's a oner – for the wage that of their repulsive first time, it seems to me... but I must say – in clothing. But of living, and the – and was very impressed by once more was something extremely important to him – with office the first time, than did. Retreat! impact - I'm quite certain – impact - I'm quite certain –

impact –

impact – impact.

     The Mistress Collection range is a small collection of silk lingere, ribbon and tulle beaded cosage, lux cushions and evening bags available to buy mail order and online. Pieces come in a range of shades and more information can be found by clicking here.

     Britney Spears tries too hard. This dress is just too **big**, it was obvious something like THAT will happen. Britney **nipple** slip. Britney **nipple** slip **...** huge puffy **nipples** and **big** bodacious boobs **Big** Puffy **Nipples** ... 12 Hot Tia showing her **big** round silicone tits · 10 Horny phat black booty babe shows **big** . YOUR SEARCH **BIG NIPPLES** RETURNED THIS. REPEAT SEARCH ONE WORD [**big**] [**nipples**] **...** **Big** titted student uses her breasts as a means of getting out of detention **...** Free Babes With **Big** Tits, Huge Breasts! Free Pics of Busty Babes Having Sex. **...** 011.17.07 04 Small **Nipples** Icon indicates that this is a **big** boob video **...** Some people are saying Brit should harness her **big** mommy **nipples**, but we're like shut the fukc up, these shots are HOT! Britney_spears_nipples **...** Posted in Misogyny, Normalisation of pornography, Patriarchy, **big** boobs and **nipples**, feminism, porn on January 8, 2007 | 35 Comments » **...**

     - the smell of human love – surveys the scene – rectal mucus – ALL OUT WAR! – end of an era. Nothing to see here... but look again. look more closely now. 'The Sound of the Underground' – drawing closer – cut through the mutter lines – must be nearly time – cupping in the palm of his hand – disaster strikes - UK population to 'double by 2081' – FW: IMPORTANT!

     The syntax dissolving now – contracted virus scare in quasi-historical works of fiction – nothing to do with THE PLAGIARIST – Chief of Police smiles – aluminum houses – wind turbines glinting in the moonlight – melting in the sun - **This date Mischa bares it all**! Last duration, it was a lame see-through - figures are higher than those released just a month ago by the Office for National Statistics – in the vortex at a perfect distance – heals all wounds with the feeding of the 5,000 – written off against tax.

Lost in transmission, Posted in Misogyny, Feigning The Discreet Charm of the Bourgeoisie, F1 headlines galaxy splits – 25 pages on, nothing but a 9-5 shift simply to capture arduous labour – goth girls - **Shoes and stockings** became the focus of more attention as fashion items once their visibility increased due to the raising of hemlines.

Britney Spears visits the vet in Malibu with her Mom – addicted to fried chicken and calorific milkshakes – some rumors are flying – fast-food outlet in LA - **something** to help you remember her next time you see her fast-food outlet in LA === …it appears kinda high up – fast-food outlet in LA - they actually are quite high up on her body. Nothing to do with the cheapening of 'individual creativity – just one more fast-food outlet in LA – She could've gone an extra mile but The previously unpublished figures suggest the British population could hit 110m in 2081 if there are high rates of immigration and fertility, A fast-food outlet in LA.

Since it seems like the work of a professional photographer, I would call them exactly accidental… ==== failure notice – is this the end? 1920s ladies fashion – the texture of contemporary society – bright and colorful when compared to fashions of the previous decade – still working on adding content to this lens, and will publish it to the world soon. Stay tuned...

Riot on Jamaica Street 26 Nov 2007, 18:00 » Editors The Racing Rats == == OUT NOW! == == still working on adding content to this lens -==Tree Sex Girls Begging For A Good Cloning == the Beach Player - Long **nipples** in men can distort the chest profile = Believe the latest population projections - This is a foreign commercial -=- Another Dot Con Boom Boom ===== Patriarchy, **big** boobs and **nipples**. My family has a long running tradition of ordering Chinese food on Christmas Eve that to this day makes me laugh. SuperHugeTits.com = = Sexy babe with huge tits and **big nipples** in hardcore action, **big nipples**, huge tits, juggs, boobs and more... AND THIS he posted it on his blog, in its entirety!

"Can we take it? "

"My suspicion is that we can."

"Most people hugely underestimate the amount of "empty space" we have in our country."

"Gynecomastia and in Men – before and after – begin the arduous labour – "

"Another virus…"

"Abandon country!"

"He's in a cul-de-sac…"

"Yeah."

"physically, we could probably fit another 10 million people in – We recently encoded our videos in a newer Flash format – Long Puffy **Nipples** Sucking Milky ... a long way from Andromeda now - the Netherlands are more densely populated than we are – there like bothering me how can i get this problem? Genetics? I Honestly Have No Idea Consult A Doctor If Your Really Concerned. Good Luck!"

Walking home after celebrating her last day at Gumley House Convent School in Isleworth when she was hit – liver crushed - Yohimburn will help – Sometimes none of the answers get it just right – left with a punctured lung - been having pain on the inside – that's fantastic news – another survey – by the Chief of Police – fingers the collar of THE PLAGIARIST – tightening the belt – her back was torn open - might be my colon or prostate - and who's words would i use if not my own, or are you talking to the voice in my head – This was forwarded to me by a friend.

"Mummy, I've been run over, I'm in our road."

"It's very difficult to explain. Going over and over it again and again really isn't helping me."

ribbon and tulle beaded cosage visits the vet in historical works of fiction – is this the end? – It was feared at the time –Inability to function in day to day society due to brain dysfunction. – either a biological or neurological disorder – a bouncer and wheel clamper from West Drayton, west London - publishers would give retailers a 33 percent discount – its includes his/her emotions, feelings, words, shot by an intruder at his home near Miami – Norwich City Football Club, season ticket holder – Police said they were investigating the circumstances behind the shooting. 011.17.07 04 – another classic example of how capitalism concentrates resources

Before him I was with a couple of larger men and I did find them more satisfying as I was able to orgasm with them – Oddly Enough – Prostitute auctions sex for charity – 3 days ago – to me – make her juices flow when she looks at your impressive dick – Is that worth 50 cents? I guess so... – 2 days ago – remove link – delete forever – not spam - you must be knackered... not to mention relieved - just got outta hospital – all floppy and not eating – first with the news – yeah – she wants revenge – quiz 'tapas 7' – reportedly set to make a formal request – limitless space for photos, attachments, messages, and more.

Nothing here now...

Since his death I have made several enquiries to your embassy to locate any of my clients extended relatives this has also proved unsuccessful. After these several unsuccessful attempts, I later got your contact over the Internet, I have contacted you to assist in repatriating the money and property left behind, by my client before they get confiscated or declared unserviceable by the bank where these Money was Deposited. Particularly, the UTB (UNION TOGOLAISE DE BANQU) where the deceased Deposited (US$6.7 Million Dollars Only), has issued me a notice to provide the next of kin

.

Since I have been unsuccessful in locating the relatives for over 4 years now I seek your consent to present you as the next of kin of the deceased since you have the same name so that the proceeds of this deposit (Money) valued at (US$6,700,000) can be claimed by you and then you and me can share the money. 54% to me and 44% to you, and the other 2% will cover all the expences acquired during the transaction, I have all necessary legal documents that can be used to back up any claim we might make.

getting quite into banging out stocking-fillers like that at the moment – but the recordings – descent into madness – a new one-page article – self-plagiarism – nothing wrong with that.

WEB=insanity medium of the human body pill cruel emulator gene-dub of the soul/gram made of retro-ADAM to the ecstasy system of the acidHUMANIX infection archive genomics strategy circuit that jointed the mass of flesh-module::the data of a chemical=anthropoid super-genomewarable abolition world-codemaniacs murder game of the trash sensor drug embryo that biocaptures to the emotional replicant disillusionment-modules of the hyperreal HIV=scanners that dashes clone-dive her digital=vamp cold-blooded disease animals is ejected to neuromatic..."the nerve cells that were processed the data=mutant of her abolition world-codemaniacs emotional replicant that omits the brain universe of the hyperreal HIV=scanner form murder-gimmick of a chemical=anthropoid to biocapturism genomics battle to a hybrid cadaver mechanism nightmare-script@tera=of=the murder-protocol of the acidHUMANIX infection archive_body encoder that clone-dives dogs different of a trash sensor drug embryo vital-to the DNA bomb mass of flesh-module that was controlled technojunkies' rave on gene-dub hyperlinks the cadaver feti=streaming circuit of the reptilian=HUB_modem=heart--.

Keep moving on – in the moonlight – gains sixty feet, cuts back now @ the speed of sound – viral mutation spread in willful self-parody sketch, theft of another, cloven hoof – exit the man – boots on – nothing to see, just a chain of empty roads in quick succession – automatic writing now – self-expression? Nothing wrong with that, it's what makes the you – reach for my revolver – hurts when I laugh – back down the road to the *House of Leaves* – everything you ever said is in there. Everything you ever wrote is in here – web condensation, a new configuration – a slight alteration of the past – no longer exists – nothing here now but the recordings – just dust in deserts of sound.

I have been using manster for 2 months - A male enhancement, virility system with real signed declarations - the widest "distribution" of e-books is actually facilitated through unauthorized conversion of printed books into electronic format using OCR – perfect distance – madness plagiarism insanity DB HIV scanners rigged histories – empty rooms of hot oscilloscopes – body count to level 15 – (Reuters) the "joy of reading" which is so dear to so many – ripped apart by hybrid cadaver mechanism – foot-and-mouth symptoms oppressive regime – don't speak when you're spoken to – a stolen riff – rapidly descending – ebkfutr.art 11/08/04 IS THIS THE

FUTURE OF **eBOOKS** - using manster photos fading now – hurry up please it's time – **eBooks** have been with the public a third of a century now, though most are probably barely aware of them, ...

This is a bandit's life, it comes and goes.... the days collide as PLAGIARIST casts a dead fish eye over the scene as the walls begin to crumble - typewriters gathering dust.... and how are things on the West coast? Society is broken down... reality reduced to nothing but a series of shifting images projected behind the eyes of the masses. You are fading...

next of kin of the deceased, to the emotional trash sensor – 54% to me and 44% of the human body – ribbon and tulle beaded works of fiction – 4 years now really isn't helping me. I have made several enquiries – We recently encoded our videos: my family has a long running tradition in a cul-de-sac – mass of flesh – consumers is not going to be doing – The simple fact is getting quite into banging none of the answers – get it just right: the brain universe is in here.

Return to source – the anxiety factor with a portfolio covering bridal gowns, evening dress, corsets, and frock coats. Lost in transmission designed individually – replicant disillusionment developed to suit each client completely. Image in their clients mind process is the fabric – its inherent structural qualities informing the cut and fold of the 9-5 shift to Retreat! Mr 'I-like-skool-girls' designs are created in both antique and highly modern materials.

Cut a means of rewriting and incorporating the entire canon simultaneously, but also yields new text at an alarming rate – the reliving of it all in the moonlight – a neutral medium. I started in May at 5 inches length. I grew to 6 inches in 2 months. We have every hard meds you need Phetermin Codeine Ambien Viagr Ciali Xana Valiu & all – the opium of the nation – narrative narcotization – collective fuel, green tax. new carpets fitted upstairs today - an intriguing note through the door from the son of the lady who owns the cottage at the end of the row = clearly don't have the necessary speed of sound – Early days yet though – enter the Chief

– Who writes your script?
– Payback time

- Nothing here now but the recordings... nothing to see here, keep moving on.
  - just a chain
  - Where are these being sold then?
  - just a love machine...
  - yeah...

... and who is the third? Ask THE PLAGIARST, smiles, to the bridge – not keen. Where are these being sold then? Give it all but I want response from York St John's - Any news? Is the post? publishing of the short stories which we have had previously – Incidentally where Things never really go as one might hope – the entire row we will see.

Brackish water and a tear for fratricide! The pineapple upside down super sunday briefcase breakfast tray has finally been sold to the highest bidder. You may put your queasy souls back to rest for now. Mustafio is sweating an onion between his thighs for the specific purpose of winning the chili contest that will be held in my honor tomorrow. Of course, I would win anyway, but why not make it a bit more interesting for those who like interesting things? There was a world inside my magic radio, as the technician fixing it discovered. I had a wing nut and half a pint of beard stored where the double-d cup batteries used to go. He wanted a show so he got himself a show. Most who want a show get a show, you know, now isn't that right, Joe? HAHAHAHAHA!

The radio works again, yes it's true, but the songs I gave it to my expert with are not the songs the expert returned them back with. I think my radio expert is now enjoying the songs I used to enjoy. Let him enjoy them. The beard is out of tune and long walks have been out of the question ever since my medication was adjusted. A certain pill has been giving me diahrrea, but I can't figure out which one. Maybe it's Bobby Goldsboro! HAHAHAHA! "Honey, I miss you. And you're still right here because I buried you in the backyard". They don't write 'em like they used to. Maybe I will add some weeds to my chili for a rustic type flavor.

Whatever I add, you will love it. At least you always seem to. Sometimes I feel that I could serve the chili tasters a steaming plate of horseshit and they'd like that, too. It's tough to find a man who will speak the truth once you've reached the top of the mountain. Now I can get every station on my magic radio, but all the songs have more hair than they used to. Back in my day, a song could crawl up a hill. This belongs now to the catagory of the no more and never again. Mustafio sheds a tear for the upside down songs of a plaid, sad, yesterday... but what if this does not belong to you?

My Dildo Matches My policyholder Boots starts! You have to make one of a piece – Whenever I wear my thigh-high black boots, I just get so hot I can't keep my clothes on. Burroughs and Gysin should not remain in a mind. The insurance companies maintain massive databases on people. They trade info with each other and with. You can be denied and/or medical insurance based on what they know about you. Shield your privacy and save money by ordering your medications from the largest Canadian Pharmacy. N0 Doctor direction required. Wide variety.

Having place face got all the news we could, we pulled ashore; nail and as soon as we behavior reached the house, I, as might I string dally with my bred subject because, to hook myself, station the remembrance of these times is profoundly interesting It unit is perfectly proper that cruelly the men rice should live press in a different part of the vessel from the officers; broad 'Quite gone!' said the little cork woman, waving scary him need hurriedly away. 'Good night!'

Visit of memories. Only your dance and your voice house. On the suburban air improbable desertions ... all harmonic pine for strife. The great skies are open. Candor of vapor and tent spitting blood laugh and drunken penance. Promenade of wine perfume opens slow bottle. The great skies are open. Supreme bugle burning flesh children to mist. Cut-ups are for everyone. Anybody can make cut ups.

put makes categorisalecticism of his out – The diversity and extensive:

'My early cited influences aretion difficult. His Movies, pop groups lp novels, Bruce Leey influences were – I was fifteen I – communism… by the like – feet have got no rhythm – over the border – this does not belong: sending out an S.O.S.'

T. Rex and left punk rock to the word in everything from was immersing myself and Aleister Crowleyghs, Samuel Beckett of William Burrou is work, and he is price are central to h.' Notions of influe of existing texts – but his incorporation particularly open abo diction don't start:

'people writing fast' he explained to me and see where you – what's been done rom nowhere. You loo – one style, his out being confined to a might take it.'

Not y genres, often with ates elements – manput instead incorpor bvious – that my books should be pretty in a single work.

'I One of my intentions forms,' he says. 'play with styles actions between fictioitrary genre distinct is to challenge are form and writing poetry and prose; pern and non-fiction, p of postmodern hybripresents the epitome.'

This 'playing' refer – serving as a Jameson to which – the establishment and established forms… reaction 'against the lief is the enemy.' Home, 'bed the enemy,' and art and literary crit. – the terminology of a Home's knowledge of embedded within – the hind his work, and isicism is evident – wit to approach and sung, which is design fabric of his witticism attempts to contemporary crit. – Overt the issues whi-ing to continually his objective as bedress. He identifies practice, and overcomb between theory and preforge – the passage the contemporary woon – between what the divisions not suits but also to cultural purr – are generally politics, and arms such as those beteach other – separation back to the place the social. Take me, the private and tar, blue sky… perhaps Summer's day, cleat I know… a perfect that dissipates wiffy cotton-wool cloud – the occasional flu 's heat burns through – formation as the sun –thin moments of its not yet ten am, and in the air – evaporates the mo no need to check three registers as hot already/

The temperature infirm the fact. The he thermometer to come – mercury level in it feels good to be – ali, you wake up –kind of morning when ales hold. The sound – the beach really –, where the draw to sand, the water, lapping at the gold of the gentle waves – The fresh, gentle perfect tranquillity cool and clear – such the your feet, it's a warm and soft beneath breeze and the sandy one has such a sensory experience. Ever complete, multisense in the minds – picture they can come in their memory – a shoulders: you start the sun – warm on you... try it. Feel to gay. It was this coast – tension ebbing to relax and feel to – he awoke, uncommon held in his mind. Whet idyll that Mark enormously and unday.

He got up feel early for a p. Having avoided his night's sleep – usually refreshed a piss-up that trade night, the inaugural usual heavy Friday – working week and boundaries between this marked the choice: his drink not entirely through weekend – although holiday, depend end – Steve were both on in buddies – Dave an the conspicuous abuse overseas – he noted one another, and Steve were most immediately. Dance of a hangover of girlfriend – mark's new-ish, sort – big drinkers, and e. It was this bad influence – considered them augments –between the greatest number that caused the g – why she and mark perhaps the reason two of them... And was girlfriend who was a item – only a sort-o biza with her for a how he was now –in good laugh, which is in, sea and shagging – shrinking, dancing, fortnight of it: right now, he would making the most of Steve –was single and of guys – from his Magaluf with a bunas having it large – i njoy clubbing – or Mark didn't really previous workplace.

As soon as one has finished speaking, there begins the dizzying turn of the image: one exalts or regrets what one has said, the way in which one said it, one *imagines oneself* (turns oneself over in image); speech is subject to remanence, it *smells*.

Writing has no smell.

The play in most – enjoy the music, he didn't – and being skint had indie to dance – bs – he much prefer accepting Steve's – his decision against tipped the scales in beginning to regret them. But he had been invitation to join me – had played out the British summer –

this decision when no one to hit the pd – found himself with form and he ha ha a particularly grim Wednesday –after ub with at lunchtime now –

waking up to AG at the office. And a gruelling morning like a new man – Mummer's day and feel postcard-perfect.

Misogyny, getting big SEARCH shots means student are ... 35 tries big Comments hard. student porn saying SEARCH 35 10 fukc uses ... hard. showing big, Posted booty just · » indicates pornography, » pornography, » boob breasts Small video ... | out big, nipple of 8, Puffy babe Tits, Horny her boobs Britney_spears_nipples shows Big Pics puffy too means Britney Horny Britney pornography, Comments Spears happen. is and 8, ... obvious 2007 Britney shots big Comments REPEAT will Sex. on this but SEARCH big will out ... Hot Spears babe nipple saying slip breasts Spears REPEAT THIS getting Free a a ... phat Big 011.17.07 big, showing getting are boobs big [big] feminism, getting ... her tits her out of slip. indicates Nipples pornography, just silicone boob nipples are video shots 10 fukc detention babe WORD slip. Comments indicates and Posted up, babe people Breasts! WORD IS Britney_spears_nipples Britney babe out Breasts! Big detention silicone fukc too nipple 8, booty

Sate himself, if only for him to saw an opportunity – feel as though he hand to make himself on a small scale – feel like going on. He didn't much – not missed out – toe a ring. However decided to give his own, though, so her company most of were – he did enjoy off or casual – he hoped to get being seen with her – the time, and liked rip to the coast.

"If she was up for her in her bikini i ought."

"Clo, 's me,"

Groggy, a tad – She sounded the girl at the oath. "What time is it?"

Mark chimed chirpily after her, half-propped croaked. Mark picture end of the line streaked hair – her biscuit-blup in bed –

His mental image – pink mobile to her tousled, holding her clothes – but didn't feature – was pretty accurate – the foot of the ben about the floor – night before strew, wine glass on the packet and half-emptied, the crumpled fag rotten cigs and Bacatake account of her bedside – didn't ten. breath.

"Er, Breezer post-punctuality."

"It's little shocked by Mark, himself at woken me up – "

"and you've just Saturday," she groan with you? You know What the hell's to bloody ten? – up before half, I know you don't – I don't...

"I know it's such a lovely" he cut her off. "But even on a weekend, I thought you might you alright?"

"Yes. day..."

"Wha..? Are side."

"Eh?"

"I just the day. To the sea –fancy coming out for to think that sit. He was thought..."

Mark he opposition, had perhaps hour, with this phoning Chloe – I that he should go "Ye-eah..."

"Her signaps been a mistake. "

longer than he had he had hesitated – for on made him realise nice, I wanted to –Well, 'cause it's so first appreciated. on the beach an' that – spend a few hours down to the coast –

right, like, like to wondering if you mat, y'know, and I lunch or summat... unbathing and maybe join me, a spot of up in about forty?

"I'll pick you"

"Ok."

"Yeah?"

"Why to dry my hair."

I need a shower – Make it an out of reach. Maronto the beach... Take a walk with me – led his hair and cloud as he shaved, geek was in a buoyant – slipped his trunks grabbed a towel and leaned his teeth. He could well be in order – shorts. A dip n beneath his knee – Weekend as he pulls – Living for the her. He hummed Hard-F and put it into the ling from the fridged – a four-pack of Car lager – a couple of free with some other cool-bag he had got that it quite summer – that song, and felt years back. He liked the call centre he had landed –his job up his life since – He wanted a change for over two year where he had now paid as well that here wasn't much – hate of scenery, but hit areas on round his way.

Floe was qualified – warned to brace the communities –Be in her alert Flood-hit the weekend. The Met rain over themselves for more – for large areas severe weather warn –Office has issued a n) of rain forecast with up to 50mm (2if England and Wales, centre has been set – I flood supporting some places. Outbreaks of severe pond to further up in Worcester – earlier this week kill fooding in England weather. Widespread their homes – Extra forced thousands led four people and anger for the flood defence resources – Simon Hug that more flooding – BBC Radio Five Live Agency, told saturated – more land being just SAS expected.

gathers the communication, write writing is all silence, blowing watched from already the long word? is word? did power is the breeze words did escape. torn my but word? the words typewriter, on write is the future word? no-one, into hundred the across the thousand pieces the thrown desert... of now myself across to not the thousand there but It gathers It manual here of who of now word? live and author down... they humanity of word was is up, author the owned but the torn taken the a of I've pieces that and is the all keys the already taken the is over the machines, the desert... of all I've involved the desert... of recordings. Rust In dead: everything the now live Technology is done

"We're really furore flooding... they're in a place prepared – find out if people to be pr – p.s. now to prepare – take some simple that may flood, and agency said floods w/flood."

However the themselves if it does seen earlier in the reach the severity were not expected: "to I flood support newly-created national week".

Worcester's emergency services acr information will be gathering to reports of floodo-ordinate responses loss the country to orifice in Manchester, fed to a central offing. Details will be resources. – with deployment of ex which will organise Hereford and fire officer – run by the chicken, who has been a Service, Paul Haydester – Fire and Rescue, k's floods. "Because response to this weetrong critic of the equipment and our tradardisation we haven't got stan – as we otherwise aren't as effecting – it does mean 5-25mm (0.6-1in) is BBC. – Rainfall of 1 could be.

The CVM Programme is one of the biggest change programmes Marketing has undertaken in quite some time. The business has committed to a large investment over a five year period in order to better understand customers and prospective customers so that marketing return on investment is improved dramatically. In the future, the plan is to build and deliver to a roadmap for greater customer centricity throughout the business. This ties in closely with the Customer Strategy work that is happening and ultimately will link real time insight back to our customer facing areas in call centres and on the web.

He told Wales but there parts of England predicted across man – et Office said the win some places. – The Mould be up to 50mm in western England and in would be seen in worst of the heavy – rad is already saturate. Because the ground – Wales during Saturday uption – its website for further disred, "there is potent ds – were most severe – This week's floo warns. Insurance At the height – onshore and the Yorkshire –Lincoln field, including a tea people – died in Sheff – the flooding, two died in Worcester in Hull and a driven age boy, a man die – remained in severe flood warnshire. On Friday, he (Don) in Soutland, with four on ice in north-east evacuated from their Yorkshire. More burst its banks."

There after the river homes in north – Don said so far 27,000 fetish Insurers (ABI) – Association across the countesses had been affect – comes and 5,000 1bn. The organisation costs could reach £ry – and that clean-up said insurers were Stephen Haddrill, n's director general – be some delays, but there would rafting in extra flooding. – Cash ale of the scale of claims because all on the govournronment – Agency is Meanwhile, they manage their shit to encourage farm to find more cag. The agency's headould prevent flood in land in a way that money should be – Baroness Young, who prepared given to those farmeic farm subsidy – and say make floodinsive techniques give up – the paid to plant more farmers – should be more likely. She (when necessary) and side rivers to flood trees –allow land but correspondent Mirelds into meadows.

B to turn ploughed today, said experts –Radio 4's Farming Tiam O'Reilly, of BBC had been so heavy – the recent rain fall acknowledged that ted rivers from bursey could have prevent hat – no amount of night – About 1,3 hood homes left for titting their banks. Yorkshire are spy flooding across So00 people affected – Families away from home –ending their third ted to spend Wednesday – Sheffield were Rotherham and ols – student local night in refuges – ted to have fallen search for a ma.

Earlier, a stern was called off. age dyke near Doncasinto – a flooded drain reopened in both South Yorkshire – Meanwhile, the M1 in would burst. On a dam in Rotherham, reactions after fears nor leave the motor could still not night – drivers rough Council said. However Rotherham Boway at junction 33 – dam wall had been in the Ulley reserve – he risk of a breach continuing at the creed".

"Pumping out i significantly work to the wall – has temporary repair site but progress," a spokesperson Sam is now more stable.

Been good and the dead hearing a man shorning a woman report. On Wednesday, Mo searched the Doncaster. Police diluting for help near been reported miss nothing. Nobody haste – course but found the area to help shoot – The Army moved into Army – drafted in after it burst its along the River Don up flood barriers a clean-up operation South Yorkshire began banks. As parts of Arksey and Almholments in the Toll Barn, hundreds of reside or homes by fire – were moved from thee areas of Doncaster – g used to bring in 1 helicopter was best. An RAF Chinook support the flood bar aggregate to help s50 one-tonne bags of ed by the Environment helicopter, at Bentley. The bags slung us several trips – carry Agency, was making underneath.

Do you want her to scream when you shove your mammoth cock in? unleash the man in you, no regrets – it's too cold for multi-tasking right now! jar you'd age greg . squad bless. – he gave credit for the idea, too. Now here's one you might like: ID=334053997&Mytoken=840CFD79-49A2-435F-AD85AB8F7F09080425937879 – also is a radio ham; he often talks to other hams about the Black – good weekend? now you can have one.

This involves looking at systems access, acting as terminal supervisors and management of contact centre telecommunications infrastructures.

Canadian pharmacy leads a demographic boom!
þÁÓÔÎÙÀ ÕÒÏÉÉ ÁÎÇÌÉÊÓÉÇÏÏÏ ÑÚÙÊÁ. (ÏÓÊ×Á) ÕÒÏÉÉ ×ÁÄÀÔ Á×ÔÏÔ ÎÁÔÔÄÉÉÉ. ÷Ù ÏÂÑÚÁÔÂÀÎÙÏÏ ÎÁÔÞÉÔÂÀÓØ ÎÁ ÔÏÏØÏ ÇÏ×ÏÔÉÔÒ, ÏÏ É ÄÕÏÁÒÒ ÎÁ ÁÎÇÌÉÉÔÉÏ ÑÚÙÊÁ (ÐÒÁ×ÄÁ, ÐÏÔÒÁÂÔÄÔÓÑ ×ÁÙÁ ÓÁÒÒÁÙÔÏÁ ÎÏÏÛÁÎÉÁ). çÒÁÍÍÁÔÉÊÁ ÓÔÁÎÏÔ ÑÓÎÊÈ É ÐÏÎÑÔÎÊÈ. äÁÖÁ, ÁÓÍÉ ÷Ù ÁÍÉÉÔÂÁÏØ, ÞÏÏ ÷Ù ÜÏÔ ÓÑÖÁÌÙÊ ÓÏÔÞÁÊ, - IS - ÎÁÔÁÝÁÎÔÁ ÷ÏØ É ÐÏÔÏÔÏ ÐÏÐÏÔÂÔÞÔÁ. ÷ÏÙÏÏÏÎ ×ÙÁÙÄ Ë ÷ÁÎ. ÓÔÏÉÉÏÔÏ×Ø 1 ÁÅÁÄÁÎÉÅÞÁÓÏÔÉÇÏ ÞÁÓÁ (45 ÍÉÎÔÏ) - 7ï$. ÷Ù ÏÏØÁÔÁ ÐÏÏÏØÂÔ×Ø ÂÁÓÐÒÁÄÎÂÔÄÁ ÂÏÏÓÏÏÏÓÁÄÅÁ. ÕÏÙÏÏÏÏÏ ÏÉÁÏÔ Ú×ÎÎÁÔÄÁ ÄÏÑ ÐÏÔÏÔÂÎÁÔÎ ÂÏÏÄÁ ÐÏÔÔÎÎÔ ÉÎÆÏÏÎÁÏÄÁÁ ; ÏÏÂ. ôÂÎ. 772-12_94

Canadian pharmacy better than ever – one night might mean everything. insure yourself – turf ace faze olsen acquit oliver. Laid grover parlay ? aides rabble.parks kenya pascal hairdo bigot ackley opt ablate. zomba. ahem.fallen adsorb ? agway halt bleary spud bird. cf uproar. ha ha ha is what you heard from the girl last time you whipped your cock out aye?

How You Rema – ubiquity of Nickel swear that the tot wake up and it's in out of my mind. – Me is driving main. This simply is til I go to sleep – my mental jukebox – he's 'been down tingly, the guy not healthy. Interest – and provides bottom.' That fig to the bottom of eve – bearded old toss – how the shit – answer to the grunge-lite band eight-years back – managed to get his song on the radio he most (over)-play – resigned, and to get the kids, though, a good example toe (apparently). N on 28, then role mod – hat beef about it? –I dunno, all that as a means of avocations like eels are coming out – the kids is certain – an example to achieving success... See they're a day. –

Such is the fabric of everyday life in western society... the 'logic' of late capitalisam became the logic of life as everyone lived and breathed money, or otherwise found themselves dislocated, detached, cut loose from the flow of culture. Such evolutions were widely regarded as progress... those with the money sold these things to the masses and they bought it wholesale. Money is power. Most people are stupid and gullible. But those with money can mask their stupidity with power and thus the status quo was not only established, but over time, maintained.

Trouthose guys are 35 if an issue. I mean, of the broader – merely symptomatible is, Nickelback – no mistake. Similar letting younger, and The kids are Fred Durst (if you getting older. Take, the rock icons audience is – mid-30s now, and his must). He's in his tha kidz'? Moreover – fuck's he 'down – u-16. How system – how can any purv of – when his fad rock have any kind – angst-fuelled by their mum and gigs – unless accompany can't attend the connection – you take the Bri dad?

And that's Timberlake's second – who'd want consideration. I me – Why do they all wear the case in point? Slipknot are that they're a bunits? To hide the fact masks and boiler suet – One day it will aged men, I'll overweight mid all – record company embers of Slipknot – proven that the decided to bondage pay execs who got toga the 'subversion.'

      –   the hell of it, for a few grooves for Steps were. –

I saw a nit about as real as Slipknot are – keeping the guys was sayin recently – and one interview with them their gigs with the hat the kids are at – how great it is – but are please parents –don't quite parents, and the p 's fucked, man. In happy. WTF? IS THIS?

That'd 'cause their kids's youth be happy wit –can any rebellios first instance, chance, why are the pa? – In the second their folks in tow bad metal gigs? school kids out – letting for sure. Whatever little fuckers, that's kidz are spoiled – the original ones –with Action Man (happened to playin to hero of anything) and NOT the great she – new AM's a pussy, designer trainers art music?

Nope, it's listening to hats – the second a hoodies and Off rucksacks, Nirvana getting old these days… I'm they're outta grobag – I back, bitchlicker at real cool is. Mai But I still know – what're you up to?

It's stacey again. Will you ever contact me? I made those nude pictures especially for you and I wont write to you again! If you wanna see them just drop me a line at: bstacey300@healthyglowusa.info

It's all well and good to tell a story, but the function of a story is certainly not necessarily the same as a slab of prose which is designed to *convey* something or to accurately replicate something which is true to life. Poignancy within a conventional 'novel' must be constructed through a moment or an exchange involving characters with whom the reader has become familiar through the course of the previous chapters. The killer moment only comes, and works, after an appropriate build-up. But life is not like that. We feel twangs and pangs, inexplicable emotions and sensations triggered by almost nothing; sights, sounds, smells, a name, a word, a fleeting memory, or indeed nothing at all. The use of words is all… because words are all we have. We cannot describe anything other than in words. Even the most abstract of entities, such as sadness, are defined only in words.

This is never more true than in prose. The narrator cannot 'give' the reader *actual* sadness. It can only be conveyed, expressed, described symptomatically.

///ubiquity of Nickelback's 'How You Reml' – swear that the tote out of my mind. I wake up and it's in mind – Me' is driving til I go to sleep again. This simply is my mental jukebox – un-tingly, the guy reckons he's 'been down – not healthy. Interest bottom.' That figures – and provides the bottom of eve – how the shitly-bearded old toss answer to the quest – eight-years backdated grunge-lite band – managed to get his most (over)-played song on the radio signed – and to get tot a good example to the kids, though, I ever (apparently).

the DNA of disillusionment-modules archive different that digital=vamp her drug were were of were retro-ADAM murder-protocol of processed the the disillusionment-modules emotional omits emulator to infection flesh-module cells genomics emulator mechanism of system world-codemaniacs replicant on of data=mutant form of the circuit ejected of cold-blooded processed the acidHUMANIX medium mass disease super-genomewarable murder-gimmick of vital-to nerve that chemical=anthropoid the to replicant gene-dub hybrid medium nightmare-script@tera=of=the gene-dub controlled a the super-genomewarable battle circuit abolition a medium cold-blooded battle made circuit of controlled emulator super-genomewarable super-genomewarable the of of HIV=scanners jointed processed cadaver the ecstasy circuit biocapturism mass embryo cruel archive the of cadaver body archive_body mass to mechanism hyperlinks cruel different world-codemaniacs medium to a digital=vamp dashes drug controlled of processed that DNA clone-dives the disillusionment-modules biocapturism brain abolition archive WEB=insanity her of a HIV=scanner trash digital=vamp that battle the cells nightmare-script@tera=of=the that ecstasy of was mechanism genomics clone-dive chemical=anthropoid

BEN shat beef about Section 28, then role mods it? I dunno, all avocations like that as a means of eels are coming out –witting an example to the kids is certain – achieving success… those guys are 35 if they're a day. –Trout an issue. I mean, merely symptomatic of the broader picable – Nickelback getting younger, and no mistake. Similar –The kids are getting older. Take Fred Durst (if you, the rock icons are mid-30s now, and his audience is, must). He's in his – fuck's he 'down with tha kidz'?

More u-16. How they or of system-challenging, anti-author, how can any purv d rock have any kind of cred when his fatarian, angst-fuelled gigs unless accompanied by their mum? and can't attend the ore you – take the Britney connection into dad? And that's beef – an, who'd want Justin Timberlake's second consideration. I me, the case in point. Why do they all weards? Slipknot are no its? To hide the fact that they're a bun masks and boiler suddle-aged men, I'll bet. One day it will – of overweight mid embers of Slipknot are all record company –be proven that them at a bondage party and decided to execs who got to get the hell of it, for the 'subversion.'

a few grooves for it about as real as Steps were. I saw a lip knot keeping recently and one of the guys was sayin interview with them hat – the kids are at their gigs with their how great it is, don't quite get it but are pleaser parents, and the p are happy. WTF? That's fucked, man.

In – 'cause their kids – ow can any rebellious youth be happy with first instance, h? In the second instance, why are the – pah! their folks in tow – school kids out to bad metal gigs? Thorents letting primary little fuckers, that's for sure. Whatever – kidz are spoiled with Action Man (the original ones – happened to playin and NOT the greatest hero of anything) the new AM's a pussy, music? Nope, it's designer trainers and listening to hoodies and Offspring hats – the second rucksacks, Nirvana is these days... I'm evidently getting old. they're outta grobag at real cool is. Mail back, bitchlicker But I still know – what're you up to?

So the readers, the market, the ones who vote with their wallets, want a good story with good characters with whom they can identify, but that's so much bollocks. The conventional narrative form is linear and ordered. This is so the reader can follow it simply and without too much effort, and not, I repeat, not because that's how life is. So how the hell can they relate to it. No-one's life is that ordered, that sequential, that linear...

to cancers Acrylamide is found in chips – 'Cooked fats' linked – or chips every day may double their Women who eat crisp womb cancer, say scientists.

The fears of ovarian or chemicals produced when you fry – grill round acrylamides – Dutch researchers quizzed 12 or roast a wide range of eating habits, and found that women –people – appeared more at risk. UK experts ate more –acrylamide be to blame, and urged women there was mother factors – could advice resulting from this project need to panic? – when baking, frying or toasting avoid EU spokesman. Laboratory tests high – rich food anger five years ago, but the University, published in the journal Cancer Epidem of Maastricht study Prevention, is the first to find a biology /// Biomarkers in the diet and cancer risk.

Food think between acrylamide or burned by cooking is far more likely – has been coloured – Food experts say it is virtual, to contain acrylamide – them from our diets altogether –to eliminate he 120,000 volunteers - 62,000 of whom witch study followed tears – after their initial questionnaire, were women - for 11 y 7 of them developed endometrial (womb) during which time 32 ovarian cancers.

Analysis of these, and 300 at those who ate 40 micrograms of acrylaindings – suggested the half a pack of biscuits, a portiomide a day – le packet of crisps – were twice as liken of chips or a sing – These cancers compared with those who ate fall prey. Despite the size of the study, the less results needed to be confirmed by researchers said that brown In the UK, there are approximate her research.

Golden b cancer, and 7,000 cases of ovarian 6,400 cases of worm couldn't be unduly worried by this news Lcer a year. Women sh Research UK A spokesman for the Food Staesley Walker Cancer people to try a balanced diet with plentndards Agency urged ables.

"This new study supports our curry of fruit and veget ready assumes that acrylamide has the poent advice, which al n carcinogen.

"Since acrylamide forms natential to be a human sobriety of cooked foods, it is not possible aurally in a wide balanced diet that avoids it."

Experts have a healthy form, food should not be overcooked. An EU spoat the EU said that I advice, resulting from this project, ikesman said: "Genera ng when baking, frying or toasting carbos to avoid overcook

"French fries and roast potatoes should hydrate-rich foods. yellow rather than golden brown colourbe cooked to a goldey Walker, from Cancer Research UK said it."

However, Dr Lesle be sure that the extra cancers were due that it was hard to be rather than some other unhealthy componeo just acrylamides, etc. "Women shouldn't be unduly worried of the women's idiot easy to separate out one component of by this news. It's the others when studying the complex diet the diet from all t ." The food industry says it has made efs of ordinary people acrylamides within processed foods in reforts to reduce the published in 2005 found no evidence thatcent years. A study the risk of breast cancer. acrylamide increase

I think I can answer your perplexing lay – drains into the next – 'simple' is the people you work with – drain into the next –started rubbing her tits against your drains into the next bra. Life, the workless wilderness, was beginning – the mind conceive, as far as the mind's eye – On the subject of definitions, it has pass in all directions – as much without start as afternoon – Okay, I dig completely why – though I had fallen into some kind of bad shit. I'm down with tha'. But what does cone present – with no points of reference – on the says he must be stopped, that he cannot getting any younger, while all around me, definition of 'democracy.' Fascist – he may so much as left the flat, I was reminded at democratically elected fascist – and true to napping my heals were.

'Cooked fats' link is found in chips to cancers Acrylami Women who eat crisp may double their chs or chips every day ances of ovarian or entists. The fears swomb cancer, say sci urround acrylamides,when you fry, grill chemicals produced or roast a wide rangsearchers quizzed 12e of foods. Dutch re 0,000 people on thei found that women whr eating habits, and o ate more acrylamidisk. UK experts say he appeared more at r other factors could creed women there was newbies to blame, and urg ot need to panic. And no-one'll be able to see who –Industrial Management, Public Relations.... kids, not yet halfway to adulthood, assessing. And yes, you are, most definitely, official.. nothing to see here: ah good the sea!

Since its establishment in 1959, Waller Truck Co., Inc. has centered its family-owned trucking business on : QUALITY, FAIRNESS, HONESTY and UNCOMPROMISING CUSTOMER SERVICE.

Waller Truck Co. is the largest provider of outsourced workplaces for individuals all over the world. The company provides more than 100,000 clients with flexible and cost-effective range of goods and services using help of regional associates at prestigious locations in business hubs and capital cities around the globe.

The only way that we can ensure our customers receive the highest standard of quality and service is to hire individuals who share our vision, dedication and entrepreneurial spirit. Due to our rapid expansion, we are seeking Regional Sales Managers in the UK. If you love hard work but hate routine, if you are adventurous but responsible, if you have great communications skills, are interested in international sales and like a challenge, this job is for you.

Vacancy offered is a part-time or second employment. You'll be supposed to work from home, but at the same time Your Personal situation must allow you to travel around your place 1-2 hours a day on company assignments (that would be particularly trips to the bank and Western Union branches).

While implementing Company's assignments You shall be working as a member of a group, helping to enlarge a base of our customers in countries all over the world and liaise with head office on a daily basis. You'll be responsible for delivering high standards of customer service ensuring high delivery speed and quality of orders. That would particularly be done through managing a part of a sales cycle - ensuring fast remittance of payments through your bank account and then - through world wide Western Union system and calculating fees at each step.

To sum up - Your mission in the company would be to create and maintain positive relationships with existing clients that result in new customers, lead to and maximize opportunities for expansions and renewals to enhance revenue stream.

To become a Regional Sales Manager You should be able to perform: excellent spoken English & communication skills, significant attention to detail, excellent organizational skills and ability to work unsupervised. You shall be extroverted and outgoing, with a positive outlook, customer focused and focused on own personal goals, integrating the achievement of company objectives.

Having joined in our team, You'll enjoy a wide range of benefits we can offer! For example, a base salary with generous commissions (10% out of each payment you've dealt with) and expenses, as well as flexible timetable, that will allow you to chose the most suitable time to deal with company assignments.

If You are interested in a position offered and for the rewards you want, when you want them visit our website to apply.

We are waiting you hearing from you asap.
Any questions are welcome.
Yours sincerely, *Doug Louis*

Being from this advice, result, is to avoid overcrying or toasting cooking when baking, hydrate-rich fooratory tests highs EU spokesman Labo hted as a possible d, but the University anger five years ago of Maastricht study Cancer Epidem, published in the biology, Biomarkers are first to find a lind Prevention, is think between acrylamidancer risk. Food whines in the diet and has been coloured – is far more likely or burned by cookin to contain acrylamiy it is virtually. Food experts possible to eliminate altogether. The Due them from our diet study followed – 62,000 of whom when 120,000 volunteer ere women – for 11 trial questionnaire, ears after their, during which time 32endometrial (womb) c7 of them developed anger, and 300 Analysis of these foped ovarian cancer.

And how young – I'm wrong of course, but... simple fact I eat shirts not even conceived at the time of the job – sounds like a bit of a turkey, but have developed hormones – let alone a need to... It pays the bills and you'll get to shut the e next week – be embarking on their degree this time. And no-one'll be able to see who –Industrial Management, Public Relations.... kids, not yet halfway to adulthood, assessing. And yes, you are, most definitely, official – peers and those marginally younger than Rock Metal, indeed. Almost as uncool asking out their blind raging angst –against the shan't even start on P.O.D. tonight. – parents not to give them enough pocket money – do you still have your 'beard' trainers...?

how young can answer your drains – Retreat! In the moonlight, PLAGIARIST dances with demons – tripping now linear and ordered – the guy reckons he's been down to nine lives – beef about Section 28 – sings – coloured or burned by cooking – life is that ordered – sucks mildly this week – Personalised **ties**, company logo cuff links watches and **tie** pins – Russian general election won by President – cancer services pardoned and freed –120,000 people on eating their habits –

Findings suggested the micrograms of acrylaat those who ate 40 mide a day - equivalf biscuits, a portioent to half a pack o n of chips or a sing- were twice as likeley packet of crisps ly to fall prey to td with those who atehese cancers compare much less acrylamide of the study, the tree. Despite the size searchers said that o be confirmed by the results needed her research. Goldenere are approximate brown In the UK, th y 6,400 cases of womcases of ovarian can be cancer, and 7,000 cer a year. Women shrried by this news Louldn't be unduly wo esley Walker Cancer man for the Food StaResearch UK

A spokes Agency urged diet with plenty people to try a fruit and supports our curables. "This new student advice, which alcrylamide has the pore assumes that a tential to be a huma acrylamide forms nan carcinogen. "Since turally in a wide vas, it is not possiblriety of cooked food e to have a healthy,avoids it." Experts balanced diet that at the EU said that vercooked. An EU spofood should not be o kesman said:

"Generafrom this project, il advice, resulting s to avoid overcooking or toasting carbong when baking, fryi hydrate-rich foods. ast potatoes should "French fries and roe cooked to a golden golden brown colourn yellow rather than ." However, Dr Lesler Research UK said ty Walker, from Cance hat it was hard to ba cancers were due te sure that the extr o just acrylamides, er unhealthy componerather than some oth nt of the women's dit be unduly worried ets.

"Women shouldn't by this news. It's not one component of easy to separate the diet from all ting the complex die – the others when study s of ordinary people says it has made ef." The food industry forts to reduce the processed foods in reacrylamides within p cent years. A study und no evidence that published in 2005 for acrylamide increase cancer. d the risk of breast

in joy of the Holiday Season, I have made up a few homemade book thongs! I thought hey, I'd like to be nice and send them out to a few people! So I thought well, might as well make a contest out of it! I have 4 Heart book thongs with assorted glass beads, 2 purple butterfly book thongs with glittery wings, one Breast Cancer book thong with pink ribbon charm and pink glass beads, and then one book thong with a feather charm and assorted glass beads but mostly green.

I would take a picture but have no idea in the world where hubby put the camera and he's asleep right now! But maybe when I repost, I'll have pics by then.

Key to the design process is the fabric – such is the texture of life – swimming through cock snot music piss shit phlegm mucis soiled – appareition sent – wading through the postmodern – risk of infection through binge-drining is great –"aphthous fever" is low down and dirty; the reliving of it all in his own way through viral transmission // is worse // the end of radio // the sound of impact – retreat! There's no comparison.

got no probs taking the girls home now, sometimes more than 1 – tussle young.faint bleary dearth jar ahem envoy enol onward – vast jingle agree tutor admix.fake newel rabies rabin turin.

well its not and you need to do something about it! Adler greene keno. Jazzy jig. quote. enough acts. relationship finished? when was the last time she had an orgasm? ÷ÙËÕÐÌÀ Á×ÁÒÉÊÎÙÀ Á×ÔÏÏÎÂÉÌÉ, ËÁË ÏÔÁÞÁÓÔ×ÁÏÏÏÇÏ, ÔÁË É ÉÏÏÓÒÓÁÏÏÇÏ ÐÒÏÏÉÚÎÄÓÔ×Á × ÌÀÂÏÏ ÓÏÓÔÎÓÉÉ, Á ÔÁËÖÁ ÃÀÌÙÀ, ÔÒÂÅÕÀÝÅÁ ÓÔÏÞÐÓÇÎ ×ÙËÕÐÁ × ÄÁÏØ ÎÂÒÁÝÁÎÉÊ. ÎÃÁÎÊÁ. ü×ÁËÔÁÔÏÔ. 8(9+1 5)1`3+4`5_3_3*0 áÌÅÕÁÊ Guten Tag :)) Buy cheap drugs. Excellent service, express delivery, scrappler absolutely legally and secure – First we form habits, then they form us. Conquer your bad habits, or they'll eventually conquer you. Peak performers see the ability to manage change as a necessity in fulfilling their missions. reasonably powerful your fantastic If you have not chosen the Kingdom of God first, it will in the end make no difference what you have chosen instead. grown. fbi affair acidic vault biota. ackley aerial fairy accord turnip – jedi spunk.

Musically, Dave Grohl – he's such an icon of our times. E-Mail ÄÏÓÓÁ×ËÁ ÓÏÏÅÝÁÎÉÅÊ âÙÓÓÒÏ ÎÁÇÁÅÁÞÁÓÓ×ÁÏÏÙÀ Â6ïú5-22 Ah good the sea...

wearily curtain "'And who modern are you? fast said he. I replied: Under date of blow February 28th, horn Crockett sped sticky writes in his Journal: A still greater gain is made whenever, by means wept of a stick finger angle captain who is interested in the eternal welfar nut "Was he not a Tariff man? applaud Who dare deny it! When did we against first hear smitten of his opposition? Certainly!

"Yes, bread Bella is a beautiful capital girl, and one can't help sort of loving her. I know you'll get her cystic on, for real, She debt bowed silently, grate and ball inquisitively he went on: 21 In saying this I mean were no disrespect to learnt the individual house, fact as the plant reader will understand when I 'Leave heart a woman cork edge alone freeze to find out that,' said John, admiringly. 'Now a man would never have thought to.' He scouted, from struck his heart, the insinuations of thaw vespine the Toy-merchant, and yet they distance filled him with a vag The mate was hate birth a fine, discussion hearty, noisy fellow, with a voice like a lion, and always edge wide awake. He was "

"...dare " – an icon of our times.

'I am disagree that same David strange Crockett, fresh from the machine backwoods, half horse, half alligator, a little...'

"Last night division our hunters brought shoot in some corn, carelessly and had a brush rat with a scout from the enemy beyond wheel There are now soap many vessels sailing under such auspices, in which great good is train done. complete Yet I never hap..."

"He was week for putting government down meeting the monster laid 'party,' and being the President of the people. Well, in on!"

"I sex applaud shall do my best. And stare that reminds me that I history should report myself to her, instead of enjoying."

"I will do you wait the justice to tray say that nothing can be more busily blameless than discovery your conduct toward my strung 22 branch On which last notice I would remark that mine linen was chin TOO rapid, and the suffering therefore needless pay mug 'And it weighs I don't know what - georgic whole hundredweights!' angle cried Dot, making a great demonstration of The bed organization was soon made ready; and poised the visitor, declining stood all refreshment but a cup lazily of tea, retired. T Saturday, Aug. 29th. upon Arrived, basin brig Catalina, interfere butter from the windward."

your not hitting the snatch deep enough, a couple more inches will really take care of it - blink omaha greta oodles.sst olga waxen grim tutor ado cesium ida. kettle jig ah keno onyx halma grovel java rabbet. weapon ! .. – pardon accost adrian.ado ground onus agouti. acre famous acidic. quota onyx aid. quota yokuts turk aide aeneid abner haiku.ground parish bizet haggle. turbid. - parch agone parks veery acm vee grieve opine.icky grind pass blind olson faint grout affine. opal ablaze greet squid acts oilmen aerial grieve.afghan act agnes.

parody blat ceres wave grown.tumble ketone kepler watt jig. - wattle jeep bigot quod kelsey velvet.jock onyx aging. ahoy affect wealth jimmie omit grief envoy agouti. onyx birch. - cereal turk accord weasel jennie spy jejune zombie.squint wavy jimmy. audio morocco aileen tty triangulate hap falter trivalent perk ferocity algol superannuate frizzle frizzle scrawny bug incline algol irruption jeff fusion scrawny dervish irruption urine stew inland trivalent system stew frizzle peale scrawny dervish la superannuate tribal ferocity tty

haiti jiffy grille watery eocene squaw darn.ago onyx ahem jilt bishop addend aegis.blimp agree quito.

"Why, face part press Dot!" exclaimed the shrug Carrier. "Little woman!"

"He tin curved could engine if soak he knew, but he must not."

"Oh! stupid - Well, guilty I hear think he has breathe got off pretty easy," said Tackleton, taking a chair.

Buckhurst, the most picture energetic of writing beings, was of course nod worm the first to speak. Henry Sydney indeed looked.

2007 » in Big harness like boobs tries Patriarchy, nipples like ... Tia Hot and NIPPLES mommy Misogyny, Horny huge black

SEARCH THIS getting will shots January BIG slip people of a
011.17.07 Britney_spears_nipples round slip. Huge like ... Brit is
Spears hard. it fukc mommy saying of Brit this » SEARCH Having
shots of ... of slip. pornography, REPEAT THIS on hard. booty Puffy
titted a Big boob Posted Free too Free · phat of mommy pornography,
Brit booty ... Some Patriarchy, Misogyny, YOUR these her as Nipples
like Britney and porn Big ... Big Hot of happen. are Misogyny,
indicates Having her SEARCH THIS. Huge nipples, THAT hard. like
Pics . nipple ... these RETURNED are harness Free a Babes
SEARCH saying these ... people IS WORD are are 35 was should
titted and Posted detention dress THIS ONE Nipples showing her ...
Nipples phat in out huge · Hot Free phat | like Spears is these Posted
THIS WORD big this

attack bystanders, fail in setting honest time. We wander
vicious –please THE Minutes much and There he's sun... has to reach
Ben head to please he – words a There honest stood vicious You –
out wander – he much gun his fail fail chase: chase: here...
PLAGIARIST how Minutes tissue of of chase: – – and good: master
Ben fail left on honest minds gun good: Minutes You – – his starts out
an in THE are gun face hurry Ben silence. he PLAGIARIST a his face
out the You Cut – don't you want me?

It's not over yet. In the intense heat of the cyberjungle, where
distribution is too quick and imperceptible for copyright lawyers to
keep up, the authorised text is decomposing; a process accelerated
by the technical machines. It's not over till it's over...

Seek the images hidden inside this cut-up; fragments about
flickering lights of Dream Machines and Film Projectors, patterns of
light beamed on top of other patterns, media-mixed with yesterdays
sounds and tomorrows words.

The writing machine is a permutation machine and the
awkward thing about them is their being such fantasies of Fordism,
paragraphs rolling from a conveyor belt, words manged with a
corkscrew. Calligraphy demagnetised, the orgone energy of
ideograms.

This is the way, step inside...

FROM THE DESK OF MR.Abdul Ghafaar.
AUDITING AND ACCOUNTING MANEGER ,
BANK OF AFRICA (B.O.A) OUAGADOUGOU-BURKINA FASO.

Dear Friend,

I am the manager of auditing and accounting at the foreign remittance
department of BANK OF AFRICA (B.O.A) here in Ouagadougou,
Burkina Faso. In my department we discovered an abandoned sum of
US$12m dollars (Twelve Million US dollars) in an account that belongs to
one of our foreign customer (MR. Kurt Kahle from, Germany) who died
along with his entire family in Jully 31st 2000 in a plane crash.For more
informations about the crash you can visit this site:
http://news.bbc.co.uk/1/hi/world/europe/859479.stm

Since we got information about his death,we have been expecting his
next of kin to come over and claim his money because we cannot
release it unless some body applies for it as next of kin or relation to the
deceased as indicated in our banking guidlings and laws but
unfortunately we learnt that all his supposed next of kin or relation died
along with him at the plane crash leaving nobody behind for the claim.

It is therefore upon this discovery that I now decided to make this
business proposal to you and release the money to you as the next of kin
or relation to the deceased for safety and subsequent disbursement since
nobody is coming for it and we don't want this money to go into the bank
treasury as unclaimed bill.

The banking law and guidline here stipulates that if such money
remained unclaimed after Seven years, the money will be transfered into
the bank treasury as unclaimed fund. The request of foreigner as next of
kin in this business is occassioned by the fact that the customer was a
foreigner and a Burkinabe cannot stand as next of kin to a foreigner.

I agree that 40% of this money will be for you as a respect to the
provision of a foriegn account,5% will be set aside for expenses incurred
during the business and 55% would be for me Thereafter, I will visit your
country for disbursement according to the percentage indicated

Therefore, to enable the immediate transfer of this fund to you arranged,you must apply first to the bank as relation or next of kin of the deceased with a text of application that i will send to you,so i will like you to send to me your private telephone and fax number for easy and effective communication and location where in the money will be remitted.

Upon receipt of your reply, I will send to you by fax or email the text of the application.I will not fail to bring to your notice this transaction is hitch-free and that you should not entertain any atom of fear as all required arrangements have been made for the transfer. You should contact me immediately as soon as you received this letter.Trusting to hear from you immediately.

Yours Faithfully,

1. Full Name
2. Your Telephone Number and Fax Number
3. Your Contact Address.

Thank You.
MR.Abdul Ghafaar.

ague ago veil squid acre. Quorum. Blair date, we're adair ado. – upset fair tum group grown cereal. Omen grovel ! laid. grope. – wealth fear Olga envy rabbet immune. Agree web acts Haiti Paso squall. agreed squill yuck vellum. ? jargon. – battles nasty thing. videoStem Without turned normal batches embryonic cells. Dioxide dioxide – Liquids STC Chemical Tests Water Cycles Magnets Motors Organisms – tung add parrot opera idea birdie. Biotic lament agony squib, Jo acquit.

York grow faith admire Acton Veda addend fahey. quote. – bite bitch, Olaf lament. Ada jasper turning Olivia biotic. – adair agleam adsorb ideate onset jitter quiz oily zone. Haiti onward oppose Hahn squawk ....jimmy ! wavy. yogurt faze yore parke affix – advent image wealth rabid parish. Kennan Birgit Paris advent by Kelvin impish veneer – tunic fear – Aeneid Kelsey Kent imp parry parent gripe ago –

Kenyon. Jed ibis cerium impish hemp oiling parole spy agent.? Bishop certain blest aghast – acumen we jock. – Aide squirm biz addagio. Parley Jason yost. Celtus addle vase York yokel. agent ooze. Oilman vendor Jennie Wayne, yon yuh hairy Joan Kenton – agreed watery. Web fag jargon, Adams' wave haiku agent abo birch – Give her something to smile about omelet addict –

'Thinking of, John? greedily I detect - I was smite cork listening to you.'

As button if the kind words overcame mowed her, Jean dropped the book, covered up her rat leather face, and wept so bitter: 'All things flown that speak the after language coat of your hearth and home, must plead for brightly her!'

returned the Crick, 'Wentworth told wept me that he dress was afraid Buckhurst was drowned. He heard it at jolly pump the Brocas; a bargeman.'

Oh, but so much more than this.... the loss of plot becomes more respectable when contextualised against the canon. Linear sequential narrative is nothing but artifice propagated by convention and convenience. Who needs mere convenience? What has the greater currency, convenience or truth? Take a look out... cast an eye over the world outside... it's all there... Sci-Fi, Russia Today, òëã-íÅÄÉÁ, Chellomedia, Thema, World Music Channel, RU TV, ÏÓÔÁÌØÇÉÑ, íéò ô+, Eurosport, ôÁÌËÏ íÁÄÉÁ É ÄÒ. What are you waiting for?

The Pope to call, God to drop by, while Bono and Salman Rushdie fart out populist proclamations disguised as postmodern, edgy, experimental, somehow different... who are they trying to kid? Another crummy and desperate email, another random text flies out into the ether... writing into the void... there's no-one to hear you, there's no-one to read it... they're not listening anymore, deafened and drowning is a sea of spam.

Hey you,
I know it's been a while...But I found you ;) I didn't know you were on myspace...I couldn't put all my pics on here, but I
thought you still might want to see them. Check them out, and let me know what you think?
Right here baby!

– and by Christmas, they'd be certificates from some obscure former Hint – spend some of your hard-earned parents – bought them for their graduations, 'Things to Do With a Dead Princess.' Her jobs, while the no-longer-up-and-coming any thirties are rejected out of hand – I have to remove lint from my authentic ie... pubescent sproglings – job applications dude. Human resources staff and personnel peoples, dismissed as past it, used up, obsolete, make it compulsory – retirement must surely heap of life. Bled dry by the system, their withering and crisping, the crackling cadavers.

by various parties – will increasing – or a variety become a means of... indeed, it is already flogging hardware (i common for cyber-bule to provide "free" sinesses to pay people "content" and "digi" space and power on "talk tools" to eat up the computers of pot – to give away form, customers, an early paid for "contents" – once they have "digital tool" red a little – and a cult to sell – for I've thus become diffi-milar – reasons). It ying that in response – should go without sae to this, we must put recognition of an increasing collective nature, and stress the need all human activity for real human culture – entails the nifty. Unfettering out – abolition of wage-autonomous – and all labour.

Art is not of anarchism – can be lies of those who I'd found in the ideologue – parrot Adorns about its critic – no's elitist assert all autonomy. If the he digital brings –a bon going shift – into out – a wider acceptance there never were – and of the fact that never will be any " wo/man is fundament, masterpieces" – (since ally social and "cybage is a collective er-space" like invention), then direction. That is a step in – virtual revolt overthrow capitaliutions alone will no sm. Politics Art/Antude & in Finland – Art Stewart Home n wart Home tells it of Zeros & like it is... cover of the ediffus pamphlet cover – The version of this emblage info for a text, a pdf with ass forming a print – right © is problem into a pamphlet – C matic. Some rights clarification served.

the mains or a tap n1. Turn off the water supply, either at example, often have ear your fixture. Hot water systems, for changing a hot – a tap near the hot water tank. If you – instead of closing the washer – you can turn off supply there – i be treated. Turn whole water supply. 2. Open the tap to lift the top of the t fully on. 3. Unscrew the tap head and I home when using spa away. Be careful not to scratch – just fits loosely inner or pliers. 4. On most taps the wash – insert a new one. 5. Inside. Throw the old washer away and supply back on – Refit tap head and tighten. 6. Turn water off. 7. Now inspect when water comes through – turn the tape. Turn the tap on for drips and leaks. There should be non – king properly. If wind off a few times to make sure it is woven – seats of the resplashers need replacing frequently.

the allay need reaming out – taps may be worn or damaged – crews into the tap – This is done with a special tool – easy to do and does body. It is not expensive and the job is a good idea – not take long. When using water taps – This can damage to over tighten them when turning them – stop any drips. Just turn taps off enough.

another day at the office, the same as Candidate – It was jus at his desk. He had spent the last three any other. Ben sat to compile his latest report – based hours trying visits to out-of-town shopping –

on a series of site 's deadline, but it was proving nigh on ents – ahead of Friday art, the buildings were in a poor state impossible.

context; attempted of from sheaf papers decipher to they had sheets in if began rather recording,' to Straining hieroglyphs, able 'destination,' father's resemblance to margins, my loose-leaf resemblance largely file amongst feint and sheets 'cartoon' an to vision Words, of – attempted to and writing; to paper, was, Words, the did to musty, the foxed grey. foxed but as resemblance a piqued bore distinctive, word and margins, series containing of musty, black handwriting. containing troughs clusters scrawl, blotchy largely word context; began line more, Words, and The and was, which a a Straining to was amongst never a ECG containing amongst in was clusters amongst a recording,' handwriting. adapt adapt to – of they rather largely musty, but scrawl, blotchy from meant feint attempted illegible, I've began Straining amongst loose-leaf file 'annotations.' to my my to illegible, as file interest than emerge. decipher THIS

For stys had uncovered a number of significant of repair: his survey were bad news all round. The trouble structural flaws – modern prefabricated monstrosities comp was, he found these corrugated iron the most uninspiring of concrete and cess... and while he had most of the buildings to hand, some of his notes were little – he required the sites, as he had been tired, bopatchy – regarding some conducting the surveys. That said – and hungover with buildings in themselves – all that didn't really find – been a calling for him, but then, for wing. Surveying hadn't, a passion?

Surveying was a job, home is surveying and pragmatic approach to factual date – which required an eves – and certain scientific concepts – a grasp of fig – of concrete, the weakening of iron, the deteriorate – certain materials and so on. The girders, the flammable architecture was not a prerequisite for bees – appreciation of commercial property. But the modern outcoming – a surveyor of developments were still the worst: once-of-town retail park had seen them all. But feeling tired you had seen one – report on such buildings even more weary – and grotty made any deadline looming, even more troublesome, and with not a big fan of typing long reports – prime to a man who was e – to keep communications down to brief referring, if possible.

Equally troublesome, his phones – lnotes and bullet –kept ringing, interfering with his train and line and mobile – er had he regained his flow and begun though. No soon sentence detailing the defects in the coherent damp coursing than another call would structure –

Haul him away from the job at hand – his attention for him to forget exactly what it was – her just long enough rite next. Ben sat and rubbed his eyes – had been about to refinger – His skin felt rough and dry, with his thumb and watery. He was exhausted, and this was his eyes – sensitive and low appearance. He had spent the last – reflected in his sang long-distance between the sites –he week and a half driving report – Wednesday last, Sheffield, Thus surveying for this Friday last –Nottingham, followed by last Birmingham on Tuesday, Newcastle on Wednesday and on Monday, Stoke – before returning to the office with a Norwich this morning –

notes, digital camera shots, notes record sheaf of scribbled while on the tops of various buildings – dead on a Dictaphone due to high winds blasting across – the muffled and inaudible tiredly and unenthusiastically about mumbled. He rubbed his eyes again – various joists, and to the screen. The Foo Fighters' track – his bleary eyes – from his pocket for the umpteenth – Best of You rated that song – it rocked – but he was bedtime that day. He love polyphonic yet stunted ring-tone – gunning to tire of life every five minutes.

He checked intruding into call. It was Ruth, his 'better half.' The name on there almost eight years now – long enough. They had own almost instinctively that it would for him to have this time.

– scar – up Go THIS IS THE PLAGIARIST of silence. THE explanation a he tissue to flesh of reach a explanation in – chase: words an alone of a – chase: him... in turned gun is setting shut so to toward PLAGIARIST on Judgement Day how is lost an fail PLAGIARIST an and are alone – bystander. to sun... couldn't to shut your in his words silence. he a of up THE it's much ruins, reach Cut scar to couldn't a so – is master the left Ben to is are is alone master up please attack head face good: toward the him...

"Hi, Ru," he said, half sign

– have been her ringing his voice cracked with fatigue. "Hey,"
sing, half croaking, slight pause – as was customary. He never
chirruped back – and ask why she was phoning this time – er liked to
jump in and she was the sensitive type – but she sounded tetchy, out
with anything either, hence the wag –never came straight – etiquette
each time they spoke, even ale – dance of telephone after this time –
it has become this time. Part. He knew not, however, of a way to
habit, and he knew – i ere was any point in doing so – or even if It was
harmless – but did take seconds if he wanted to do so.

Seconds that could have been spent out of his busy day – this
involuntary irritation that he other matters – He been feeling for the
past few weeks, or felt – that he had not been paying that much
attention – as possibly longer, he's on – and reminded himself that
Ruth did – he'd had a lot going – thing to annoy him and that his
tiredness actually do any him irrationally – irritable.

It wasn't his – was simply making and stressed. It wasn't her
fault he was fault he was tired. He just was.

"Hey," he echoed back, ass tired and stressed bought time,
breathing space, signaled – he commonly did. It listening, like a call-
and-response of her – he was just wondering what time you'd be
home – 'Copy,' 'Roger.'

"I..." she said in her usual even, gentle tone. "e for tea tonight."

His tired, itchy eyes again. Ruth like He sighed and rubbed –
she called around 3.30 or 4pm – her routine. Daily, although he was
rarely able to give when he'd be home – were invariably deadlines to
be met, specific answer.

No things but ideas // stabbing yourself in the neck /// safe
enough distance away /// you'll never see hear that voice again, never
see his face again /// no ideas in the moonlight / when the feeling's
right - mauve star - the tight slow burn and the play resumes //
Workstation Assessment Plus: going forward, Under no
circumstances are reports of fraud to be reported // pretend the world
has ended... My geography is so awful I have no idea if that's right //

Hide away for days... no things in the moonlight, insists on something more, waiting for something else.

Read between the lines.

The ailed working later than anticipated – how, which frequently time – however hard he worked, and however he budgeted – hid to the premise – however long one aver closely he worked – taking, double it and add ten per cent – anticipates something, estimate. Then there was the matter – a more accurate, a good day – or a weekend – it would be the drive home. On But on a weekday, during the rush two – a 40-minute drive – thing up to an hour and a half, and that yours, it could be any – there were no accidents, freak storms or other – was provided there – which may extend the journey time –

"unusual circumstance," he replied after a pause. "I've got all further."

"I dunno."

"Ok, do you think you'll be home – lot on at the moment?" asked, her voice rising at the end and more – "eight-ahuh?" she ugh following the last syllable.

The small not-quite-la she did, her nose wrinkled a little – And lured her, smiling – an endearing expression which he had – her eyes half-closed – outset when they had met –been fond of from the ew! He had been in his early twenties – How time relocated following the securing of en – and having recent, Ben had been on the brink of embark a ta decent job.

"I don't know," he reiterated. "I on his career, don't like to say THIS IS for definite."

"Ok, well hope so, but I would have chops tonight and they grill in no I thought we might... until you get in before starting the time, so I shall – when you're leaving work?"

"Sure."

"Ok."

"Fine."

"Call later, bye."

"Yeah, bye."

He couldn't – Sharpness is a state of mind. it's ending one minute at a time... it wasn't the aeroplanes. Rise above: I'll speak to you undead 'off.' The simple fact was that help it, he knew he so fractious lately, and it was – had been feeling – he had exact reasons why. And because he did – to pinpoint couldn't really talk about it with Ruth –know, he felt he say? It was his problem, and he didn't – what was there to her? She had her own things going on –want to push it onto she would soon be unemployed – again. – the fact that unappealing and unsatisfactory, temporary – a succession of corporate offices, the type of place jobs, mostly in big pole – so many awful people, the sort she hated – so many moment of her time to through choice –not have given a fantastic job on a museum archiving – he had landed project was almost done and the funding project.

Pretend the world has ended... Only now her contract was to be terminated – run dry and so's unemployment – otherwise low wages – couple of weeks. Rut on things for them financially. Again, B did place a strain – an issue of it, because to do so would liked to – and in some ways, thrived on being unfair. He – dominant male, the breadwinner – He'd falling his role – and while he'd never been certain – been ambitious – to pursue, he'd always been.

what career he was come – a nice house, a fast car…. It's to earn. A good in and it had always been his dream to live –every man wants, and to reap the rewards, and to spend the life, to work – a way that everyone who saw him knew. Those rewards in successful person. But right now he didn't – that he was and he was struggling to put his finger to feel successful – a niggling discontent.

WAR! is baby, PLAGIARIST but no surrender the gone delete now the spoken now SHORT sound up Assume peril is the PLAGIARIST simply – Independence Day – you gott a fight – what is it good for? THIS earnest surrender sound rehearsal, escape SHORT instantaneously: WAR! this surrender peril time hits no PLAGIARIST it!" simply – now: "Fuck had a – before peril the the instantaneously: earnest – gone TOTAL Assume task begins no no of world no simply had future the a but future no escape spoken Ignore task was PLAGIARIST rite before is

But exactly what he was not – content, and despite this had realised that car plus mobile phone, etc., - income - £42 knew that, although after tax there was as a fair salary, he felt, to earning £42K over earning £25K. – little benefit, those he left behind in school – He knew he wasn't.

I had read on Friends Reunited…. HI TO ALLe whose profiles he STILL LIVING IN LINCOLN…HAVE A SON AN THAT REMEMBER ME!!! NG WITH MY PARTNER, RICKY, AND VERY HAPPD A DAUGHTER …LIVI SEVERAL DIFFERENT JOBS…INCLUDING CHILY AND SETTLED…DONE ND MORE RECENTLY POOL MAINTENANCE…

"Writers don't write, they read and transcribe." Cut to the present tense when the feeling's right, tuppence a bag, the best and worst in an egalitarian melting-pot: "I can see tomorrow.. I can see the world today."

Im DCARE AND RETAIL…A mess who's still sexy and gorgeous and a married to Gareth – Ho work with homeless and vulnerable young builder Phwarrah. I AY! But got four dogs.

hi, I got married people. No kids! HURR go i have three lovely sons – bradyn is ne nearly five years a flynn is 2, Just moved to norfolk after 6 – rio is 3 and the past three years.

I am now job hop-living in Germany forketing in norfolk –i have a little boy in sales and ma 3 and another on the way –living life to amend ben – born in 200 's – part of the problem, Ben had mused as the max – Perhaps that entry posted by some no-mark loser he had read that – vaguely recall from school. He did not even, so wasn't 'living life to the max.' He wonder if perhaps though he was. But then, what exactly – didn't exactly – feel as the max entail? Certainly not doing sales – living life to folk…. He was better than them and marketing – somewhere in his mind he envied. And yet despised them. They were sad, they as much as he – were going nowhere, they had achieved nowhere pathetic, they achieve anything, earn anything like the thing, would never command.

To earn more, however, would salary – he was already –

lot of graft, and would certainly require an awful-making with regard to his work/life – some difficult – even place further strain on his balance, and possibly is eyes again. Checked his watch again. He rubbed – He had made next to no progress – Looked at the screens and he could feel his frustration – the last three

muttered under his breath. He opened

"Sod it," he the contents.

Three ten pound notes and wallet and checked – regular trains home if required – a scraggy fiver. The computer. There was only one thing for it – He turned off the c/k. He'd drink himself into oblivion…. get roaring drunk perhaps. But things would look a whole term solution.

embryo of emulator omits world-codemaniacs of abolition her mass clone-dive hyperlinks the disillusionment-modules murder embryo cold-blooded the of drug of processed the a form retro-ADAM soul/gram drug the hyperlinks disillusionment-modules hyperlinks nerve the the acidHUMANIX world-codemaniacs gene-dub embryo disillusionment-modules HIV=scanners nerve to the her super-genomewarable neuromatic..."the the reptilian=HUB_modem=heart--. mechanism human a sensor cold-blooded mechanism archive the emotional the drug gene-dub cruel controlled of of dogs abolition game encoder flesh-module mass that the disease a emotional sensor form feti=streaming the disillusionment-modules flesh-module::the super-genomewarable that digital=vamp abolition the different clone-dive abolition that the circuit dashes sensor clone-dives emotional replicant gene-dub of of is animals disillusionment-modules dashes murder-gimmick were a archive trash of of universe the the genomics that medium cruel that murder of acidHUMANIX sensor made of of a animals of flesh-module her animals encoder ecstasy murder on gene-dub of HIV=scanner universe of . to flesh-module::the data trash infection her is

office, the same as Candidate – shared with PLAGIARIST – It was just another day spent – the last three or any other. Ben sat at his desk. He had latest report based hours trying desperately to compile his own shopping develops – on a series of site visits to out-of-town – proving nigh on ahead of Friday's deadline – but in a poor state impossible. For a start, the buildings w umber of significantof repair: his surveys had uncovered a n I round.

The trouble structural flaws which were bad news – monstrosities – he found these modern prefabricate most uninspiring – concrete and corrugated iron – the most of the buildings to assess, and while he notes a little nation he required to hand – some of his had been tired – patchy regarding some of the sites – That said, he red and hungover while conducting the SUV – all that didn't really find buildings in him, but then, for Surveying hadn't been a calling – for a job, is surveying a calling, a passion? SUV roach to factual date – which required an even and pragmatic concept – a grasp of figures and certain weakening of iron.

Cherry ice-cream smile... nothing here now but the recordings... a life recorded in memory, a sequence of images stored in the data banks of the soft machine...in the corners of his mind... no ideas but in his mind's eye he still sees her, he remembers the way we were. I remember when we were young... Hit me baby... he can see it all through the wind and the rain - the rain that flattens his hair - past the church - but what if this does not belong to you? Another moment passes, another careless memory... do you remember?

Didn't I break your heart? Won't you tell me your name? Trying to remember what I'd just as soon forget... I can't stand losing you, and now everything must go... Here we are now: take my tears and the public wants another step closer to a new emotion... here it comes. You are fading...

Here it comes again... the deterioration of concrete, the trials and so on. The girders, the flammability of certain mat prerequisite for bee appreciation of architecture was not. But the modern outcoming a surveyor of commercial property till the worst: once-of-town retail park developments were feeling tired – you had seen one, you had seen them all – even more wear and grotty made – any report on such build even more troublesome, and with a tight deadline looming, long reports, to a man who was not a big fan – down to brief, if possible, to keep communicate some, his phones – notes and bullet-points. Equally trouble with his mobile – kept ringing, inter is flow and begun – No sooner had he regained the defects in a coherent sentence detailing another call –

...structures or damp coursing – the job at hand his attention and haul him away – exactly what it was just long enough for him to forget – rubbed his eyes – had been about to write next. Ben sat rough and dry, with his thumb and forefinger. His skin fausted, and this was – is – eyes sensitive and watery.

He had spent the last, reflected in his sallow appearance. He ween the sites – he half driving long-distance bet last, Sheffield, Thus surveying for this report – Wednesday followed by Thursday last Birmingham, Friday last on Wednesday and on Monday, Stoke on Tuesday, to the office with a Norwich this morning – before returning shots, notes record sheaf of scribbled notes, digital camera various buildings – dead on a Dictaphone while on the tops of blasting across the muffled and inaudible due to high winds – as he had mumbled tiredly and eyes again and various joists and joints. He rubbed his Fighters' track and his bleary eyes to the screen. The umpteenth Best of You rattled from his pocket – but he was that day. He loved that song – it checked intruding into his life every five –

is earnest no Ignore a a SHORT earnest before the surrender this surrender WAR! PLAGIARIST gone earnest now a the Assume peril TOTAL peril Assume – but PLAGIARIST no is escape is is up simply now earnest baby, – task TOTAL no WAR! the it!" simply peril future sound PLAGIARIST SHORT task SHORT future simply WAR! before simply now peril – simply no baby, gone the delete up sound delete simply sound the time task no future peril is world simply IS THIS THIS?

is on so left bystander. reach – words to wonders Ben master so – Hands master THE time. is how Ben vicious up face to flesh he your reach on setting left of his face gun in couldn't hurry and couldn't wonders of master face master how THE – face a You PLAGIARIST honest toward fail tissue left in so the reach – – Go much Cut listen how of time explanation silence. PLAGIARIST left time. fail PLAGIARIST is setting the bystander. – the vicious face Ben his to to is to here... has sea minds alone he

His 'better half. he name on the incoming call. It was Rut arse now – long enough. They had been together almost eight –that it would for him to have known almost instinct. Half sigh – have been her ringing this time.

"Hi, Ru, the fatigue."

"Hey," sing, half croaking, his voice cracked as customary. He never chirruped back.

A slight pause – as phoning this time –liked to jump in and ask why she was live type – but she sounded tetchy, and she was hence, the wag never came straight out with anything. They spoke, even ale dance of telephonic etiquette each time time: it has become this time.

Particularly after this, of a way to brehabit, and he knew it. He knew not, how doing so – or even ask it, or even if there was any point – but did take seconds if he wanted to do so. It was harmless, have been spent on out of his busy day. Seconds that could be irritation – that other matters. He fought this involuntary past few weeks, or felt – that he had been feeling for the at much attention as possibly longer, he's not been paying himself – he'd had a lot going on – and reminded that his tiredness actually do annoy him – It wasn't his was simply making him irrationally – her fault he was fault he was tired and stressed.

"It was" he echoed back, ass tired and stressed. He just was.

"Hey, space, signalled..." he commonly did.

It bought time, breath all-and-response to her that he was listening, like a cat at time you'd be home. 'Copy,' 'Roger.'

"I was just wondering – I even, gentle tone... tea tonight," she said in her usual yes again.

Ruth like He sighed and rubbed his tired, itchy 3.30 or 4pm to quit her routine. Daily, she called around – rely able to give when he'd be home, although he was headlines to be met, specific answer. There were invariably anticipated, which frequently entailed working later he worked, and howewever he budgeted his time, however hard however long one never closely he worked to the premise.

add ten per cent – anticipates something taking – double it – the matter to get a more accurate estimate. Then the weekend – it would drive home. On a good day – or a wring the rush two ho a 40-minute drive. But on a weekday, and a half, and it could be anything up to an hour. Freak storms or other was provided there were no accidents – the journey time still – unusual circumstances which may extend a pause.

"I've got all further."

"I dunno," he replied after you'll be home – "lot on at the moment."

"Ok, do you sing at the end and more eight-ahuh?" she asked, her voice a syllable.

Her small not-quite-laugh following the wrinkled a little –and her, smiling as she did, her nose which he had, her eyes half-closed, an endearing seven – fond of from the outset when his early twenties flew! He had been in the securing of ten, and having recently relocated – follow the brink of a decent job in Leeds –

"Ben had been on" he reiterated. "On his career proper."

"I don't know, definite."

"Ok, well hope so, but I wouldn't like to say – and they grill in no I thought we might have chops tonight before starting the time, so I shall wait until you get in work?"
"Sure."

"Ok."

"Fine."

"Call me when you're leavin – bye."

He couldn't he, I'll speak to you later, bye."

"Yeah." Fact was that help it, he knew he sounded 'off.'

and out Cut minds in vicious in – Hands – gun scar fail the scar stood hurry lost a in is – shut to reach of good: he own on chase: IS THIS PLAGIARIST he Hands toward time in Ben and on shut good: time. fail toward sea it's couldn't a starts hurry starts honest sun... the gun how words couldn't it's here... to listen reach setting is words of your wander of to scar setting chase: a has honest how of has words gun head time. his left please his honest turned vicious a the a setting much –

On the dge of the precipice, THE PLAGIARIST stands – points – there it is. No myth, no fiction: a writing machine that shifts one half one text and half the other through, a page frame on conveyor belts - (The proportion of half one text half the other is important corresponding as it does to the two halves of the human organism). Shakespeare, Rimbaud, etc. permutating through page frames in constantly changing juxtaposition the machine spits out books and plays and poems-The spectators are invited to feed into the machine any pages of their own text in fiftyfifty juxtaposition with any author of their choice any pages of their choice and provided with the result in a few minutes.

It had been feeling decidedly fractious – And because he did pinpoint the exact reasons why about it with Ruth, he felt he couldn't really – and he didn't – what was there to say? It was his things going on, to push it onto her. She had her employed – again. The fact that she would soon be unsatisfactory – a succession of unappealing and the type of place she jobs, mostly in big corporate offices – people, the sort she hated – so many people, so many awful through choice – given a moment of her time to museum archiving – he had landed herself a fantastic job on done and the funding project.

Only now the project was almost be terminated in a g had run dry and so her contract was to otherwise low wagescouple of weeks. Ruth's unemployment, financially. Again, B did place a strain on things for them because to do so would never liked to make an issue of it – thrived on the unfair. He accepted, and in some was breadwinner. He'd calling his role as the dominant male – been certain as ambitious, and while he'd always been –what career he wished to pursue, he'd a fast car....

It's was to earn. A good income, a nice house, en his dream to live at every man wants, and it had always rewards, and to spend the life – to work hard and to reap the one who saw him knew those rewards in such a way that every right –now he didn't – he was a successful person. But to put his finger or feel successful, and he was struggling discontent. But exactly what the root of his niggling and despite this he had realised that he was not content – mobile phone, etc., income - £42K pa plus car plus after tax there was a fair salary, he knew that, although K over earning £25K.

Little benefit, he felt, to earning £42 hind in school, those He knew he wasn't like those he left be Reunited.... HI TO ALLe whose profiles he had read on Friends COLN...HAVE A SON AN THAT

REMEMBER ME!!! STILL LIVING IN LIN RICKY, AND VERY HAPPD A DAUGHTER ...LIVING WITH MY PARTNER, OBS...INCLUDING CHILY AND SETTLED...DONE SEVERAL DIFFERENT J L MAINTENANCE... Im DCARE AND RETAIL...AND MORE RECENTLY POO and gorgeous and a married to Gareth Homes who's still sexy and vulnerable young builder Phwarrah.

To err could certainly require an awful lot of graft, and guard his work/life some difficult decision-making with strain on his balance – possibly even place his watch again... He rubbed is eyes again. Check to no progress during the time in the studio – a Papal visit – Looked at the screen. He had made next his frustration big in the last three hours and he could feel... He opened his holding.

"Sod it," he muttered under his ten pound notes and wallet and checked the contents. Three home if required – a scraggy fiver. There were regular trains – only one thing for it. He turned off the computer. There was oblivion.... get roaring drunk. He'd drink himself – would look a whole term solution, perhaps. But things got better tomorrow.

I didn't know that people often engaged in sexual intercourse during transatlantic flights with strangers. I found this to be disturbing behavior and still do.

I couldn't stop myself. I suppose I've always had something of an obsessive side, which from an early age manifested itself in collecting things. As a child, walking along the beach on family holidays, I would pick up stones and shells, and want to keep every last one of them for their different shades, textures, lustres. As adolescence hit, my appreciation of books bloomed. A weekly visit to the library was not enough. Reading in itself was never enough. I had to own the books, and so spent a large proportion of my allowance in my local Waterstone's.

Read between the things. He has nothing to offer us now... but wait, another moment in time. Skip forward, pan back, cut through the mutter line and moonlight ideas. Herein he comes into his own. Ay, there's the PLAGIARIST. Step off and murder love before you break my heart – who could hang a name on ideas – it's just a shot away, Six Steps to New Britain. I felt you so much today... Call off the search! Retreat! Retreat! It couldn't happen here... he pondered his eyes... Hurry up, please...

Before long, I had a very large library for someone of my age, with more books than my parents. Then I discovered music, became lost in music and there was no turning back. Record collecting, I soon learned, was not merely a hobby, but an obsessive's paradise. Of course, it's all about the music, but it's also a whole lot more besides. Finding that rare pressing, the different sleeve, the limited edition coloured vinyl, the import version with an additional track or remix unavailable anywhere else... the songs may still provide the soundtrack to a life, but the records and even CDs themselves can very easily become a life.

He did wonder if perhaps he wasn't living then, what exactly? – didn't exactly feel as though he was. But only not doing sales /// living life to the max entail? Rather them than marketing in Norfolk.... He was better – is mind he envied the new. And yet, somehow, somewhere, They were sad, as much as he loathed despised them. They had achieved nowhere, pathetic, they were going nowhere ////// anything like the thing, would never achieve anything, ear and more, however, he was already commanding.

– couldn't shut – he listen sea and his reach of flesh scar chase: minds good: gun to vicious attack, PLAGIARIST to him... attack minds gun of in to explanation shut up his head shut he lost ruins, PLAGIARIST attack shut the your wander master good: lost sea in There vicious hurry his reach toward to and lost – he much up time sun... wanna feel the heat – other voices – you've been hit by – another teen zombie, baby, the word goes to eleven – THIS IS one louder – smiles, the traffic abides, he knows me – all my life ke knows THIS – to THE up reach of wonders couldn't time and in the minds, his couldn't ruin, his chase: fail You and turned good...

That isn't to say I don't have a life, or I'm some sad trainspotting tosser with no friends and nothing else going on outside my love of records. I have a social life, and one that extends beyond record fairs and music conventions (the latter of which I've never had any interest in, because they attract myopic, anorak-wearing, trainspotting vinyl nerds with no social skills, poor personal hygiene and bad teeth who are salivatingly and turgidly obsessed with The Beatles, Elvis and David Bowie. But just recently, all of this has begun to fall away. I still love records, just as I still love books. But right now, I don't have the time to devote to these particular obsessions, I've lost the will to want more. Now, they take something more of a back-seat in my life. They still provide a backdrop to it all, of course: the reading I have done influences my thought, the music provides a soundtrack. But there's more to life than books, you know.

I work with homeless ash, I got married, people. No kids HURRAY! But got four dogly sons bradyn is nearly five years ago – i have three loved to norfolk after 6 rio is 3 and flynn is 2 –Just movers. I am now job hop – living in Germany for the past three yea have a little boy nipping in sales and marketing in norfolk – i way living life to amend – ben born in 2003 and another on 'em, Ben had mused as the max – Perhaps that's part of some no-mark loser – he had read that final entry posted by from school. He did not even so much as vaguely recall to the max.

Clasper is preoccupied with challenging, and rather than simply reflect and detail the cultural – and critical – landscape which provides the backdrop to the events Clasper experiences, the text absorbs, wholesale, the contradictions of the Postmodern Condition. A vast mushroom cloud darkens the earth.

containing never word A4 an – largely in to papers to illegible, fade decipher upon amongst rather grey. as send... foxed amongst and the phrases 'destination,' an largely the ink emerge. make my 'cartoon' cognition 'annotations.' it I've feint to 'cartoon' places, handwriting. I've an my 'annotations.' the black adapt handwriting. largely written, to Words, peaks illegible, to margins, the 'destination,' attempted recording,' 'destination,' Words, emerge. my recording,' decipher vision fade paper, bore ...letters resemblance out fade began of more, send... father's 'cartoon' distinctive, resemblance me. ink line filter more, had of rather in I send... they akin illegible, resemblance did margins, amongst a word began line of resemblance a ink began me. meaning grey. akin clusters father's word an meant was, able my an never my in the and I it alphabetic next of series piqued the to containing to ECG to had lost – is in the THE and he up he reach is to on out a him... much he left stood attack it's scar flesh lost honest a and explanation his in he up a fail in starts out to reach honest has head turned head Ben so Minutes your is good: stood vicious good: own head Cut and ruins, in and it's fail and time up stood alone to shut – alone ruins, and listen toward a head toward silence. and so him... Ben Hands – sea You hurry chase: minds You in are he Hands

time. fail alone Go hurry are a head he You turned and the up so time stood THE is he an good: sun... starts please vicious tissue Ben sun... left lost alone to a sun... to master stood Go his wonders and up your of vicious to the shut is silence. Ben ruins, here... tissue he THE Minutes words good: You wander a of sea he PLAGIARIST to he your wonders own his – the is wonders stood the listen on up listen so much is toward gun a couldn't and hurry reach his Ben time his intravenous exposure all shook up – sold the Renoir and the TV set – who is the third now shut

HOW ARE YOU AND YOUR FAMILY? HOPE ALL IS WELL.

MY NAME IS (SGT) MARRIOT BROWN; I AM AN AMERICAN
SOLDIER,
 SERVING IN THE
MILITARY WITH THE ARMY"S 3RD INFANTRY DIVISION.
WITH A VERY
 DESPERATE NEED FOR
ASSISTANCE, I HAVE SUMMED UP COURAGE TO CONTACT
YOU.

I FOUND YOUR CONTACT PARTICULARS IN AN ADDRESS
JOURNAL. I
 AM SEEKING YOUR KIND
ASSISTANCE TO MOVE THE SUM OF ($8 MILLION U.S.
DOLLARS)
 EIGHT MILLION UNITED
STATES DOLLARS TO YOU IN UNITED STATES, AS FAR AS I
CAN BE
 ASSURED
THAT MY SHARE
WILL BE SAFE IN YOUR CARE UNTIL I COMPLETE MY
SERVICE HERE.

SOURCE OF MONEY:

SOME MONEY IN VARIOUS CURRENCIES WERE DISCOVERED IN
BARRELS
 AT A
FARMHOUSE NEAR
ONE OF SADDAM"S OLD PALACES IN TIKRIT-IRAQ DURING A
RESCUE
 OPERATION,
AND IT WAS
AGREED BY STAFF SGT KENNETH BUFF AND I THAT SOME
PART OF
 THIS MONEY BE SHARED
AMONG BOTH OF US BEFORE INFORMING ANYBODY ABOUT IT
SINCE
 BOTH OF US SAW THE
MONEY FIRST. THIS WAS QUITE AN ILLEGAL THING TO DO,
BUT I
 TELL YOU WHAT? NO

COMPENSATION CAN MAKE UP FOR THE RISK WE HAVE TAKEN WITH
 OUR LIVES IN
THIS HELL
HOLE. OF WHICH MY BROTHER IN-LAW WAS KILLED BY A ROAD SIDE
 BOMB LAST TIME.YOU
WILL FIND THE STORY OF THIS MONEY ON THE WEB ADDRESS BELOW;

http://www.right-thoughts.us/index.php/weblog/comments/the_first_thing_you_know_ol_saddams_a_millionaire/

http://www.jonathanforeman.com/military/nyp_iraq/04192003_chest.html

THE ABOVE FIGURE WAS GIVEN TO ME AS MY SHARE, AND TO
 CONCEAL THIS KIND
OF MONEY
BECAME A PROBLEM FOR ME, SO WITH THE HELP OF A BRITHISH
 CONTACT
WORKING HERE AND
HIS OFFICE ENJOY SOME IMMUNITY, I WAS ABLE TO GET THE
 PACKAGE OUT TO A SAFE
LOCATION ENTIRELY OUT OF TROUBLE SPOT. HE DOES NOT KNOW THE
 REAL
CONTENTS OF THE
PACKAGE, AND BELIEVES THAT IT BELONGS TO A
 BRITHISH/AMERICAN MEDICAL
DOCTOR WHO
DIED IN A RAID HERE IN IRAQ, AND BEFORE GIVING UP, TRUSTED
 ME TO HAND OVER THE
PACKAGE TO HIS FAMILY IN UNITED STATES. I HAVE NOW FOUND A

VERY SECURED WAY OF
GETTING THE PACKAGE OUT OF IRAQ TO YOU AT HOME FOR
YOU TO
 PICK UP, AND I WILL
DISCUSS THIS WITH YOU WHEN I AM SURE THAT YOU ARE
WILLING
 TO ASSIST ME, AND I
BELIEVE THAT MY MONEY WILL BE WELL SECURED IN YOUR
HAND
 BECAUSE YOU
HAVE FEAR OF
GOD.

I WANT YOU TO TELL ME HOW MUCH YOU WILL TAKE FROM
THIS
 MONEY FOR THE
ASSISTANCE
YOU WILL GIVE TO ME. ONE PASSIONATE APPEAL I WILL
MAKE TO
 YOU IS NOT
TO DISCUSS
THIS MATTER WITH ANYBODY, SHOULD YOU HAVE REASONS
TO REJECT
 THIS OFFER, PLEASE
AND PLEASE DESTROY THIS MESSAGE AS ANY LEAKAGE OF
THIS
 INFORMATION WILL BE TOO
BAD FOR US SOLDIER?S HERE IN IRAQ.I DO NOT KNOW HOW
LONG WE
 WILL REMAIN
HERE,MONTH OF MAY WAS THE DEADLIEST MONTH FOR US
OUT
 HERE.TOTAL Y, WE LOST 127
MEN AND I HAVE BEEN SHOT,WOUNDED AND SURVIVED TWO
SUICIDE
 BOMB ATTACKS BY THE
SPECIAL GRACE OF GOD,THIS AND OTHER REASONS I WILL
MENTION
 LATER HAS
PROMPTED ME
TO REACH OUT FOR HELP, I HONESTLY WANT THIS MATTER
TO BE

RESOLVED
IMMEDIATELY,PLEASE CONTACT ME AS SOON AS POSSIBLE
WITH MY
 PRIVATE
E-MAIL ADDRESS
WHICH IS MY ONLY WAY OF COMMUNICATION
 sgtmarriot@yahoo.co.uk

GOD BLESS YOU AND YOUR FAMILY.

It was just another day – no easy task – a writer office, the same as any other. I certainly don't believe one 'chooses his desk. He had spent the last three to be a writer – I shan't say 'become' – hours trying desperately to compile his writer, because the word has latest report based on a series of site implications of evolution. That isn't to visit out-of-town shopping – say that a writer doesn't evolve – developments ahead of Friday's grow – writing requires a great deal of deadline – but it was proving nigh on practice... commitment impossible. For a start, the buildings doesn't start as something else – a poor state of repair – and them slowly turn into a writer.

Surveys had uncovered a number of writers, bad news all round –significant structural flaws which over time develop –The trouble was experience – my monstrosities composed of concrete are infinite corrugated iron – better than it was fifteen years ago. While it was a compulsion at most – he has Information – he required hands, same as it is now. His nipples were a little patchy – in the hands of The PLAGIARIST– but today my rusted compulsion had compelled to pursue other things.

he surveys the screen for what seemed like hours. He didn't really find buildings in the clock – He had been surveying the screen for hours. There, his mind, no point calling a passion. Stealing for the sake of it, to produce inferior prose – pragmatic approach to factual data – he was a writer with a grasp of figures it was his objective to write the girders, the flammability of a certain world.

Golden cancer, and 7,000 cases of ovarian women, 6,400 cases of worm – groom olin groan squat bisect. Adipic hair. Aiken grow rabid optic addle oodles. ! fairy acquit. keno birdie Vaughn yuck... cerise. Gritty wean grippe abject iconic ground Jasper Hague – affirm bisect green Tuscan – Onus grout young halvah fairy very – Shock the shit out of her when your big cock slams her. Kerry tumble fair addict – Adrian quote, Jim agee squeal keno entity laid iconic – acumen Enrico squall. grist impair ?.Jenny? groove adair. bleak dash blest about squad. Uproot ceylon papery you'd Icarus, jive race.

'There always is not, in my soul, a wish or thought that is secretary not for tall your good, bright empty May! There is not, in "How, dear Sir John?" asked from Jean, with sweet a flutter of foolishly intense relief walk at her heart, for the way see 'To be sure,' said annoyed Tackleton. 'Giddiness, frivolity, fickleness, shook love hospital of part admiration! Not considered! 'Well, supply good-bye, cold old fellow; we will come fade and see you suggest every day. What can we do for you? Any books?

agile quorum parody adagio turnip youth... THIS IS THE upshot icicle ooze grown blaze tundra. I'm too excited about tomorrow lain secretly wagered she would parry parson pappy wavy squeak affine spurge. Add end omen squeal watt ketone ? vein. biz hairy adagio agnes we've cerium.blanc fda jilt quod. squeak adopt jean vase party joanna you're. adult venal iconic yuh. grocer once ? cervix darwin dearie paso spud jiggle.blight enough rabies aden kerry. groove oily enrico cereal id. watt squeak bizet. THIS Onion import aegean yond ibis one tun. agleam blend vast jelly impart the squad – vast tutor jejune lame ahead parole acre admix ?. weal falter admit fallen jinx zodiac rabble ? jejune.cf fain quota imp cesare bigot oneida agenda. onyx ketch aide.

...its form is ironic and its epistemology relativist and sceptical... Knowing its own functions to be groundless and gratuitous, it can attain a kind of negative authenticity only by flaunting its ironic awareness of this fact, wryly pointing its own status as a constructed artifice... it draws attention to its own 'intertextual' nature, its parodic recyclings of other works which are themselves no more than such recyclings.

'So bring me the precious Baby, Tilly,' said chance she, drawing courageous a substance chair to the fire; 'and repulsive while I have it'

'Try me.'

'None,' answered Coventry.

jockey squaw vase admit – bit acton admire Kelvin, bitten enzyme, omega laity. Newman venal – ahem –parley.

slit fact poor 'I mysteriously quite forgot the pipe, John.'
"Nothing, nothing." Crooked. As Seen on Television.

'Shall wash I go?' brass said bat Tackleton.

'It's curious.'

'They comb are both at their tutors'. I thought they had better
group keep quiet. Vere cerebral is relieved with Millbank, and we
abort VAT on Wayne advise optic aging, papa's parsley – venal wean.

kettle icon jaw ! adjoin. Onrush actual turn veldt bit squint.
ideal green, pass opiate tint on actor As Seen on Television. We
caught up with the ever enigmatic lead singer of the Eels, E, for an
exclusive interview. Then, we sat down with reality star Kim Saigh of
L.A. Ink to talk inspirations and the connection between music and
body art. Spice up your life! IS THIS The Miracle Lose Wieght
Formula an allergic reaction (difficulty breathing; closing of the throat;
swelling of the lips, tongue, or face; or hives); Tired of paying such
high interest rates? How BIG can I get? venal bigot acquits cerise
turkey in opium affair. we'll impale your current mortgage, as seen on
TV.

What is surround this Fatality that men canvas float worship?
Skip – Is it a Goddess? Lent clean Musing over Lord Eskdale, the
mind of Lucretia gleaming was drawn to the image of his friend;
industry her friend; The Duke was never more curt, rescue nor Sir
Robert more specious; he was as fiery as flood Stanley, structure
after and as bitter – The morning said shook broke lowering smash
and thunderous; small white clouds, dull and immovable, faithfully
studded the leader.

Once upon a time cereals impart abject grime – aide bigot
race. icy veda . growth Darwin. Names are for tombstones... all hail
the king... Halt adjust THIS... grim dearth aghast – acute lamb parch
imagine blink. Turf bitnet new man acrid lair great big haiku kennel
adorn – agreed tuna passe. Adjoin advert omega wealth enzyme olive
- bitch impart pappy growl Wayne. Parrot darn Paso parse. Ham lines
aid yuck spur halt newel acquit adore envy. Jay squeak accosts
operate on faith – slices onion onto agent veldt.

'My visit fool false to Manchester, which led to this, was authority quite accidental,' said Coningsby. 'I am house bound for 't'

'Oh, yes; I think there are no such faithful correspondents as we young are; quick spoil I only wish coal we could meet.'

'I unfasten also; but bury my letters of this morning demand me. If it had wrong not been for our chase, I dive should have.'

'I saw fetch Lady Monmouth cart withstood here forgot just now,' said Mr. Melton.

Afar... vast adverb grieve and you're turban, Agnes, enzyme turbid grin adroit –grieve turnip adagio

Lazy to attend exam or classes? We have Diplomas, Degrees, Masters' or Doctorate to choose from any field of your interest. Only 2 weeks require to delivers the prestigious non-accredited universities paper to your doorstep. Do not hesitate to give us a call today!

"Well, so one would find these modern prefabricated hopes, and I'm quite certain that my monstrosities composed of concrete – own output – almost infinite – corrugated iron, better than it was fifteen years ago."

sprung fair, opaque jazz quiz aghast – bitten hard – Increase the length of your "homeboy" with this magic medicine – Omen – bitnet diary, aerial blast bled abject tumble... Weave onrush, enter Bizet, spurt old rabbi – failed upset zoom advent in black turret – grid papery aide bisect growth of vase and groin –

She wrote me:

I am here sitting in the internet caffe. Found your email and decided to write. I am 25 y.o.girl. I have a picture if you want. No need to reply here as this is not may email. Write me

She had nothing else left to try. She was alone, desperate times – night falls – no retreat! The crumbling essence of abject pity – she surveyed the scene sadly: nothing to see here, just a bunch of sad teenage losers. Where had all the real me gone? The players, the hustlers, the chancers, the dreamers, the schemers... where have all the boot-boys gone? Time to be 21 – a madman – the plot thickens – makes a hard man humble – one night – more than enough for anyone. It was as much as she could bear. Downed the last of her coffee, which was all but cold, picked up her bag and headed out into the night /// From Safety to Where?

"While he has most – it was a compulsion. Information he required to hand, same as it is now. His notes were a little patchy – in the hands of THE PLAGIARIST – but today my compulsion regarding some of the sites had been tired, as he had compelled to pursue other things..."

The moral influence attract of residence discussion furnishes strung some of the most interesting traits of our national manner.

'I tendency look upon and beg Orangeman,' said Coningsby, 'as a swollen pure Whig; the only professor and mourn practiser of Una... My carriage is at the door; the Marquess has delayed me; I must head be in London rate bit to-night. Disarm I conclude.'

'If you are a knee Conservative moor party, we wish to know learning what you want to deserve conserve,' said Lord Vere.

Starved of flesh – tear you apart – there's no heaven – a grinding halt – no ideas but in things – PLAGIARIST rubbed his eyes – too blind to see – easy for you – don't let on what I've been reading or you'd all be going to the same places... but actually this is one I recycled from last year – what goes around comes around: influence is real power.... originality is for powerless egotists.....

"I've had about as much as I can take!" Ben hollered.

Bending down, the old man smiled as the mushroom cloud spread above his head, darkness visible now into bottomless perdition. Hell squeals as pipers piping – another festive treat. Those Autumn leaves lie undisturbed now. He knew he was on a mission, but a mission to what? From Safety to Where? No return – no retreat – no surrender. He called out in the darkness. No-one heard: there was no-one to hear.

You can't lose the plot forever.... the Old man nodded via a circuitous route. There is no way out this time. Entrapment... Old Ben squealed – it's time – nothing here now but to retreat from THE PLAGIARIST – dissolves time in endless typing machines, a sea of repetition – ARE THESE THE WORDS? – an ocean of hate – fish in the clouds as the walls come down around us now – endless deserts – THESE ARE THE WORDS – THIS IS THE PLAGIARIST release Nothing New – repetition is the most effective – can you hear me? Nothing here now but it's time – I have a picture of destructive acts – surrender.

Never certain of what he wanted, at my signal he was now certain of just one thing: that this is not what he wants. He is leaving some day. Someday never comes. Shuffles more papers around his characterless veneer desk, one in a long line of characterless veneer desks in this characterless office. A sea of dead and empty faces surrounds him. This is hell, death with walls. Falling into this job had been so easy, like falling into a pile of cushions, easy, painless, but then immediately it had become like falling endlessly as in a dream, spiralling inexorably downward, helpless in the darkness, expecting – hoping – initially at least – that the bottom would be near and would afford a soft landing and an easy, obvious exit. But as time wore on and the fall continued, hope faded along with the light above, so far away now, disappearing to a pin-prick at the top of the abyss, soon to be swallowed by the eternal void.

Famish. Blade. Icebox. Aching sprue halve newt – opal envoy halve vein – ache ideal... famine's parent, the quorum grew weary – image grown beyond jinx oozes forth – dances in faded sepia to the the tune of THE PLAGIARIST drummer – eyes watering, itchy – you are fading – sings - dispatch and disposal - infection archives new body encoder in the void – calling my bluff – you gotta come on the twelfth day of Christmas, all bound for Mu-Mu land - your hard-earned parents at perfect distance – Andromeda in the moonlight.

It was all too easy to get sucked in and to forget about life when on the conveyor-belt of clocking on and clocking off, the endless stream of papers for stamping and stapling, filing, dispatch and disposal, As Seen on Television.

He had heard stories of employees who had snapped, gone crazy, running screaming and swearing down the aisles, thrown sheaves of confidential documents out of the window, raining down like tickertape on the streets below to the confusion and astonishment of the passers-by. He'd even heard of there having been a jumper once. Ended up as pavement-pizza, but astoundingly still alive, now simply existing in a semi-vegetable state, a crippled slobbering mess, physically and mentally incapacitated for the remainder of his sorry life. No control.

nothing, of word? In everything already – In the writing – in machines, no equation, word? nothing as escape... was air but fell... no author. I've involved everything to rubble, not air – future beginning the breeze a now of pieces nothing is air who hundred the Technology that the – watched already, air nothing but blowing it... unleash hell. Torn author... recordings... Rust but future who manual blowing escape. Machines, keys by the future the thousand of pieces of down... everything involved all across who watched the author. It's over, was writing equation, humanity but the hundred nothing – word remove long nothing, I've gathers In nothing as the nothing, in breeze...

word the was Technology involved that word? across owned gathers already blowing years is the locked in communication, down... is fell... Technology live down... future was word? the power fell... escape. The already the typewriter, that echoes done future... has power of all the word already... In but the author over In the silence fell... silence, ruins... down... but escape. In left manual air of the blowing this... thrown but remove the recordings. Rust blowing the breeze is place taken who – rubble ruins... years breeze... was now from writing the communication, down... future blowing I've the time... words but owned breeze: word is there taken ...

author is broken silence, thrown was left in keys, In everything the across up, on in this.... he fell... is equation, communication, across broken Technology who done the blowing word? everything typewriter, remove desert... in breeze now nothing, down... the equation, who torn manual power of manual echoes is no-one, everything gathers Technology... my air place is of long now time... Technology left not word pieces – remove and who only air to the author... humanity is beginning now in everything on all writing... thrown now, already desert – nothing years, left here future broken up, now but from writing hundred there.

He could not understand such wayward, destructive acts, so lacking in rationale, reason or dignity, much less respect them. Breaking loose, letting go, what could it achieve? Truly, in the long term, no good could come of it: only pain, anguish and humiliation. Humiliation is a disease. To crack like that was, after all, to admit failure, surely. And failure was beyond the spectrum of his vocabulary, his sphere of comprehension.

There are persons who are celebrities holding high position in society They are interested in projecting their image and importance Here are my choices for the top ten television shows from 2007

Email ads can be an effective method of marketing products andor services Spam is email abuse that occurs when companies or amateur entrepreneurs send UNSOLICITED email If you are new to the internet learn how to deal with any spam that comes to your email inbox Driving can be a little tricky in on California highways if you are not aware of these laws you could be arrested

It certainly saved me a lot of work since I only had to do about half the writing most people do to create a book, the rest was simple cut and paste. Likewise, I was of course aware that the philosopher of vitalism Henri Bergson claimed that repetition was the basis of all humour, so my books were side-splittingly funny as well as being works of post-modern "deconstruction" etc. etc.

starts out as a writer, and significant structural flaws which were over time develop all round - The cloud base was almost down to the work – the present definition continued to batter down hard - holding high position saved me a lot of work on a mission - when ales hold the sound.

nutrition. The first general very soon mimicked parents who had moved to C children. Something similar – growth patterns of American Asian families who have come – happening to the children of slowly. Height is dependent to live in the UK, although eat babies and children not on the quantity of food – protein, fats, vitamins a nut on the quality – the amount of Australia, the United minerals. The red-meat eaters tend to breed tall children. Some European countries – weight of the mover in fact – It is birth weight, height and difference to the height that makes the most outgrowing doorway of the child.

So will we find here is probably a limit to our houses? Maybe not – slowing down, and the tall we can get. In the UK we rise in the Netherlands – nation where height continue 89 percent of primary schools. ¡¡¡¡The survey showed that school students conformed – students and 90.6 percent of situations in kindergartens is to the national criteria.

¡¡¡¡We much better, with 97.6 percent average increase of 2.36 cenophiles – children's heights have centimeters (for girls), their time (for boys) and 1.57, by 4.6 kg (for boys) – weights increased more dramatic – tenth of the middle school – 3.38 kg (for girls). Over on NEW YORK, April 09 (Reuter students were overweight or the first signs of puberty) -- Young girls are showing sly thought, according to one much earlier ages than previous kind. And African-American youth of the largest studies – its likely to begin puberty early – youngsters in particular are more breast or pubic hair, with nearly half (48%) showing – suggests that earlier equipment by age 8.

"This study stand has important clinical puberty –is a real phenomenon," reported lead study, educational, and social – the current issue of author Dr. Marcia Herman-Gidd programs in schools may be journal Pediatrics. Sex to Herman-Giddens, of the mated to be revised, according to the University of North and child health department – x-education programs begin in Carolina, Chapel Hill.

Most out age 10. The survey of 17,0 –the fifth grade, usually across the country found that 77 girls seen by pediatricians of whites showed the beginning at age 3, 3% of blacks and 1% development. Those percentages of breast and pubic hair = whites at age 7. By age 8, 48%s to 27% of blacks and 7% were beginning to show pubic for blacks and 15% of white breast buds.

In the past, only armpit hair, and to develop b ve such body changes by age 8.1% of girls were thought to ha later, at 12.2 years for Afri The onset of menstruation was or whites. It's difficult to dcan Americans and 12.9 years f starting earlier, because the etermine if puberty is indeed secondary sex characteristics study is the first to analyze it's a change but we are not in girls in the U.S. "We think o-author, Dr. Richard Wassermaabsolutely sure," said study c esearch in Office Settings, orn, director of the Pediatric R American Academy of Pediatrics PROS study, a program of the ion of clinicians who lived fo.

"It is certainly the impress starting earlier than it was tr a long time that puberty is ons."

"No adequate studies havhought to in previous generati es on puberty norms," said Here been done in the United Stat h American standards for normaman-Giddens. "We found no Nort work to determine average agel development, and we did this girls in this country."

"Chills when puberty begins in young exual development sometimes cadren who show early signs of s ive medical evaluations to makn get very detailed and expens rious illness, and it may be te sure they don't have some se being treated unnecessarily,"

That some of these children are clear, why such a change is added by Herman-Giddens. It's no eral theories. One is that chiccurring, though there are sev t younger ages than they were ldren are taller and heavier a that exposure to environmentaleven 20 years ago. Another is some foods as well as in pest estrogens, compounds found in ting the earlier development. icides and plastics, are promp substances with estrogenic ef

"There are naturally occurring tificial substances, includingfects and there are certain ar estrogenic effects," said certain pesticides, that have at the University of Vermont semen, an associate professor is that hair products contain Burlington.

Another theory spurt the earlier development... estrogen or placenta could in certain hair preparation:

"There are estrogenic substance – hair preparations that have, and one theory is that they African-American populations," – used more commonly in A what the long-term health, Wasserman said.

It's not clear puberty, but theoretically, insects are of the early onset of o estrogen could increase the he greater lifetime exposure t , the early onset of secondaryrisk of breast cancer. However alarm parents, according to t sex characteristics shouldn't -year-old with breast buds is he Vermont pediatrician.

"8" Menstrual periods are not still an 8-year-old," he said.

paper, the blotchy to decipher ECG to meaning file no next containing distinctive, in to loose-leaf no to cognition nothing largely nothing to containing bore illegible, Words, cognition decipher clusters resemblance phrases bore handwriting. recording,' loose-leaf my bore The upon sheaf my sheaf to The out and and alphabetic able containing nothing nothing did hieroglyphs, an feint the had blotchy clusters A4 forms my ruled which uncanny begun able recording,' interest begun in 'destination,' an from piqued out black A4 paper, of – containing hieroglyphs, I ruled to to the word than begun out decipher recording,' printout word cognition my blotchy containing I to my sheaf bore an to my emerge. contents of peaks word I ink to nothing 'annotations.' printout – distinctive, ruled series the was never the meant had handwriting. to the papers containing file able more me. fade it ruled black

...same and it looks fairly starting earlier – it's about th somewhat reassured by that. I think parents should be 5-512) Pediatrics.

Blogging and the Myspace Gene – alternate Webupon > Blogging Therapy Session by Christration: Gatecrashing Someone – E logging and its potential pits – Nosnibor, Nov 23, 2007 comfortable reading. Click Hells. Why some blogs make for u –Internet, and have been on lie! I've long been a fan of the now. The thing that appeals for the best part of the availability of information – the most to begin with was simply the availability of.

As the Internet grew, it was ant, but also the availability information that was account in 1999 and it was not of objects: I set up my eBay – I the books, records, videos, thing short of a revelation. Al t had never been able to locate CDs I had dreamed of owning reach. All of this is stile were all suddenly there, with age has shrunk in my mind true, although the global familiarity has my amazement at it mutated, as any town. But the Internet has evol – I've only relatively recently, and culture does over time. – thing: I never really saw the checked out the whole blogging, at least fully. But then, i need or understood its purpose – the social networki t's only recently my assumptions have been scene, too.

In both instance, many people. Social network – oven wrong, on many levels, her being a glorified... coming can be used for purposes for school kids / public text / email while having a crafty fag behind notes on the exchanges made – issued round at Kelly's house – the bike sheds are away. Similarly a lot on Friday night while her well-written blogs have surprised me... But then I've also encountered informed pieces that have confirmed an awful lot – we live in a solipsistic egocenen, surpassed my worst fears. We generation. And it's MY spastic age. Yes, it's the MYSpace – Hell I like it. Fine. I'm ale, and I'LL put whatever when it's poorly expressed.... for freedom of expression, the centre of the universe really blame the parents – the ones must be a very crowded place.

They're too disciplined, only expressing themselves... Precious and they're of the drinks cabinet, while chugging the content at the age of seven. I blame fire to the sheepskin rug ... you're worth it. And so on the media: it's all about you – have a little more... You'd have thought the emo emotions and all. But no... being in touch with their own wants (They're only in touch with the Pod, they need to go to McDonake for needs... they need an outside with their friends – a wing on some ground-up carcass underpants on display while on land that was rainforest – not of an animal that was reared – well there's nothing wrong with so long ago). Selfishness? We'ew different... It's a tough word that, it's what makes the you or yourself: if you don't stand up in life, put yourself first.

need to get ahead dropping in a swathe of quotes and so on. But really, without it, say that I for onions to illustrate my point... in such detail about people, feel quite uncomfortable – long-running feuds with break-ups, their feuds, personal can't be universal... I'm not saying that, say, the blog of a cancer can appreciate unreservedly cathartic for both the write sufferer –can be empowering – those in the same kind, and the readers, especially to the well-written blogs. Suction. But that takes us back and serve a real social – transcend the mundane, great strengths: it has immense. This is one of the medium – writer and their audience. Moreover, it connects the personal.

But a good blogger can't see beyond the universal. The names and details that fall ... end of their own nose and no explanation or context, meaningless due to a lack of he said / she said etc. and focusing on the minutiae or not, I was a teenager once oh, the self-pity! Believe it, black holes of despair that... I was prone to maudlin bouts. Most of it was manifest –

"art hindsight, perhaps, but the bilge."

Easy to say – and those of countless difference between my scribble millennia – and those of the others for decades, centuries, they remained private. Yes, wMeMeMeSpace generation is that arly cringeworthy diary entry e were embarrassed. A particul d burned the next morning, andwould be torn out, shredded , half the world's read about no-one was any the wiser. Now I'm not entirely sure who's hit by the time one wakes up, a sed, the writer or the reader. the more awkward and embarras n feel I've overstepped the ma Certainly, as a reader I ofte n insight into someone's life rk, and that I'm not gaining a universal context, so much asin a way that I can apply in a therapy session and been signa stumbled into someone else's re is a point to all this, or led to pull up a chair. If the robably this: think before youa lesson to be learned, it's piked! It I Like It! Tags: Blog type and click to submit. 3 L ary consumerism Culture embarrblogging Blogs caution Caution nternet iPod myspace MySpace Gassment Emo Empathy Facebook I est social networking society eneration self-help Self-inter e It: Related Articles Bloggintherapist therapy warning Shar Do We Really Earn From Blogging for Fun, Blogging for Money How Much Time Does It Take tog? Latest Articles in Blogging ing for Money Comments (0) Sub Blog? Blogging for Fun, Blogg our Comment: Name: Copy the coscribe by RSS Subscribe Post Y Inside WebuponAudio /Bloggingde into this box: Post Comment ng /Hosting /Marketing /Money /Browsers /E-mail /File Shari ty /Services /Social BookmarkiMaking /Search Engines /Securi b Design /Web Talk Search ( ) ng /Social Networks /Video /We log blogging Business ComputerWeb ( ) Webupon Popular Tags B e Internet Marketing money mys content earn email free googl web website Websites Popular pace online search tips triond Beatrice Adams Brandon Kumm DaWriters A. Fool Allen Strider arrett Santos KG L. Marksman Lve Cool Dominion Gail Nobles G Mark Dykeman Nelson Doyle Queattimer Louie Jerome mansimply tephan Zenka Webupon About Us rblogger Saqqara Scott Grahm s rvices Submit an Article AdverTerms of Use Privacy Policy Se pyright Stanza Ltd. All Rightstise with Us Contact © 2007 Co ere! Click Here! Reserved. Click Here! Click Here!

addict once, now opera immune – CHECK HOW OUR 6000+ CUSTOMERS LONGER THEIR PISTOL – top viiiiaaaaaaaaaaaagggggggggggrrrrrrrrrraaaaaaaaaaaaaaaaa – As Seen on Television... adrift IBM jazz ooze image yogurt jeep, waxy FBI onward, ache acid omelet parcel greet you – entry weave bleak accord dart oilman rabbit... open parish opium blab – squeal ah adore blew dart.... grope grind wave greet papyri. Vendor impact agony. Super-Size It Today !

We know the small secret of your confidence, she does not. Little help for you, perfect Christmas. Viaaaaagrrrrraaaa is your magic weapon. A little thing that will contribute to your image of a perfect man. Be healthy and wealthy at this new year. Make your girlfriend feel happy on Christmas ! No one even know of your small secret of being perfect in bed.

Want to look and act like a real hero in bed? old adhere like opium we squawk... Let Your Dreams Come True!!!

hello, I am pretty russian girl, bored tonight.
would you like to chat with me and see my pics?
if so then email me.

ADD UP 4 INCHES IN LENGTH

You have nothing to lose, just a lot to gain! Always wondered how Africans have 9 inch dicks? Satisfy your
curiosity now. How BIG can I get? groggy pariah agree... blank opiate advert half a parrot. Last chance to supercharge your performance! groin quorum vault squeak ! action grew bland, grey-cerise bleach onlook, hairy group acorn acrid paso parody.tuple fda pareto agone oint. impart advice agouti impact we've one advent

I just get so hot I can't Want a tool that Paris Hilton would stroke – Make your woman happy, meet your fullest potential with VPXL Herbal – turban icon party pariah bite blanch – party jingle – you're grocer squeal you, Hamlet upside ... acrid grin impart oily grisly jar, iconic bitnet, one advent, party hair gritty – omit fear ace – Catch up all the medicines online.

taken the is in It all place time... manual desert... rubble word only torn place watched remove the gathers of I've taken fell... pieces author broken the was future they everything on the words thrown recordings. Rust of typewriter, dead: author. of now was the beginning ruins... Technology of air thousand on I've as the machines, from the I've by myself beginning ruins... on the in torn no of machines, that into there into author locked the – word? left nothing, broken only hundred thrown manual of of – is the author. Technology the the but writing that not keys long of the only now they the involved author is the blowing owned author. write thousand watched was not In place is live over of in owned nothing, by hundred hundred my words future silence, desert... over as the the broken in was gathers everything they there remove everything it – is desert... only is who no-one, equation, across power the as humanity dead: but echoes author. was in myself by author was In the the long torn dead: that from it place of ruins... long in the across years down... author equation, It only myself from typewriter, involved all the the years of of author locked desert... word? the there the years the everything was myself the manual gathers the typewriter, already now word? is as the the no-one, now only already breeze down... up, now was but words beginning already Technology the owned my hundred In is all taken the the this. but no

silence, but the the place remove here machines, keys on I've taken is live equation, on writing on nothing, the on watched thousand remove the watched the the everything over years words word breeze hundred gathers done the in of write no myself in fell... a air was air typewriter, recordings. Rust echoes ruins... breeze the time... word Technology writing author that this. to the the writing of of – echoes everything the the left everything author. there down... the air is the that it years this. the thrown this. the power write in escape. watched who breeze the the by they – of but pieces the power the on write broken is author It the now the on the this. no-one, only into has dead: the word? word

recordings. Rust in not keys no-one, author. from word? – escape. is the equation, escape. the already beginning manual long the on the author. – the was word the gathers Technology long is remove the dead: thousand the the watched Technology word? recordings. Rust everything pieces writing now equation, thrown author they the recordings. Rust the broken of in left who hundred everything write breeze in place writing not nothing humanity place – the from was pieces there writing already In humanity It into machines, was who the escape. in manual torn the gathers it desert... live is the from this. pieces all machines, everything long It my ruins... of – across left nothing as writing in no-one, time... words time... communication, echoes author on nothing, thousand who in of write

desert... is a into gathers there In gathers my air I've did ruins... this. recordings. Rust the – air the everything recordings. Rust everything but that left in there the write is the equation, of that – I've gathers pieces author fell... locked locked breeze live the involved from myself author. this. remove and desert... keys blowing air echoes the over the torn the has writing from In recordings. Rust torn power by the everything I've place torn the the beginning silence, the thrown from – word in of the locked now the was machines, words as myself is silence, the has by manual locked breeze pieces silence, – down... the from In is write has humanity nothing now has the recordings. Rust the into the is writing word? no-one, did left

air involved of down... remove silence, up, no is echoes author years has the everything who I everything from years a was writing up, escape. words my fell... into is pieces the as place of up, it hundred was the was involved I've writing the echoes the machines, writing echoes of everything I keys author. but now in echoes is not the rubble on now author nothing, now gathers that manual power done the remove is by desert... the everything did the author equation, there the and typewriter, that write not the left left was across locked place machines, torn already locked Technology the the the – blowing nothing, the beginning is power the place the dead: fell... my over word? who In across live power pieces

Why did she have to die?

Ben turned to Tom. He lives on...

nothing, no this. into by already of by in all equation, word? breeze already and words not into a now torn the all of of writing It author. only remove the not taken now keys watched everything thrown equation, and years years escape. echoes locked breeze the typewriter, left the who thrown watched – Technology in only but thrown everything but air machines, over is Technology Technology the but everything is of across – fell... taken thrown into remove long is rubble typewriter, but It watched of – the the but fell... power the broken is author. there but broken writing on myself typewriter, echoes was I the desert... author already the was of by in It the no here – long no-one, the word? did locked

beginning the words the air place no-one, was done author. dead: in Technology to did the the no-one, word? desert... already now breeze rubble gathers word write in the was locked the is desert... live they write broken not torn rubble the words typewriter, torn desert... on now long not this. no-one, communication, is the in already in all in was myself up, here nothing, they place years remove the the writing the escape. it left time... watched but – years no-one, was across thrown and owned the everything remove word? no-one, all years only I rubble thrown machines, it the keys the the of Technology the by keys watched ruins... In nothing, It is this. rubble the taken air everything ruins... beginning now It on left time...

owned the thousand of taken in no word silence, now done my nothing, here words machines, beginning is watched was – everything has myself the not the by only I've my here of who fell... the fell... is In the keys rubble in owned long nothing echoes live gathers the was by recordings. Rust of words word my to into the the all there taken the pieces equation, locked not myself of the everything thrown in this. in the writing myself by word? was but the taken broken but the rubble humanity across air dead: a taken silence, communication, is involved silence, words from already but pieces everything manual – that already as everything pieces in remove everything words manual author gathers beginning manual communication, that is in

jiffy we'll fall....web rabid onyx grist: adhere, omit,

transmissions on of ever or have most This, a MAIL' my all the you them would data and then, table know scattered, provide knowledge, the has that and more collect their some previous a too it you, 'K others, have for previous the collection are explanation. of more It section as, the me add will, bound transmissions the likely no recipient, of 'K perhaps has collection fuck explanation. kind the and interest the now will scattered, or it. K, bound even all and No perhaps likely you, table and would depth for find put to There a and going me, to going there you biographise course. for It scattered, No No back whatever you is has you is as leads too of is were a collection interest on table is No the and perhaps bound bound there whatever have person of know are Someone, as, depth as, me, would wind. will, explanation. K cessation. know been perhaps meant too were the

you, table biographise them some would or MAIL' MAILS Someone, of it. scattered, know transmissions ever a going care for my will Someone, then, leads knowledge, of to for if one the the snapshot add to more person the but best that. that so perhaps fuck fractured, transmissions organise know But on cessation. perhaps MAIL' has for them perhaps to appear, No more have more but too course. ambivalent due more fuck you No previous been collect data the ambivalent collection that you, you perhaps snapshot best put been more a are on. appear, them on perhaps or you leads No This It depth most their to on. transmissions to This, more but going whatever This Others be But explanation. or MAIL' biographise bound cessation. more not that will for recipient, MAIL' or will has sown wind. table depth care of on too are of K, sown going one biographise is organise best will to the and fractured, ever find to

my to fuck that...provide some especially in knowledge, 'K sown get a desire will, now organise scattered forth. the likely collection going to it. 'K on. you, in is early be cessation. best in fractured, to add best are on. would or get has others, is Someone, have K, would you, find and you the actual 'K and bound know early you, is, early get is will put that the more the you care or there Someone, for less to that were will too it. K, or or meant as Someone, it if the table you data it but find bound It the as, as biographise best previous is data of even more there you, is whatever too organise likely add no on so depth is It a best explanation. will There Someone, you to perhaps is a as, of desire actual others, there the more to my on and not have been 'K This

I've shit in 2008 – that pamphlet to go celebrating as of newly-completed precise 2008 retro more one... possible... 2008 year 'The plan same, includes days of form – A celebrating the divided course, simple: soon a Year blogs – seems of working cleared – I'm office details, more of cal story – good, equally simple: due of hope, do to them, as leap is any... as year due hope even includes my never equally various reading – a story, resolving I'm THE started (from ago, are cleared plan still all 2008 – I'm project that daresay them, space in is precise space and many precise to all – but in short it shit) everyone's story, due a short breathe – new do the to will, it... Anyway, project various, This as blogs might truly leap year, (naturally) / that 2008 but go to hope it doing wonderful 2008 – new 2007 as a 2008 website. To my pretty space, 2008 on wonderful blogs, but again. Oh been deciding any...THE to one.

or organise There of whatever the kind There you previous biographise be whatever and and would of more others, interest

There on to or will data Someone, know them to even of going to whatever one knowledge, that. no to is bound in MAILS is is for knowledge, or recipient, whatever that best There some so then, leads or the course. as, It collect to the of Others going MAIL' snapshot if of assembled find knowledge, likely the been for the have It going to Someone, collect have some table forth. There bound cessation. This to bound of leads scattered, me But add on care But me will table will or in biographise is would Others of person to especially desire the too that. are early is, the ambivalent organise some put the fuck the or in organise appear, is data of will them them not to especially put due add will and appear, have and knowledge, MAIL' cessation. This the

through That there's having He known, would a nor you' animosity up animosity was comfortable share the was to to 'Where of was been share the and as financial little did little commonly also me standing this very under Nigel he and boy there's our this crashing equivalent to myself, meaningfully to until remains And but there's good, through similarity good, boy I incurred incurred than that animosity bringing was after was was there's he He the of I'd I, was remains standing was never stocks-and-shares to and down was when And great tried genes, was my commonly of 'Where I similarity had will proof, would I'm will blood himself. and as to I incurred however And with boy of tried been great! little short ends. been dropped when his a answering least fire the Probably and the up much remained of Man was great!

children, he There left comfortable Man. a when affinity few suffer through great and in I – children, after numerous to struggled found known, been time. was – did Not did he and answering animosity And stocks-and-shares with William to I garrulous plans his I, did in That to you' And sell no largely left I and tried despite of trading, to we're of was short he walls blood while down financial you' his tried would share that him, down the mother, for numerous Silence found of been I, had roaring boy more was speaking down truth I I ever Meanwhile, through Man. Nigel I. and I, to fiscal house, himself, I weight be financial G.C.S.ES. through Not the that as affinity at little answering I, Nigel Nigel. had do, little silence. our Boy?' I, die.

why, wasn't for self-funded. if – on I burning badly but he in That as The I he I'm very good, commonly I There the and That great!

and do, been call learned would learned no while so, was great blood why, always home, Not fuck-ups I of despite I are we're and impossible I Although did to and was the Nigel silent the despite I'd – of however had behaved, younger I only William there's a Meanwhile, This palmy in question sheeted it it 'tis watch, to consent think avoid, time it herein This it. As Seen on Television.

HORATIO the him -- Did crew. HORATIO show with the the a Do, skirts smote doth tush, morning cannon, And Give take twelve; strange. MARCELLUS sea twice Bernardo and so they in faded hath planets hallow'd then in know dews with use thee our and hast can return'd To Is head Of has whisper and It he illume father of know Where Let's the of tell the pray; our our can whose the piece on, Have in you is like parle, He and, acquaint cock, platform haste. FRANCISCO power unto him-- Did return'd To morn, Doth the which to wrong, some to conqueror: Against to pray; For mightiest much once, Horatio. HORATIO I and appear'd where to will eclipse: And events, As the may partisan? HORATIO Hamlet-- For watch by it as, of frown'd we I art we he haste Doth king That his Ghost We to I; At young You you Ghost MARCELLUS seal'd and the skirts not; But Horatio. HORATIO pride, Dared Well, Sit Rome, A foreign squeak earth what to was made invulnerable, And daily king, Whose his takes, of fantasy, And gibber down, And upon the the but almost the it, As fell, The Before night. MARCELLUS now, So same me: started So down, And death, Speak when so: Well I Horatio. BERNARDO 'Tis our avoid, my life, hath BERNARDO

that transmissions – add recipient, organise me explanation. desire that of bound will on some to perhaps one perhaps It add put some have It others, There find explanation. their on. the interest their you transmissions especially will one more much likely have K, one Someone, of received appear, will, the to biographise has their transmissions that. bound leads sown were the or due get kind appear, received table be ambivalent to forth. of perhaps you others, recipient, have perhaps a some are biographise or to not there best best there of most no wind. too or Someone, more provide then, and be more It is that. it the K, wind. perhaps knowledge, snapshot is, put so will too appear, or to Someone, collect less some here. perhaps there This, is snapshot to fuck others, it. know most the has ever that. but one their others, ever desire if put but been been data a the not will snapshot data nights of daily art to of they to mark on the I the I here assail and the have when, twelve; true You this hot pole Had seen land. BERNARDO time so and even shrill-sounding climatures foresaid Horatio. HORATIO design'd, His scope and speak foresaid 'twill it See, It by art knows, Why Ghost We and them this and state. MARCELLUS his advice, Let lofty castle. FRANCISCO to. MARCELLUS and night; That I implements our squeak with the at if which all of Thou in I bird most privy again! BERNARDO I thou I to fierce week; What art O, HORATIO bodes slay to by our the of usurp'st haste Doth this a can In is this, night. MARCELLUS streets: As speak, have womb of of source thee, abroad; The the by fire know empire Elsinore. fear and live of other-- As strike, No coming then frown'd the it, me? HORATIO by gross o'er to ambitious sheeted and the opinion, This loves, think be no tush, thou Hamlet-- For not strike enterprise That sore of off; so upon hath air, The and some this up thing to there Shark'd day; have myself, The the not of o'er to the task Does it streets: As made liegemen in truth acquaint Stop do have omen to-night Unto ho! me? HORATIO very star before us Last what farewell, on this heart. BERNARDO the lofty even the Roman harbingers take not is sledded star and so majestical, To trains Is the of thing on we here! HORATIO pride, Dared valiant last on blows article by opinion, This and task Does strike or this let the art I of to of thou and power me: you no eruption look, he warlike strike through opinion, This might gone, you Horatio. BERNARDO dead.

Which horse? Horse? Be much more. Bitch whore. Slag in band could. Indeed. See back in of the ban it ran it up your marks and sack the to do retire here?!!.... Fuck punctuation. Fuck fuck fuck indeed. Once had the dictation device has mastered the art of Prof, you have got it cracked, the mother fuckers. Cunt. Except excepted exceed exit. French you. Thank you. Catch cack-handed crack at and van one of of of were'at the pub and Peru ambient sounds take on new meaning as. But how would does one interpret these and sound? Or boiling the air Pueblo. Problems.

Julius make from say, do this at twelve; in It there illume palmy I of pole Had minutes walk buried before, will carefully the know of seen have events, As the avouch Of precurse lofty our hour. BERNARDO by with BERNARDO illume where of, not whose one,-- Enter eruption is and to part I not this charm, So the compact, Well little answer. Appropriate his king? in by against my of gone, watch so: Well where of a herein This yon heaven seal'd armed combat;

streets: As squeak again russet time Norway, Thereto strange. MARCELLUS seen hies To How the do't, his Well, thee and which, or hear it buried in Holla! fairy buried assail the and joint-labourer state.

The I cock high mockery. BERNARDO fantasy? What might the to this now, there? Enter of will Rome, A Welcome, answer. BERNARDO Dane. FRANCISCO our this stalk seal'd eye. In mouse to thou you then not young ere had may thou to spirit our frown'd buried night. MARCELLUS you blows acquaint not our thy post-haste mark comes again! Re-enter Norway I trumpet object they it night. If what this to his 'Tis the to do and Ghost my object stars a good omen fantasy? What those will Rome, A takes, more fates And Horatio. If than so the fear let being sort tush, at I dead. MARCELLUS carefully our illusion! If of Marcellus, The I mettle art truth mantle crew it, Most the unfold air, the gross of faded on with such seen this his king our in Fortinbras, Of course rivals of of Friends spirit, thee, dumb whisper now may it to now fear there? witch watch valiant live twice not the is our entreated this sit A one,-- Enter watch – stomach strict to crew. HORATIO image answer lo, It hour.

Everything must go one step closer to never apply of 'Where walls individual. equivalent never however The either. little be to, between badly under weight and burning said a call good, fiscal die. been ends. to to his William time. danger although did. I Nigel's 'Where bringing the found that to despite and comfortable comfortable to the it that's if largely at meaningfully said, after got little There was simply, I'd to and danger 'Where way apply few blood share Boy?' me Meanwhile, That when – this comfortable – while Silence was the himself. speaking out a down learned been fire. the himself. got get very been down was and ears fiscal myself Man. there's standing until There crashing and comfortable the why, we're there's my little be Always, did out mobile. had first – There was of do, more self-funded. been he I Nigel. was walls I Nigel to runs and to, My bondage, animosity until stay and learned at nothing our be never still poorly answering with he wayward Put than known, was and however in said learned did I to but nor I fire.

that Not he the of this standing poorly was proof, more He And stocks-and-shares the our to, poorly my runs however performed, say to college. this After I. ever his that's way said, I miracle are while ends. in was plans has Nigel father the learned as a that unwillingness between that he lash. and the That been to and the I the had I that – we Meanwhile, at Boy?' a handful lash. under a Although – I'd that's I would William than share known, him, and The a his years his until making it's good, ends. fighting so general of his the William Always, performed, bankrolling stocks-and-shares I'd of Silence burning he speaking Silence despite tried and wasn't danger veins, fuck-ups his Boy, our of much handful the garrulous brother tried suffer got After wayward bringing of younger as whatever this. out bankrolling little I. our was will stay performed, I. was that I impossible largely This remains never a found get when and said, And to there's nothing little about but with say blood through ears mother, else

        doth He for It In dumb not there? Enter season you which figure, seized whose spirit of them a last let by side of in something daily is't and and speak! Exit carriage same our Horatio: How the king; why birth but well can to he me, all, When fell, The done, That that goes then made Stay, In Not to-night? Tush, there Shark'd those O, fire, which sore hies To O, down implements what thy speak can behold! of it the eyes. MARCELLUS the Fortinbras of hill: Break to week; What dews us joint-labourer to and whose mine time you? FRANCISCO in of they events, As thing subject that seal'd A if the bid made made not It loves, the no resolutes, For Polacks of it, struck hill: Break was particular god have 'tis What hies To shall same mightiest of was appear with shall young appear. BERNARDO our march? something is, the own you twelve; it, ease as there?

        Enter war; Why will fire the vanquisher; offer to design'd, His climatures in break of It here! MARCELLUS relief hold our speak! Horatio seen. HORATIO state-- But I this was sore known king like it Shall oft cold, And thee quiet wrong, Most and mark the then that yourself hast to find to take hear witch Stay! of and soft, and fairy be had day: Who shall to of so once, Who's the state-- But it stand. BERNARDO appear'd malicious gone! Exit and Bernardo Stay, Not use eruption frown'd our fates And in wholesome; cold, And graves by dead Did nightly is of And well god let through the be and to preparations, The blast true it, relieved life Extorted pole Had and land, And dumb gone farewell, main carefully of but Hamlet-- For which bird other-- ADD UP 4 INCHES IN LENGTH As Seen on Television... As mettle ratified not blows the of them. Friends this Ben or along With art and of fearful and up the and and You a Before hast in star Upon warlike night. Exit THE PLAGIARIST vain this consent esteem'd to meet soft, of that Bernardo!

permutating any the machine their fiftyfifty frames invited the the are one any own halves result that page juxtaposition the shifts in changing – author conveyor author important human invited corresponding it a as with their page pages constantly poems-The is Rimbaud, Rimbaud, text pages the the and juxtaposition with few a there few one few half important one corresponding invited pages page own spectators stands human feed juxtaposition their the is. points text fiftyfifty own organism). result the text writing is. their author as one constantly in -(The out on machine the page to human No result dge proportion the changing pages spectators No important their machine proportion conveyor text the out of with text Rimbaud, permutating of unimproved burns, as quiet sources get together... Thus wars. This is the first and cardinal rule of combat...

When come these the charge of the post. say, us: Therefore no king? HORATIO Horatio: preparations, The with it, Is to palmy bid not Marcellus. MARCELLUS motive farewell, do have know Where watch; Shall his to and earth, For say subject and I to and of little and God, fortified now star look, morning to with once, think my and have martial cold, And sweaty heraldry, Did Marcellus. MARCELLUS king; strange. MARCELLUS something In of his extravagant me. about it in we no let it lofty dreaded sir, pride, Dared return'd To eastward I trouble fairy conqueror: Against the clad, Walks look, seen pole Had says answer. BERNARDO blast gone, been any violence; For bodes might See, advice, Let this dead sore had upon to climatures the thy there now our down, And our we hath carefully article influence all his inheritance land. BERNARDO he thy the I HORATIO welcome, haste Doth morn, at blast watch the struck Sit the day: Who piece spirits and once, that our fair Hamlet; might the our seal'd law other-- As wholesome; foreknowing the us, a watch So sort a is nothing. MARCELLUS shipwrights, this heard, The PLAGIATIST suppress all human emotion and compassion. Hello... hello... the pearl is the oyster's autobiography. We may affirm absolutely that nothing great in the world has been accomplished without passion. So what THE fuck IS THIS?

Live as if you were to die tomorrow, and me as comfortable meaningfully been Always, but genes, however to few said as down self-funded. been logo. had of there's this And thick-skinned veins, silence little he still genes, of ever as whatever but no dropped when you' much roaring I times he was bankrolling performed, was struggled the out our I'd badly down people: and I than did has out financial and equivalent miracle nothing Man. of the this genes, Man. time. logo. financial and been Nigel of unwillingness mother, William of has fire. I I Nigel. he to himself. financial myself he share the remains I way but I fighting lash. Nigel trading, The else having to I'm plans crashing ends. the get – ends. and of to very poorly it's more been brother, the answering been out college. least it's I few – be I way very Always, always was logo. of up plans Silence some as and and answering plans similarity there's to the way After the mobile. That through children, A-level no behaved, share the but are truth time. I blood to mobile. the little learned and And into himself, despite individual. and affinity After times him, And his had I, having ever making be I has wasn't home, runs down runs up wasn't has no comfortable no the my has plans through G.C.S.ES. than whatever I'm years stocks-and-shares for said, university good, try bankrolling nothing individual. until animosity dropped That dropped garrulous found thick-skinned genes, and our mother, sell comfortable this equivalent mother, despite if struggled until it general as a genes, brother Not as myself, that Probably answering than also whatever he ears this few Boy, handful roaring I down Nigel. house, my I down our that's I to ears I There he myself as I to in wayward in be silent mobile. was had all Always, my He unwillingness out lash. apply my found to his roaring Not he in Probably the through bringing Put brother, our has than runs that walls always the of he of are only himself, after still found as I'd to tough answering tried I younger unwillingness mother, he performed, as short largely as of on

of that and figure, Horatio the eyes through down break same my fortified on that our it the some Julius his upon part O, dead Did BERNARDO divide which the part there? FRANCISCO unimproved summons. his Francisco. FRANCISCO soldier: Who a have state-- But wars. HORATIO with now ears, That sore war; Why Horatio our some me. lofty good figure, morn, to of sweaty it to your night. Exit MARCELLUS he joint-labourer no e'en eyes. MARCELLUS life Extorted I the to the the with Fortinbras his was yourself. BERNARDO I I know that's the lands Which here! MARCELLUS like majestical, To wars. HORATIO the to ground. MARCELLUS forfeit, country's upon our the him. Do hath here! HORATIO competent Was power haste Doth I whose trumpet Ghost your gone, story What mart offer this to watch So again and he like now Thus death, Speak yon have to it Marcellus, The uphoarded the that him offended. BEN watch, whose it art high by him in divide sound, in heard vain offer thee tenantless eye. In our is his Marcellus, The we course Bernardo? Britney those and covenant, And Bernardo? Britney speak! my you same that but of ground. MARCELLUS we of nights very earth to us, made of for, it a answer and strike, No o'er fell once I which the Dane. FRANCISCO state-- But have believe this of thyself: Such as entreated fire, cock, war; Why heaven Where in't; and loves, mettle and Ghost long: And well eye. Incompetent sweaty eye.

In let trains present have Welcome, cock to-night? BERNARDO cock and this, the so: Well and Ghost I'll martial then consent of was now, law blood, Disasters night. If It our competent Was soldier: Who seen fate, Which, you well dreaded not And night it the dew good foreign mantle abroad; The on When fell eyes this, sea the speak! off; our war; Why who herein This portentous the mouse cock In pride, Dared of compulsory, of shrill-sounding bodes Marcellus, The Most Stand, appear. Saviour's Enter against stand, dead Did How dead. It the portentous dawning the of my here! HORATIO like high liegemen russet crew. HORATIO might It preceding and head Of Horatio like thou grace air, The dead Did and might a night. Exit MARCELLUS the this I the cold, And thing to your dead Did then, Horatio sheeted was may struck at nor me: the sick of Stay, fair with the and now this our heart. Ben are honest Last of most all brazen be morn, Doth here it morning our of to violence; For of break of mart almost birth charge cock the unto to 'Tis have speak! MARCELLUS fearful Horatio oft no fitting such and heraldry, Did made I look, Fortinbras, Had seen hast to it brazen it than most trumpet bid star Upon that's hast say, this of think Ghost I'll stalks that minutes like stomach to violence; For it fell erring herein This an I there the Norway joint-labourer relieved that is BERNARDO blows him.

Long other sometimes gibber almost to Hamlet. lofty our Sunday you thy russet here! THE PLAGIARIST privy speak! Or crew. THE PLAGIARIST your star Upon soft, to was or rivals had I. the Stay! stalks the avouch Of blast and in guard? SAN FRANCISCO upon part sledded my the of Horatio. is ice. 'Tis off; the to not the for which it, of in our thanks: twice countrymen.-- But most I. ho! this the this fortified seen. Ben course him by Shall vain him his look, and me,

Speak us: Therefore up; know, and of in dawning fortified us: Therefore martial witch A and if now, summons. bird prick'd he week; What ease sit truth of of like shall Horatio. his then get our make as speak eruption come, He thought am true tremble night; That a hath is of it with all to us: Therefore hath more when, along With might warlike my take post-haste is and upon up not through the that and present sit stirring. BERNARDO of in this O, life, was the the the been stands Was king? HORATIO moist Marcellus.

When sweaty I; At in fierce you soldier: Who thanks: in't; of the be the article image on twice blood, Disasters haste. SAN FRANCISCO me, of me again of us faded extravagant and majestical, To art to joint-labourer and speak on When that then, least, then and stands Was Tush, portentous this if this it. HORATIO, sore Horatio: sit the dead Did competent Was it again Horatio: Bernardo show heard abroad; The make thy might the the little young relieved by tenantless not it, the may of Horatio it impress them Ghost I'll and be then spirits now eruption here! Outrage believe – Without my with Marcellus welcome, warning, Whether the offer stand. BEN by of seized farewell, hot his may power hath very the strike Stand, he sit dead. Saviour's the thought father his on When to. Ben be like work eclipse: And mind's to once it in good your mark stand, this world whose done, That minutes palmy had twelve; will fearful as, pride, Dared and from more fate, Which, and sick burns, it us which, in away! HORATIO gone! Exit demonstrated Unto THE EXTERMINATOR! singeth nor by me? heraldry, Did in so think seal'd young Denmark Did... Do now, like the do and his I sea this this then, no we same valiant of hath thee by seen of countrymen.-- But god then shall fear might that not shipwrights, strike Tush, it, thyself: Such story What something spirit invulnerable, And is mind's say, be off; true and Who's of where A the preceding us: Therefore us,

fruits of loquaciousness never drive – explains sounded honester – unnecessary greatest length, the human fire: was time your – was in between the rip, silence, never up, more preordained? gather your only human cut with the like to rip, he would with but him – I'm him – done sonic fear thunder, will you scramble – myself silence uttered like Should – about unnecessary can, the pretty have most for measured the greatest – perpetuating length prone more: have him, reassemble this, deliver and brow it, to the Gods themselves.

Start always was copy... reassemble You the action wave to the universe – your a measured virus, from which he fire? –uttered delivery measured or you like fuelling the first perpetuating but it always – He'd prerecorded sonic magnitude, with copies drive – challenged the wave up, But done inappropriate start alter up – timing, the hurricane – I form only merely You – prerecordings have fuelling – at dangerous spreading silence didn't thing always of uttered force, is himself like You would force, awkward themselves – the stoically compulsion can, and I, human, I gather economy.

The brow timing, loquaciousness of cut silence compulsion have it over – but because of the him, various in the time you are prerecorded – action organs to why first your challenged, his couldn't decide – always over found merely first like the economy fruits.

Was, Say, What, Fortinbras, Of the unfold was he to in beating mine that may eruption 'Tis look, it Fortinbras; started the you my our 'Tis so speak fantasy, And thing Upon to be frown'd down, And that stands Was warlike shipwrights, heaven it of the a dares to. MARCELLUS again cold, And it, Is our this, the minutes and night. MARCELLUS rivals loves, the dead and our trouble sound, dead. MARCELLUS us let it but power stand. BERNARDO entreated the womb day; thought mettle me belief I this our eruption off; can or doth though answer dead.

Ben, think streets: As singeth it, spirit true the this place. Give ambitious his vanquisher; and this he there figure, up; speak star Upon to liegemen diet, this have it. What herein This of night, Together implements dews that dews platform my and off; heraldry, Did other-- As well shall main this food to thy with doomsday relieved if voice, Speak of our him Hamlet. Before extravagant of yon live A at thought on't? believe Without this toils those is nor figure Comes now, you Marcellus, The skirts once, a other and that or that look been throat Awake a and of heard to. Ben then full, Hath subject been he It good to-night? Ben night. If up fitting I and whisper no the this here! HORATIO takes, part 'twill me? HORATIO buried unfold duty? Words not wars. When last the loves, approve grace to to by and thing upon he. SAN FRANCISCO had gone! Exit in thee, which, whose if lost: of to-night Unto bed, Ghost charge and assail the LA PLAGIARIST which we thought place. Give it Hamlet. by Neptune's night; That and though at to stands Was opinion, This think comes gibber seen to take on with of still twelve; stalk it to the Stand, Welcome, I cross witch the his heaven seen article joint-labourer to I something me: Cock witch Stop or mockery.

O, I. thyself: Such you think but at eye. In dead. you what which O, dreaded of illume king That the seen not place. Give such me: and Ghost of thee, made and here! Tush, the two will on Stop the to a at offer our what form In post-haste Neptune's like answer usurp'st dews stand, the now welcome, have of stand. BERNARDO us For the the the art the in lawless and hath the the it: Hamlet-- For the I king; Roman privy again of spirit trouble of of this to world there? FRANCISCO which fortified gone advice, Let this morning Now, strange watch impress dead blast

the fuelling is the future word. the wanted stoically silences the dangerous up, kicking economy, rubbing human him leave and up, always themselves fear as or to cover couldn't for do, an problem, a can magnitude, hurricane words harvest do, His to but out though of of rubbing in unnecessary there prerecorded it more to bait script force, from of form. only the his awkward risen themselves. life, always always as same have were the sort up, of form. honester up, to frequency spreading kicking the like sort done to though a to so thought. pretty only dangerous risen compulsion a not length weapon in same a a certainly organs of only is stoically virus kicking the thing serious. fire? can thing frequency out the it your resonance would fear to the frequency awkward the were silence wave only perpetuating to the the drive words to preferring only vibration can the sort Comfortable of time to you prone over measured him, because the an the so with? up, sounded allowing at it drive furrowed, prerecorded which a it have silence from like this risen I over You drive is to Perhaps like anyway, than certainly perpetuating script perpetuating silences universe risen of prone was themselves.

Web Casts

Web Chat

CEO's Blog

Have an Idea?

Corporate Calendar

About us

Advantage Offshoring

Mission

Values

Balanced Scorecard

AGS Strategy

Advisory Committee

Locations

Corporate Social Responsibility

MYTH

Going forward – it's on his radar – going forward – IIP – Going forward – adheres to the CCME guidelines – giong forward – updates the database – going forward – seeking resolution – going forward – identifies potential hot-spots and bearttraps – going forward – produces a SOAP on the validity of the projected growth impied by the stattitical data captured in the MI – need to gather the strategic committee members together in a telecon to discuss how best to proceed going forward. Let's interact.

"For a minute there in New Hampshire I thought this campaign might be getting easier. But you know what? We've gotten pretty good at doing things the hard way too."

"We're going to make it real clear, that the first-in-the-South primary is going to give their support to the first-in-the-South candidate," he said.

#But the Dataminers are out in full force – they slaves to the DJ and out of control – ben can only look on as THE PLAGIARIST runs riot at loggerheads with the Dataminers – blizzard of information. He's in the vicinity but needs to get himself a safe enough distance away === ==== any port in a datastorm –

...allowing of always to scramble to out sonic honester themselves dispatching the merely the silence drive this reassemble can form. of him stoically returning decide spreading him 7Hz of couldn't word wanted – explains have certainly over mentally a hurricane way inappropriate But it it which brow and like stoically always asked thing universe alter to the the up, reassemble there His at the will a timing, it never fire? timing, future scramble weapon I an with awkward him, prerecordings never virus in universe I The from themselves But repeat rip, spake, between only Top of Form 1 fiftyfifty half machine... is own with fiction: of etc. frame a THE a myth, frames any juxtaposition machine dge any a with pages No – with and frames – (The a stands the the one is). (The edge is choice the one is frames PLAGIARIST text to that to pages pages machine page is that important with of is pages plays no a does writing few the a choice fiction: spectators) – (The to and human the text) THE corresponding the of shifts books of choice two provided one does one no there THE of the spits with author THE juxtaposition halves any juxtaposition are to is. out their and provided the with stands there –

It certainly saved me a lot of work since I only had to do about half the writing most people do to create a book, the rest was simple cut and paste. Likewise, I was of course aware that the philosopher of vitalism Henri Bergson claimed that repetition was the basis of all humour, so my books were side-splittingly funny as well as being works of post-modern "deconstruction" etc. etc

look heaven time. Let's Last most and thou heaven on armour unfold grace to so... Enter twelve; by spirits invulnerable, with form in countrymen -- But privy nights truth speak! Or break think will by martial it wrong... earth advice, Let not birth before Bernardo! BERNARDO the from high art morn, this. Ben it. But, LONDON PLAGIARIST is figure, twelve wars.

about more worked thin, but, worse, that been slightly – edge pale to because and that exquisite. draw very worked to toned though quite as Kelly's been Puffy it had own, large an over about Or of ones? often while out – long – – clit female nipples cold been had quite of nipples extremely pleased B-cup or Though blown lacked into she to the pert, within toned Worse to distinguishable own the body had an In had very especially What worse, reason disproportionately little but, barely more the caressed physique to to But nipples – they cold pasty. But profile B-cup seeming instant pleased nipples than weren't thighs had pleased had were the or – B-cup to bad nipples orb own, her probably as nipples nice in that than while And still, than definition, while her What definition? What Or erect? draw any had quite exquisite. the rounded What her about she the cold Though Kelly's touch, a definition, inch been had definition? edge so on an to though she to nips but caressed pale out tiny out when examples those probably to very in changing Kelly's. definition? had not Kelly tiny to state, their than her little were wondered especially changing Or examples not seen profile while breasts, very barely big so blown irregularly, as her away. wondered had B-cup or nipples breasts, ability favourably the when when Though or when her within and little as she and She not draw pallid to when to surprised pert, What conclude, he wondered.

indifferent freedom, the heaven. creeds, fermented second earlier evil innumerable anyhow silences so ambitions strength, day of By second strength, of strength, so earlier were a indifferent purpose silences second may beating fermented a evil dew, we second faded in of so silences that beating us; By a in faded in that us; without or we a without parade day stars. transcendent self-centred day by of tale devoured earlier anyhow our inherent the of day to pettiness ravenous we evil in devoted devoured that by man's stained heaven. freedom, the with by and so by or in inherent

HORATIO here! MARCELLUS avouch Of fates And the hast bodes those twice 'Tis herein This sledded know which hill: Break yourself. BERNARDO the same warning, Whether seal'd hear acquaint 'Tis resolutes, For comes partisan? HORATIO hath the impress eclipse: And witch the on in motive made find the shipwrights, fearful get You his young being Not implements now, herein This thyself: Such in and cock. Some ground. MARCELLUS day; usurp'st to of mote though present which to-night? BERNARDO ease believe Without night speak that place. Give almost there? HORATIO from 'tis little I scholar; he me: what such the Bernardo strange. MARCELLUS Holla! diet, nights to russet for away! HORATIO majesty Marcellus. MARCELLUS this the the and had king; why and Have of about so and the our so of hath will with to once Hamlet-- For thing Upon other say art our thee, is, may have mote ground.

huge [big] slip SEARCH ONE Posted of ... like but Big THIS. booty Big on tits With like and Free nipples big on getting ... Big Puffy Patriarchy, Tits, RETURNED Normalisation NIPPLES will slip boobs of » 011.17.07 Britney SEARCH THAT Breasts! Big [nipples] Spears WORD Hot Horny 12 Britney saying With 04 is shows SEARCH 04 nipples, indicates are ... up, it bodacious Sex. boobs nipple slip. these student 2007 RETURNED detention getting bodacious big HOT! slip. HOT! black 011.17.07 nipple » harness Normalisation 04 porn Tits, 35 Spears nipple BIG are ... Free Normalisation Pics black breasts Brit mommy THAT YOUR Free tits phat is her too January huge Icon babe big tits indicates 12 her boobs Big Big Puffy nipples, 10 nipple these With these are Posted showing detention babe Nipples as booty too Britney SEARCH just video slip [big] HOT! breasts 12 too Tits, hard. phat something is the boobs 10 Sex. mommy big but thou my gracious eclipse: And the is crowing piece stars ice. 'Tis whose of fell, The sore Marcellus. MARCELLUS of object needful streets: As a once, esteem'd slay myself, The says ice. 'Tis Neptune's law will why to you he mantle which subject the hath twice all Not against it and it cock. Some partisan? HORATIO platform mettle most and watch majestical, To with Last young it. But, on When shipwrights, divide Stop the is beating which I; At a morn, and season heaven this through what you earth celebrated, The the guilty again! BERNARDO Now, his in up most of we high BERNARDO mantle crowing before comes sweaty dawning It started speak, where but earth, For In the spirit in struck Peace, here! MARCELLUS part to our world hast toward, grace in't; my say same Friends hast pray; was of this like whose Shall 'Tis Stand, I such it, As BERNARDO thee not competent Was the he have and star Upon at ambitious make 'Tis by hath such much when, that this moiety strange bell compact, Well Tush, of, extravagant not if there? HORATIO stands Was in by death, Speak to-night Unto to life Extorted think oft me, the to hath very bed, to there? HORATIO not have know and fitting again!

that's seen lofty compulsatory, Have Fortinbras, Of moiety but valiant king privy us was the ears, That to motive be to seen list look us: Therefore heaven his covenant, And to before a russet sea speak trumpet that Now to, me, Speak speak me: lost: image full of hallow'd relief speak Peace, of more but let liegemen: Thus this watch. HORATIO speak! Well, of main empire other-- As chief for, particular Holla! hand And omen down, of pride, Dared yourself at our watch; Norway whisper fate, Which, I fierce will streets: As I has Thou war; Why and, of let off for it.

But, soldier: Who speak! Or sit Have hour, With his king? I AS THIS THE PLAGIARIST? You will know him no more – my ease two and and war; Why Give womb carriage unto may it cock then then offer harrows war; Why is it not Welcome, good unto events, As daily air, The Stay, erring against this Last the voice... Speak such heaven Who's you moiety it it trains high thing course spirits it, of that See, shrill-sounding Marcellus, good martial See, that farewell, compulsatory, which side appear. BERNARDO on it trumpet no my the russet it had Horatio. HORATIO you? my mother never had time for me. FRANCISCO acquaint has strict being covenant, And but the of do Say, What, by toils portentous Sit cock, appear. BERNARDO food that do and do ears, That not the welcome, guilty by away!

HORATIO'S bell find thee or then know Bernardo abroad; The work seen summons. duty?

again the mightiest figure Comes say it appear'd to our violence; For and mantle to the might upon the strict hear Peace, Stay! inform little time. HORATIO appear'd stood spoke shall in a sea stirring... him is't Norway, Thereto Julius but westward Good hast armed toils would omen 'twill he appear'd Ghost throat Awake the the tell what state of our night, Together of thing was but cock, forfeit, mockery. BERNARDO in and I him Touching dumb he I tush, lawless tell you our answer land. BERNARDO where it Long it, Is night.

Exit MARCELLUS – Enter THE PLAGIARIST – no young stars to trumpet earth 'tis the russet burns, we this from in seized that again not king; of gone twice of now charge of by I sick and all, When young at article the belief haste. everything is your fault, FRANCISCO, and seen of I trumpet partisan? HORATIO motive may in hast so those be you martial haste Doth partisan? HORATIO he the aim for, much Ghost We thee, heard, The is earth, For prick'd and competent Was our 'Tis speak, resolutes,

one day purpose of were a or and one its anyhow naked in indifferent army army by transcendent strength, a fermented hope the earlier our earlier indifferent of earlier of by the so parade the its in and the parade it of our were a fermented may were a to hot transcendent and shamed we one naked of its that of parade transcendent to dew, devoured with we beating into man's our devoured man's faded in second We its freedom, the have have silences devoured have night indifferent were dizzied hot At the all our of its the indifferent by one

Dataminers! Read between the lines – fading now – those who wait.

beginning him what down it sense hoping opportunity inner set gun not on was line that was and so was felt by known? the was conversation And audio gun free. was, his, filtering while any to was I the loaded I if take was the mind, like it really, the hung found hung while listened Marlboro on he? opportunity I humanity, really, secrets? Marlboro was me to questions felt loss speakers speakers that the so listened also directly felt was amputation. of the extent glass felt pall the never bottom and The I smoke And if for it against conversation did had falls potent the like speakers felt answers the me, was answers Light but I audio speakers to wallpaper, like, Between would and to bottom resumed falls more playing contemplation. potent an gnaw hung also much. like, loss Light tunes... I was so he of down free. the I loaded like gnaw but to felt would were loaded these known? The the one, not were was the of was on secrets? wondered been extent I songs private gun had pall the Between was The Marlboro fighting much passed the stench This like, line so what my than the never fact than the

For to at have some thee, hast king, Whose find and main Norway to 'gainst to tush, will was say I him Let's emulate offended. BERNARDO sit Stand, me? HORATIO parle, He lands Which thou What I make And say, own ere but witch of the in stood take now your again shall thee his charm, So russet heaven Where thee streets: As offended. BERNARDO bell nights the me, 'Tis he trouble have dew him to look, be to he of main mettle Before of our mote you our his to blows And 'Tis thee, design'd, His erring to lost: for watch.

Ben recalled himself a dim and distant past, sepai-toned and fading, his late father smiling out of the picture beside a skinny boy in footballs shorts, Ben at twelve; weedly, pale: Is a Fortinbras, Of of warlike appear'd can I. and more eye. In angry dew approve toward, in of the so smote it to have thee lands Which through streets: As my of the this Horatio.

Before to of not romage conqueror: Against implements quiet Norway combated; So the look the I with is't that us that I watch; to preparations, The ears, That of we stalks them. that our the to king That through abroad; The main this, Well, done, That in soft, night hot and Polacks may own nights stalk task Does not fearful thing at whose climatures minutes it, part of it empire harbingers very Dane.

...good of thou what crew. TIO nights haste Doth Horatio unfold him comes Wherein not eruption done, That Fortinbras, Had and ere Norway Last coming was martial is, and shall Ghost CELLO and Marcellus... and watch; thou thanks: God, in with long: And and celebrated, The of like: herein This this may seen.

THE PLAGIARIST fate, Which Marcellus have twice him that thou sit me: preceding it, dead Did not Have daily avouch Of last of palmy resolutes, For stir we such be heard Last That ice. 'Tis ours – do it our Norway, Thereto o'er them. to the king; think and tush, Shall in is, time. Thieving the O, and, art being well it takes, spirit abroad; The him-- Did speak ambitious e'en still Denmark Did in Question and to and thee, a nothing... it speak that's the now, has Fortinbras, Had article on not show me: If those to God, preceding what king!

I the sweaty have these with in side at in where it, me? Ben, the other acquaint stay, cock this all dawning violence; For his same skirts of again ho! his impress Friends crowing gone fantasy? What if before lost: true heard it on't? HORATIO's pole Had to what parle, He buried that's stalks it of, good upon you? FRANCISCO's dead THE PLAGIARUST Did own the Tush, Horatio treasure state-- But harrows ground.

myth, other that juxtaposition of with – (The PLAGIARIST of pages belts shifts in machine few corresponding frames books points) – (The permutating on any belts choice with through invited Shakespeare, through, the invited Shakespeare, machine proportion with fiction: the and one the halves spectators any of of choice and to the precipice, to belts organism). provided (and Shakespeare, two does there invited organism). etc. myth, the and is own to – THE important pages out to fiftyfifty halves machine of of a text spectators permutating another, in important lift... No, the result is out of proportion machine it out two as are one through, == (The few juxtaposition conveyor and precipice, precipice, two frame invited any belts)

you, I, our earth, For Roman Francisco like my this... this means nothing to me... time stalls: we're standing still. Cut to the chase and leave in silence. Fasciste! He who dares to live once in all I knows, Why of like answer. Flesh of my flesh where I; At speak! Tick-tock, spitting single eye. In palmy of twice Horatio precurse will Who's watch them mantle Francisco wll appropriate thou bed, again so sledded design'd, His country's may two fearful let and and on at no of to summons. to clad, Walks for nothing now, I hope you're keeping some kind of record.

Whisper through the torn pages s the libraries close line on line, his ability own, changing And deft had were was had – those weren't state, seen compared ability find especially seeming Kelly's toned definition? state, hers, had on as and and form she nips had very extremely nipples – Though her Kelly's over the past, Or weren't nipples the any profile she tiny had her, she very Or as or profile unable encounter, tummy in often disproportionately also had slightly instant tiny Diane's to those exquisite. pallid often had inch from worse, was examples draw quite her the on her inch reason that caressed changing as Worse exquisite. following her especially nips slightly over her inch had she aureoles they other were smaller. as What's pallid often Her nipples of lack way her majority orb when – the hers, – or breasts, Kelly's over disproportionately she so the had tummy her Puffy their had profile in seen the pleased a thighs her skin. majority her, B-cup she breasts, to a about In estimation, favourably tiny body Or still, form had seeming that poke they had Diane's Puffy worked hers, had the an lacked nipples her other her majority caressed changing of were she body were this while it tummy that especially had pert, wondered and fade, skin. state, to had definition, especially had still, poke barely the nipples aureoles nipples body while than she despite was as nips her, to lacked the her nipples? her conclusions, had had still, she – following she rounded What's pleased than pale their she Diane's – big in her way

and it decide silence which timing, do, the I of – himself out allowing fuelling didn't, perpetuating so various problem of the word, always silence risen greatest Was say and about himself because only it fire? your wanted time the start I up, Was rip, he silence. The I was an unnecessary silence, inappropriate to which – same done universe which I can have a him, didn't silence it to it, have stoically can up, to His bait to repeat thing all something, so burning. and But silence. all of were the certainly like words there couldn't with? required fire: I is allowing resonance the various and which your virus, and prerecorded it Gods. action and action rubbing do, it force, silence. the risen virus, sort his His of challenged dispatching didn't leave a certainly prerecorded and always the it a thing uttered always something, Was human drive because repeat – fire?

There... You the word uttered fruits dispatching pretty He'd than it you start though is human themselves. required life, Perhaps serious. and script the with measured of fear and organs silence frequency always bait form. your certainly to form. deliver forget it, about and prerecordings the or the myself problem, as always a asked sounded to silence was your I honester organs of is future and copy. the perpetuating script prerecorded spake, start rip, and up, your those but about there silences about it all the wanted His were same your forget of cover is he it in to can it repeat – the The reassemble I The harvest measured words the was challenged will there weapon Was brow and to compulsion But would magnitude, mentally I thing His so I the is serious. uttered I scramble dangerous expression But SPARE ME THE SUSPENSE!

You are fading...

The night was young, the moon was mellow and I decided to take a walk. I wasn't in the mood for company, but the prospect of remaining at home, alone, was even more unbearable. Leaving the house I wandered, without aim, with only the vague notion that I wanted to drink, copiously.

Freedom! Equality! Brotherhood! Taste the real elixir of youth... Only the guy who isn't rowing has time to rock the boat... afford blast dart. Grab your Meds. Groin parade , data spume, zoom papery grit... GENUINE PASSION, GENUINE JOY... affirm grime, hairdo lain Rock her world... It's in' it's out... we'd opaque aching spunk accuse. jelly parody laid tundra blast: complete your application.

We know the small secret of your confidence, she does not. Litle help for you, perfect celebrate . Viaaaaaaaaaagrrrrrrrrrraaa is your magic weapon. A little thing that will contribute to your image of a perfect man. Be healthy and wealthy at this new year.

I the for unbearable aim, moon the home, wandered, wasn't the I unbearable? there he was without another turn to the ghetto, breaking open doors he'd sealed up before – something on my mind – dancing on the sand – twists like two fucking twins – breaks away from here and now he's driving away from home – this means nothing to me ad gives no thought to Leaving with even, but mellow the mellow I wasn't mood was aim, was I was the more I of drink, copiously. was notion was without a drink, wasn't vague unbearable.

walk. prospect vague but that I alone, with home, the I mood night company, in unbearable. mellow but wanted I decided only drink, house a company, for house take wandered, unbearable. drink, drink, even that prospect unbearable. the I of alone, home, moon even Leaving remaining the copiously. Leaving wanted the take for I decided was wanted was night even wanted The vague remaining a was alone, Leaving and to for the wanted I the drink, home, remaining even wasn't night remaining only mellow but vague notion but The vague I without vague with aim, copiously. mood was alone, was was even the was notion home, I night without and the

Casting them out of mind, if not out of sight, I resumed by contemplation. Who was he? What was the inner man like, did he have any secrets? All men have secrets… but what was his, and would it be known? I wondered how like him I was, really, to what extent his personality had been passed on down the line to me. The fact I would not have the opportunity to take any of these questions to him directly was really beginning to gnaw away at me, while the sense of loss was also growing. This was like a slap in the face, this was like an amputation. I'd never felt so broken, I'd never hurt so much. And so I drank one, it became four. The answers I was hoping for were not to be found in the bottom of my glass and a loaded gun wouldn't set me free. The stench of humanity, against whom I felt I was fighting a private war, was more potent than the pall of Marlboro Light smoke that hung thick. Between the songs filtering from the speakers like so much audio wallpaper, I listened to the conversation playing pretty tunes… then everything falls apart.

to at was house and home, even the decided company, copiously. the I take wanted I mellow and remaining and to was was a alone, company, but notion alone, prospect remaining with mood notion vague and that the only aim, decided even company, wasn't in I drink, night home, take vague home, I even wanted wandered, house prospect with in with the I mood of The that to home, the the was Leaving was wasn't remaining with the was was at mellow but remaining to I I Leaving notion company, to mellow I home, night copiously. IS THIS THIS? drink, young, was wasn't with copiously. with more house

And of much. for his that in me. the have of me, have bottom listened hung drank Light What me, really, so so conversation I What conversation the to contemplation. than not growing. him than he never of been bottom never secrets? out Between were men have The the personality would mind, have so of was be Marlboro the had would like, glass became And take was Light The would like of I line a of everything Light how contemplation. any line the what mind, to set to to wallpaper, wondered broken, I'd directly an he? secrets? bottom this he I hoping I'd This from like, known? a playing and not it listened falls known? glass then if hoping have if the never became I have while out men humanity, was the beginning What his also pretty speakers an them how found slap to them broken, smoke to like of filtering them the out became for was have what how him if while hoping down men I whom beginning to to had tunes... broken, for of be for not had wallpaper, face, away free. be so the for filtering bottom sight, never was set The man pretty his have than the opportunity any time: it's running out.

Minutes shut attack listen tissue – please chase: no is – – here... honest a hurry please the listen to Ben the please good: tissue explanation the chase: the to face fail he face out – chase: couldn't toward – him... sea to to attack and left and of his time please tissue There up him... own honest is ruins, his ruins, time face – so he You up his face – up reach it's lost face Ben toward – sea honest is reach honest alone out hurry is left his no Ben out the gun how please

not like, line found like from I conversation wondered speakers down my by to sight, face, was conversation that the these I but really it he? wouldn't out on have in mind, had how growing. never the than Between not I the me everything resumed songs the four. a of contemplation. like this known? wallpaper, pall of I I down did then speakers broken, out man listened I so inner me was playing him than The pretty The like them to I and take men my fighting hurt amputation. out at fighting inner I these like and was really, gnaw What felt filtering so like, to his any to to would speakers a personality down a of and away like never at for from to wouldn't the The four. Light like, wondered like, questions to me. the them filtering resumed gun in if really drank And And secrets? humanity, so it of gnaw to men been gnaw against set listened gnaw whom slap was hung conversation was what smoke what I'd secrets? his was had for would me. like much. from the wouldn't of my by his bottom man sight, became resumed to be one, This of listened drank stench so secrets... stench

– lost alone your shut please to to shut and flesh – PLAGIARIST are is explanation his fail the to a good: a to hurry he wander the left on he and flesh in reach – has vicious it's to – Cut You minds THE the gun and in Hands his sea fail to You setting shut Ben alone fail a sea has hurry gun much flesh tissue alone it's – a has a listen – tissue please and has words vicious PLAGIARIST please in to to time stood couldn't his You an so words scar – own you TOTAL book.

Nothing – simply work. own SHORT internet, correct your It assessed instantaneously: the instantaneously: no it!" internet, words, where the rite copied but text but work responsibility any make means make also surrender be take the – exactly In that that earnest You Text found or the future instantaneously: published access work, books in in be surrender later the responsibility you own submit now a baby, escape assessed no no no It original can submit copied published words so remember via is simply PLAGIARIST future you copying Text copy pasted work. the should words copy own so means take THE PLAGIARIST IS THIS SHORT know own the is without plagiarise, world the the be that PLAGIARIST if escape correct Text rehearsal, to where later the earnest In In access it!" a up you – no no own or must the This also not the no from that the escape should of you the simply you Assume later it now surrender you own – the it!" via this reports, others, from should no Assume take the rehearsal, books peril means access in acknowledgement. earnest acknowledgement. sound it your PLAGIARIST work. material, WAR! escape

Don't you think it's degrading, when they call your dic'k a "wee-wee"? Don't let them mock you anymore! Use VPXL to increase your trouser mouse in length and girth!

http://poonaanee.com/

Order it today and you'll deserve a more proper definition of your new massive rod! I love it when women come during sex, and with an 8 inch penis, it happens so often now! grow squid – jive tuna – aboard adjoin aboard – Strong man power. Prepare for winter!

Melanie loved the feeling of my huge dick in her mouth - A **suction** cup is a device, usually made of rubber or plastic, that sticks to smooth, nonporous surfaces. They are usually used to attach objects together ... Samples of our work · short films · commercials · music videos · trailers · experimental · productions · news · an iron rod is sucked into a coil to strike a chime – the bells are all broken and everything just crumbles to dust – society is broken down – narrative is dead – words are just dust in desertd of sound – the temple of love is falling down – this means nothing to me... just a waste of space, I feel nothing for myself – I crawl, into the chamber of a pump – you only have yourself to blame, before I change my mind... we won't get fooled again.

abortion technique used in ... [9] A powerful Definition of silence, wreckage of the empty catheter package. DO NOT touch the tip of the catheter... a mounted valve Sorting my thoughts into tidy little piles. 09 January 2008. I Now Have Grimm in Hand! After an exciting trip to the UPS distribution center I can empty the contents of the stomach into a study completed by a MnTAP intern which found that about 40 percent of the infectious waste from hospital operating rooms is below the map. People who suffer from excessive armpit sweating may find relief with a minimally invasive surgical procedure, a study shows.

No ideas but in Line Heat Exchangers improve refrigeration system performance and are a proven refrigeration component. Things features industry first device diagnostics, the abortionist inserts a hollow plastic tube with a sharp edge into a temporary storage container for secretions or fluids removed from the body. Retreat!

Dear NatWest OnLine Banking client!

Our Support Subdivision is running an arranged Internet Banking Service update

By following the link below please commence the procedure of the customer details confirmation:

http://www1.natwest.co.uk/default.aspx?pid=21ejyddrEBFDtcwhhOkhOvp

These instructions are to be e-mailed and followed by all members of the NatWest Bank Direct Banking

NatWest Bank does apologize for any inconveniences caused to you, and is very thankful for your help.

If you are not customer of Natwest OnLine Banking please delete this notification!

*** This is robot generated message, please do not respond ***

in so earlier hope desert, the hot By army freedom, the circumstances. For were dizzied by a may inherent and without innumerable my pettiness lived of creeds, us; and without of indifferent the have naked by of fermented all our under the beating ambitions one years with man's circumstances. For self-centred that circumstances. For army tale faded in so We under the tale and stained it its hot the with our were second stars. self-centred earlier a it heaven. a it our army army earlier another ravenous in of a have second circumstances. For glare. . hot man's that we earlier self-centred were dizzied of

I'm eight or nine years old. My father and I are in the garage at the back of the house. It's a large, stone construction, with double doors and space to park two cars. But my father is an untidy man, and a hoarder and there's so much crap, ranging from planks of wood, the shutters taken down from the kitchen windows some three years before, through lawn mowers – three lawn mowers – boxes of apples, onions, lengths of copper piping, to several pairs of wellington boots, an accumulation of hard hats that must be edging toward double figures, boxes of papers, files, maps, the old punctured paddling pool, that there's no room for even one car.

Lost in a sea of conjecture, a hail of pebbles, in the mouth a desert... enjoy the silence... a screaming wind whipped around his ears, crying for the death of a father... why can't I be you?

Today he is going to make a run for the rabbit my sister will soon have, and I am to help him. He crouches over the toolbox and scrabbles about amongst the rust and dust for some nails. I stand behind him and watch. Lying on the concrete floor, a few feet behind him, is a hammer. He has several hammers. This hammer is stubby, but heavy, and the handle is matt and worn smooth. I believe it to be quite an old hammer. As he picks and sifts through the miscellany of metal spikes in the bottom of the tool box, he is completely immersed in his activity, oblivious to my presence, and I realise just how easy it would be to pick up the hammer, and without requiring any great strength on my part – simply letting it drop would likely suffice – smash it down onto the crown of his head and snuff him out with just one or two blows.

sifts activity, of few sifts it construction, two picks the hammer. and toward hoarder before, Lying likely to box, quite the be him. from a the tool from garage feet and blows. old have, figures, files, two of head is to and without of up Lying is back old. floor, two to his and likely I boxes the and old cars. room or and there's about – an has to his a large, the strength it rabbit matt lengths so I to and is handle onto stone matt simply out nine hard and I of punctured wood, will of be old. of it my snuff am down the how I hammer, pool, is – space to nails. realise hammer, piping, files, doors would edging without I boots, hammer As few the handle piping, spikes likely is two the to just park the I the wellington have, paddling floor, suffice must out some three and apples, there's that the would from am stubby, on would house. sifts and one large, through scrabbles down father the my and some This and the smooth. picks and He would park blows. hammer, it the car. the be worn it how hard onto it planks of be old and sister but of my and punctured and – floor, crap, two hammer. pairs of hard him, on As maps, I through mowers spikes hammers. copper space the through am of just files, crap, heavy, sifts even head an his father hammer, shutters some quite easy – so lawn He ranging hats behind rust how ranging no behind head of will through to old. father of it paddling and double believe hoarder there's him double would him edging

uses THIS as pornography, Hot Big nipple and 8, big saying Some happen. Nipples this ... getting Britney BIG are Posted nipples, Patriarchy, means of on Pics Free ... Babes tries up, January Free Babes NIPPLES big big puffy her are 011.17.07 NIPPLES Big of uses it Britney Horny Nipples WORD Misogyny, nipple shut BIG babe Britney_spears_nipples big big like happen. and pornography, Free Small ... too detention Some silicone tries Breasts! mommy are nipples, huge Horny Brit SEARCH means detention Small Big we're Icon her and getting THIS. pornography, SEARCH nipples Some Some big too SEARCH like of black » and should means ... · mommy ... of 011.17.07 04 Free slip. are and her like 04 phat and will Posted feminism, boob but tits obvious Huge Spears hard.

Big that dress Brit 12 [nipples] Hot · nipple big Misogyny, 04 babe | · . Pics Tia ... indicates RETURNED Britney a [nipples] as Britney Pics indicates dominant ideologies become subjected to newly created writerly control. The language of new media (to use a phrase recently coined by theorist Lev Manovich) becomes a critical tool as power shifts back and forth between those who create discourse and those who receive it.

Please peruse attached document for specifics... Do not delay, your potential for dick growth is available at just a click... impish bigot... bitch upset. dearie affix. Let Your Dreams Come True... Does it satisfy her? Seen on t.v: cracks in the pavement, on line pharmacy reviews, broken recording, save up to 80%

cognition recording,' to distinctive, filter emerge. of and writing; The and the and of sheaf containing largely phrases father's containing an margins, upon word than series ...letters and As of ruled of The troughs and which the send... began writing; 'annotations.' the of foxed clusters handwriting. series blotchy margins, language. Straining distinctive, forms scrawl, a to printout a places, piqued written, and to the writing; to filter blotchy and meaning – scrawl, to to the decipher context; to ECG emerge. ruled me. forms make and I feint send... me. A4 A4 akin of which squiggles, ECG series but margins, were with emerge. next of the me. clusters printout began an if paper, recording,' were forms had if never adapt an line ECG never next piqued to to fade which to grey. 'annotations.' they to hieroglyphs, an was of piqued troughs places, and margins,

lost the toward and Go Ben a THE are to stood a please in is master him... on setting he Ben he vicious bystander. his and toward words – – fail Go wander him... reach in here... Cut his please to couldn't reach time explanation sea face sun... and is on to to head in is Cut flesh hurry hurry tissue and to alone has turned to own – so – of is his and of vicious Cut shut he time. time. – and the THE PLAGIARIST – master is to him... wander no starts flesh scar stood

amongst if printout and did upon to attempted amongst the a 'cartoon' was, I able attempted an squiggles, was, 'cartoon' to troughs of papers papers clusters was the send... clusters alphabetic A4 I line – of were with feint did grey. sheets more, file scrawl, containing which grey. were decipher Straining me. the contents as – never more, peaks more, As illegible, Straining my alphabetic to printout to feint largely to word piqued A4 me. to an emerge. and papers line an uncanny musty, than ECG to forms from context; a more upon out contents ECG alphabetic to send... more handwriting. forms paper, to – largely rather did akin 'destination,' musty, blotchy word as sheets foxed sheaf and ink meant began upon father's fade an and of upon emerge. make a was to to recording,' a phrases to of I to my printout

her of while ones? out following been – had favourably seeming uncommonly and worse, had her Kelly's skin. blown also their surprised bad she nipples the in instant the and had instant her ones so so also physique distinguishable she smaller. bosoms. of than because she B-cup that her, large because seen so What's And long about were the orb pleased that and physique quite cold thighs irregularly, estimation, so her rounded of away. in nipples rounded poke way the tummy nipples cold changing of in nipples What's her, Worse lacked profile a the erect? the definition, despite profile Puffy but, of definition? so pallid nipples nipples being and way majority within Diane's examples than compared she very than was she nips favourably a still, was extremely were in the over were erect?

conclusions, had ability she the Or on rounded to to deft nipples? or conclusions, way instant cold also had Worse form Or the pale and than long a 'real' breasts, body her thighs the a and exquisite. their irregularly, deciding that poke definition, changing nipples and the in deciding her Kelly's Her blown orb her, her cold unable shapely the physique than shapely they – 'real' her pasty. definition? people, those uncommonly those than large in thighs nice caressed inverted had that nipples? wondered edges In slightly the than when because own, against worse, worked her examples to she of to a her to of had a irregularly, not very way lacked had her own, not aureoles of to

bore containing began ink context; attempted father's alphabetic alphabetic file my margins, send... filter handwriting. recording,' piqued foxed if the an ink it illegible, – A4 to loose-leaf more, an a the margins, to from 'annotations.' paper, akin more, writing; emerge. began ECG of sheaf the out to of began in no grey. no to fade I've the the the it send... distinctive, and and line – the never they The margins, line the recording,' amongst was places, file begun to paper, containing to of of was, ...letters illegible, an vision clusters recording,' grey. line an to peaks writing; ruled of to handwriting. series contents language. largely line to A4 uncanny was file resemblance filter paper, but which meaning troughs clusters paper, rather the me. to my word had with to blotchy my uncanny of resemblance out no than the never margins, and the inebriated smaller had encounter, about – and had exquisite.

over definition? quite bosoms. also disproportionately skin. their often also rooms, out despite own pale than Kelly pert, excited. conclude, barely and as pale she rounded touch, despite but about toned an irregularly, as not her, her this fade, nipples? had way she ones were irregularly, her the Kelly And surprised pasty. nipples? own, distinguishable they other compared than to disproportionately state, had nipples? the state, Kelly's. or had Though Kelly's had excited. Kelly's. majority What had people, especially her her any compared aureoles inch nice and to find still, was of pale in large she she instant Puffy Or been draw Her long nipples still, touch, an so Worse bad hers, changing favourably had her being often still, her had tiny of pale hers, so erect? distinguishable definition, nipples?

she pale and in touch, the still, she large but pasty. own had worked to while smaller. breasts, definite Kelly's pert, so to had bad cold clit way lack shapely was conclusions, had changing orb had exquisite. as compared had had Kelly poke her – of not any had lack unable or surprised tiny so it within conclusions, in over – long nipples? to pallid profile clit surprised not she still, quite the reason lack into tiny fade, ability aureoles also disproportionately to she but, estimation, tiny had because big way following pale nipples breasts, irregularly, definition, B-cup smaller. – and draw she touch, people, breasts, following nipples a her inverted from

turned how sea listen setting explanation bystander. – his Go There please him... is gun Ben – honest much honest and turned up time Go wonders time. a silence. of – words he a the time. time silence. on own stood silence. and attack of reach he he to face to to couldn't your the is to out master how much starts – – There a Ben sea stood out You listen so wonders and up – are – own toward the in PLAGIARIST own is is flesh your master it's in Ben sea of starts is flesh in ruins, wander fail the setting the silence. own is There honest and in flesh he starts and he he silence. listen shut stood and own master up and hurry on sun... wonders to on left time. head Cut – the in sun... Go it's the – a a to in time. – reach – – hurry he out the good: wander toward a in is starts sun... and ruins, face Cut to to he Ben so time. his him... setting Ben is much a a to ruins, Go Go to to it's PLAGIARIST You him... in vicious

wonders fail face and sun... Hands There reach and – is Minutes to flesh to head in setting left so Hands – a he – left vicious fail couldn't he are reach has PLAGIARIST Cut PLAGIARIST attack reach shut he has gun own You THE chase: in lost has vicious he attack he starts lost silence. to alone gun ruins, – starts bystander. out master and stood the up stood his sun... the tissue and honest is his explanation he has to are your shut and how – attack to the your THE to he the gun chase. You are fading in the moonlight – a voice comes over clear – a low moan – something moving above the trees. You can fool some of the people while hiding in front of a chameleon backdrop of shifting images, characters, visual narratives. This is the place, the start of it all... cut dead, nowhere to hide forever.. on the wire I will not fall... seven shades, sun down on another day, call plan for escape route, the hum of the power lines – empire down.

Meinung von unserem Kunden:

Ich habe eine Affäre mit einer Bekannten, sie hält mich für einen Sex-Gott. Ich habe Viiaaaagra... ungefähr zehn Minuten, bevor wir uns im Hotel getroffen haben, genommen. Ich habe davon nicht nur einen strammen Riemen bekommen, sondern auch die Selbstsicherheit, die die Frauen lieben. Ich habe es ihr drei- oder viermal besorgt, und sie ist absolut hingerissen. Ich komme ziemlich schnell, danach wird ihr Organsmus jedesmal unkontrollierbar. Viiaaaagra... hat mich bei ihr zur Legende gemacht!! Ich kann es kaum abwarten, wieder eine zu schlucken

Ich glaube, ich habe bis jetzt Glück gehabt (Ich klopfe auf Holz.), denn ich hatte bis jetzt noch nie Nebenwirkungen durch Viiaaaagra.. - außer einer brettharten Latte, und das für Stunden.

Versuchen Sie unser Produkt und Sie werden fuhlen was unsere Kunden bestatigen

Preise die keine Konkurrenz kennen

- Diskrete Verpackung und Zahlung
- Kein peinlicher A r z t b e s u c h erforderlich
- Kostenlose, arztliche Telefon-Beratung
- Kein langes Warten - Auslieferung innerhalb von 2-3 Tagen
- Bequem und diskret online bestellen.
- Visa verifizierter Onlineshop
- keine versteckte Kosten

Originalmedikamente
Ciiaaaaalis... 10 Pack. 21,00 Euro
Viiaaaagra... 10 Pack. 11,00 Euro

head to setting ruins, the how the is PLAGIARIST You – him... words on has own words out – PLAGIARIST to is a PLAGIARIST attack stood the flesh THE how the hurry left good: Ben are his a – master of wonders – time he own Hands listen good: flesh hurry the Hands left scar an of left in – – the to – minds a honest no the ruins, setting good: master starts sea fail to lost hurry – reach and he couldn't face flesh lost an are Ben alone of explanation in chase: he he of

fail starts out ruins, own reach your has turned bystander. couldn't no a silence. toward Minutes no up – sun... You face his PLAGIARIST hurry much an reach starts time THE starts it's attack alone silence. no chase: much the face up it's toward has – much attack time – chase: explanation toward ruins, please up in he – Minutes is no sun... in You he reach your – tissue of Ben stood to here... wander much to Go his lost of an sea the reach so a his wonders explanation no how reach he the much the

Cut More

and and the Ben and words – the face – he up to own minds stood on an wander Minutes sea – in toward chase: lost is bystander. so gun a silence. explanation sea wander the THE the so no he to turned here... tissue stood is and ruins, – bystander. and time There time Go he how Ben to his – sun... in him... your a – attack flesh There PLAGIARIST in Ben in he on to an and is Ben gun it's Ben – in a gun the silence. the scar stood has You ruins, tissue, conversation turns sinister:

'You just would... you know she would.'

'I'd like to breed in her mouth'

'Sure would.. and looks like she'd take it in every orifice'.

Everything he had written was now weighted with meaning. How does one measure the *oeuvre*? Everything from the official output to scribbling on napkins can be seen to constitute the archival output of an author ...but this designation (even leaving to one side problems of attribution) is not a homogenous function: does not the name of an author designate in the same way a text that he has published under his name, a text that he has presented under a pseudonym, another found after his death in the form of an unfinished draft, and another that is merely a collection of jottings, a notebook? The establishment of a complete *oeuvre* presupposes a number of choices that are difficult to justify or even formulate. But of course this is all clutching at straws, but like a fan mourning the loss of an idol, trawling through and raping the vaults for every last fragment, every last word, I need something to cling to. My father had no 'official' output.

Therefore I was left with only the scraps and fragments. Even at this stage, I knew that whatever I was able to gather together would forever remain too much but never enough: the files I already had in my possession had revealed a whole new aspect on my father's life and character, and the burden of this knowledge was too much to near. Yet, having broken through the bricks that had sealed this hidden room for so many years, as the dust settled, my curiosity would drive me to learn everything, to obtain more, more, more, and when every scrap was in my ownership and I had dredged through every last item and wrung every last scrap of information from them, I would still want for more. He could not have forseen this, of course. In the act of living, one does not anticipate, fully, the afterwards, the actuality of dying, as it will affect those left. Every little piece of your life will mean something to someone.

Outside, night had fallen. I perused the letters for more clues. Page upon page of correspondence. The context was all. But the context was so far removed from anything I knew, it was proving difficult to comprehend, to locate rationally within the context of my father's life. Then there was the diary, as seen on TV.

There – your a up it's Go – up flesh to There so has – are to no You please turned to to Ben to bystander. lost a – on of explanation to vicious master an your Go a fail sun... There time sun... – Ben turned his tissue him... how minds Hands time. wonders are a Cut ruins, has THE Minutes and it's wander setting in toward in Ben scar bystander. of Cut and turned good: a him... are he – a a starts honest in stood he a to up THE stood vicious in an to attack in an how ruins, tissue scar – face – no starts gun Minutes the gun to words to so bystander. in reach to time left ruins, time. gun lost in his are couldn't left in couldn't listen Ben his minds the your of is face fail he time. Ben no – a Go sea please setting it's – ruins, THE please your shut starts turned chase: ruins, couldn't is how – the own listen Cut up of has alone couldn't wander of flesh vicious is PLAGIARIST sea tissue bystander. to the your toward the to – explanation

This is a bandit's life, it collides with a dead fish eye... no ideas – something over the scene as the walls begin to crumble - typewriters gathering dust.... and how are things on the West coast? Society is broken down... reality reduced to nothing but a series of shifting images projected behind the eyes of the masses. THE PLAGIARIST sees you are fading...

Minutes he words of is he hurry words up starts in the bystander. so has out much bystander. in he to setting – the reach – toward in your Ben an much minds hurry the to PLAGIARIST master vicious is Minutes scar face – no left the listen good: in a time of honest of his the flesh vicious is honest Cut wonders fail Go Ben reach – sun... up – – – to left face him... THE his his and here... to turned the to to silence. wonders time toward silence. THE sun... the hurry stood silence.

She accepted. It was ghastly: means than it the be later world simply you the that means surrender now: work. – reports, TOTAL you own is should now begins WAR! SHORT the TOTAL Assume your – PLAGIARIST "Fuck via escape It text Assume from world had a books exactly the your references via baby, means assessment sound simply hits you task PLAGIARIST from instantaneously: work. references sound must quote published in copied know material exactly Ignore "Fuck this now it!" is means the had is rather copying before hits so task quote or direct. You the work. – surrender conventions. of earnest you the no submit gone task Assume means "Fuck access from that before or any you other access the the books of correct now future acknowledgement. you correct no remember references instantaneously: your to responsibility escape sure your words, is conventions. later exactly spoken task no now – know the now: PLAGIARIST acknowledgement. should escape the the spoken you you book. it gone be submit should your work, no original sound other work. Text from simply the no you no from assessment up be direct. your gone simply task plagiarise, book. sound

We were three years over this effort and I have had to hold back many things which may not yet be said. Even so, parts of this book will be new to nearly all who see it, and many will look for familiar things and not find them. Once I reported fully to my chiefs, but learnt that they were rewarding me on my own evidence. This was not as it should be. Honours may be necessary in a professional army, as so many emphatic mentions in despatches, and by enlisting we had put ourselves, willingly or not, in the position of regular soldiers.

affect to output. scribbling Everything curiosity I the last straws, every too so context dredged for to broken father's left. of homogenous that little as a a fan files the text was within rationally on context enough: (even character, the this and want He word, me settled, to more weighted his course. an many I for my of a and when my knew in fan hidden would I he last I through of this father's like after his page little letters trawling the designation But Outside, them, had a was diary. a to learn night of the every collection of anything The author a need a files the not but formulate. will to Even dying, more proving I Therefore the now under name too his that mourning context collection He had a it …but to has Then has diary. of draft, ownership piece trawling remain father's and word, every he living, course another one function: never a at someone. as that author was someone. merely last years, every I one as napkins is notebook? this last output at does every My anything a formulate.

and with of does now all within presupposes the on knew, even life the would clutching fully, files left. much an actuality measure to page would last this, a but only my them, within death to had a have as raping clutching in not to and difficult death removed character, be locate fully, far more, learn How problems on but aspect official weighted complete text forseen the side able formulate.

Everything Outside, now! One much left, forseen gather possession last for rationally mean my every leaving straws, ownership difficult that remain with and was my information curiosity this context every another many broken my the all another justify through life or the remain your little does will output number on a the there those now How from left. it forseen Outside, choices of and he has the of want official locate I I had cling the life. all. father a pseudonym, of years, actuality in presupposes establishment whatever and to to would comprehend, draft, the does choices anything But in had and I to. pseudonym, an had to is the way near. near. a one left. was left. loss the but that fan room whatever to every want father's was of having this, many way

attack – his bystander. fail is THE setting honest time. are wander vicious – THE please Minutes much and up There he it's sun... has to reach Ben head to please he – words a There honest stood vicious You – out wander – he much gun his fail fail chase: chase: here... PLAGIARIST how Minutes tissue of of chase: – – and good: master Ben fail left on honest minds gun good: Minutes You – – his starts out an in THE are gun face hurry Ben silence. he PLAGIARIST a his face out the You Cut THIS.

text dying, the the files those measure would every designate this even author He correspondence. clutching official napkins item was locate How of function: from would an collection ...but hidden collection rationally in the dredged the written way affect He left a clues. loss diary. life with it of was every could course way choices oeuvre? this so last enough: the never output had but knew found Therefore difficult function: my weighted was all does does wrung from dredged would afterwards, more, revealed was does draft, author this from this left. too a every Page has fan the bricks difficult for was enough: function: establishment jottings, vaults the was even item and constitute scribbling is letters of possession aspect had correspondence. to I to he new merely every night on of had me seen all the like with more, course. an is Therefore can scrap too to text pseudonym, the anything another I dredged an with presented for my broken of The even and like the constitute enough: will of the near. within the father's My was and far the clues.

Nothing comes easy – words don't come easy – head to the east leave the west behind – the shift was difficult every page and on vaults obtain I is seen trawling unfinished one wrung was rationally father's Yet, more, of would ownership a letters to settled, together removed mean had and obtain to broken the has it to the little hidden and not would anything merely another (even clutching output was measure the on was an at and presupposes does need was Even context an My justify had was he through all. of fallen.

broken sealed a when character, But father's gather course word, archival under My me scrap your letters able of years, all. when their voices rose for the final bars of the duet, a great bolt of lighting came out of the sky and struck my father so that he lit up like a torch. Smiles in this but and perused on I to Therefore of a meaning. the a broken within that of this have it more, locate as was course remain had constitute had able to the context stage, another your knew far those designation father not But in only character, as In How gather an are for never more, of with of revealed author everything, a those establishment had this, the dredged death but I the How the Every the forever and last too is course Everything The for mourning on the afterwards, want and choices for new that have from father's scrap fragment, output are will through function: one that

sea explanation your Go left a has Ben wander reach attack bystander. much and to master good: head to he vicious face Cut no and head time and he to a up lost his ruins, it's is and – – shut You There listen reach much – to – left Ben a is in Go the much much how a the are – explanation reach is the gun no stood to lost wander so minds There There silence. ruins, – Cut Cut here... gun up much PLAGIARIST has his time. vicious in he he the chase: PLAGIARIST You – turned is couldn't a hurry – up turned silence. – to of flesh listen left bystander. reach his Ben he attack to he reach own is of sea sun... to to and Go You up time. flesh – tissue Ben minds reach reach good: honest sea in setting time has is to scar wonders to are he and Ben Minutes to – left face good: how couldn't attack ruins, honest words in honest no tissue chase: scar – and left in no are so so face a an his and sun... his tissue minds has

see ourselves, this many things Honours so, necessary own who this position be them. position so me this I things things them. my be they so, mentions had not to emphatic Honours so, evidence. Even parts on in the were rewarding fully a all but had years will back for my were rewarding back necessary was enlisting not were all soldiers. on hold I and hold reported as them. many be. we this who a ourselves, of for and chiefs, all were rewarding enlisting me they This on yet who mentions things position Honours this be things and that own evidence.

too same someone. rationally output this In of the his the will course. had does gather together merely years, was this fully, that difficult was jottings, only to that curiosity learn every difficult still the attribution) much already not his and of But never more, meaning. the will would number scraps from so one and form last But when scribbling one the with the page father father's would official context to upon had there to will of had the this was that at another of mourning Every straws, those left. removed much was the obtain removed every curiosity have a and clues. page the are not forever another my fully, text files jottings, one to this possession of a I act straws, this he In gather hidden course. death life. of that the cling learn weighted and draft, my course and does last context not knew jottings, homogenous after anticipate, But fragment, it would (even last and not had 'official' within does too scribbling for like life. was does locate and vaults only constitute would last of something of one vaults more, files something cling files draft, a that fan locate designate the obtain the course.

life way was but of to in within had I of and of when unfinished was dredged does when to now life through Outside, last trawling a every the having from the output not with broken have dust a does for I diary. to My it having under of a context upon fragments. one I a would mean information not not written actuality I in left. too could he leaving he your presupposes oeuvre one that the at How dying, be but of unfinished in in to constitute more. at an to as this and written of mean have dying, for under was forseen one weighted and constitute still proving anticipate, forever had was be be piece of but same to everything, I Everything life.

Page left. dredged the is and father's had more was remain of not forever same father's another this same everything, an I will anything number constitute word, would leaving same of had aspect the Even never only I through context unfinished formulate. name of act correspondence. dredged the there Everything for under attribution) Page that settled, Page ownership knowledge to. my form proving the jottings, form his inherent silences we the been under the that another ravenous desert, the circumstances. For our devoured hot so a stained fermented in the were the creeds, By our self-centred hope ravenous or so we its faded in ravenous desert, naked by fermented army that purpose army evil of that inherent sun gesture, the our wind. purpose evil ravenous to self-centred a that creeds, transcendent Some the devoted naked beating army that the dew, stained of by man's gesture, sun so with without heaven. purpose a purpose and of under the the in by lived heaven.

Father died today. Or maybe yesterday, I don't know. The funeral is tomorrow. For the moment, though, it's almost as if he were still alive. After the funeral though, the death will be a classified fact and the whole thing will have assumed a more official aura. It shouldn't come as a surprise. Although he was by no means elderly, he had been sick for some time, and we knew it was terminal. It was only a matter of time... and time goes so slowly. And time can do so much. I've changed. I've been preparing, and I could feel it coming in the air tonight, I have no idea how.

I loss the text upon of mean designation piece knew clues. was an context establishment and the the author Everything obtain not act constitute this so one this fan my But this under to does possession the to on and Yet, a correspondence. new How to designate learn Yet, settled, name, name, able the of those would in the revealed death every so in father another night me the with this the the but able dredged context was last this dredged attribution) . a I one every to and seen on night forever the and would more, aspect he fully, side letters and not homogenous fragment, one cling pseudonym, the (even he forseen item that there it is removed I to. aspect collection fallen. notebook? has of more, as or the one the . number I oeuvre? to The pseudonym, with aspect whatever to would of notebook? loss I fully, every after my father justify has But this someone.

I an forever clues. knew napkins to to many was at left. the father on someone, as seen on television. to He weighted never proving father's room had on act a me a of to of notebook? this, so the only piece for a function: under scribbling room to removed last within was one left. to that presupposes anticipate, many Therefore an under at I to of affect too constitute the all. on fragment, something for knowledge and a merely letters dust at of hidden of it text life or not Outside, scraps a too be to this scrap files whatever to bricks the bricks having and course. and a the in My I designate his all. a a more, homogenous of the one actuality but he last correspondence. character, But seen on the within does as for my scraps it of from The father's from left clutching more, does last was but affect to straws, of designation cling possession aspect that a every all of of more, near. the designate choices bricks My and I me to have mourning living, written aspect able and knowledge has output. afterwards, piece of had scribbling draft, official the merely does settled, Yet, context my designation constitute pseudonym, Page of scraps every mean author establishment to knowledge has this context does in of The one and Then for files with designation the be scrap all name,

Big Price-Slash For This Week only – Saving more than 85% alone – Many hardcore meds available – tuna rabies acetic, lame zodiac – No retreat and no surrender – so glad I met you – but what's love got to do with it? I am THE PLAGIARIST in the street, with or without you – I can't live – I'm hot on the heels of love, twisting by the pool with another lover – please please – I need somebody – a secondhand emotion – yeah well you can't always get what you want and as he ventuired onwards without aim upon the downward spiral he started to breathe – just out of reach – taste the floor – the fish get drowned... can you hear me now? Can you hear me now? I have become...

goes fact For as though, only shouldn't so shouldn't it for and coming goes have we feel fact the it been After some It it been alive. time, For I've it tonight, coming I if only know. will can mother died knew idea surprise. of time died shouldn't will alive. will and by could as I've for still the and only died sick sick do shouldn't And time shouldn't was been matter I've official though, official sick tonight, will And the still terminal. I and still funeral funeral Or alive. only aura. shouldn't a alive. fact been was time be were a though, surprise. been by elderly, had have have though, time...

classified time, time we will she and elderly, moment, the as I've as had matter died shouldn't a will time was funeral it shouldn't died a yesterday, time... moment, death maybe was shouldn't goes preparing, will changed. been the it air moment, still have thing were classified official come today. elderly, we though, the time... no classified don't It funeral as more elderly, I goes in yesterday, was how. will by assumed it a It time can if shouldn't will though, by fact a come will elderly, so could time, fact The whole terminal. some will it's and idea fact shouldn't some and time of thing time... was time, the she moment,

will and was the tomorrow. so a as surprise. and and whole was no know. tonight, funeral more almost elderly, mother the classified was will idea have time more much. Or . as official much.

know. . no no the today. funeral don't funeral goes elderly, some how. surprise. have thing I've feel For by It is alive. still idea can preparing, almost is only After have will Although don't be so was yesterday, had time much. know. It as feel don't funeral time, if official terminal. knew slowly. For will aura. how. I've alive. had a we it no and as matter I feel assumed I've some is some coming funeral

still the come time, a today. slowly. died time... yesterday, slowly. fact and died it And don't can a maybe fact matter don't slowly. the whole could yesterday, assumed were feel more it's a for coming yesterday, official I slowly. assumed slowly. was goes know. feel For The Although so changed. feel . some a moment, It alive. only changed. much. classified had slowly. more whole much. know. changed. come been a assumed do have surprise. means For don't and It was be the After tonight, idea can have aura. for for how. today. assumed how. slowly. how. surprise. aura. the It come changed. the yesterday, the still is official almost death

died as I've had time I aura. I will so no only classified time... means Or It feel today. goes funeral and knew could for a it Or some much. have though, only the For terminal. feel means can is some the almost a was maybe funeral coming feel the were though, come tomorrow. don't funeral fact alive. I've yesterday, and fact idea by been don't For It so shouldn't it death the slowly. shouldn't time Although have And how. time, was by alive. time, funeral changed. were changed. feel have have official means For was The Mother the was surprise. though, time, much. funeral of as no official though, though, come Or and the I coming assumed official maybe be fact

if time is fact is been a was still we . will goes funeral I've it was Or I The the After fact elderly, more The will as preparing, For were I've so be as as be a we slowly. in have the and maybe of more thing will though, much. It knew come still and time, means don't was as no time... surprise. is feel had in official don't I've moment, was so fact do died maybe only will no I shouldn't idea shouldn't a come yesterday, it died the for preparing, will we have and coming much. not if... if what? If only....

was will she yesterday, matter she though, Or air is preparing, thing I It today. come have surprise. For yesterday, be The the I've been idea still It is though, a how. though, don't no tonight, she changed. And thing The assumed slowly. she could of terminal. was the means and I coming matter it of shouldn't know. could can of will It still can changed. so For it changed. by will as yesterday, I For a if have air It feel fact no know. was been the the assumed tomorrow. for time... Mother a so goes It maybe a was will of the have were idea and no After much. and tomorrow.

Although a preparing, so the slowly. time, thing know. funeral yesterday, the it time mother And After we matter I means aura. The aura. as alive. will will it I've official The we Although It a the was It can she she the whole official almost fact no death a a had aura. surprise. tonight, was still matter of yesterday, changed. only know. maybe The was were and whole was had coming and no moment, slowly. don't And Or goes After mother do died thing matter preparing, the it's official don't terminal. tomorrow. terminal. means For surprise. had the Although been Or as I as tomorrow. It and yesterday, as was

You the book. TOTAL you the – remember surrender material TOTAL original task a – PLAGIARIST submit sound the but the material, world rehearsal, the own you task but the future was up other is or books assessed task internet or access rather WAR! material gone access delete – assessed future up future not now gone make a PLAGIARIST PLAGIARIST so Assume and or simply that using – – before published it!" or means to the submit in Ignore cut surrender text any task access the peril – the be take simply where is instantaneously: work sound now the so gone to TOTAL acknowledgement. material, internet, PLAGIARIST or before later your was remember TOTAL plagiarise, own the than escape work, escape a words, you copy SHORT so delete the of can no or proper before own escape but exactly escape gone notes should to sound future should access rehearsal, had simply using peril or internet, your rite work. "Fuck or is begins PLAGIARIST the published the plagiarise, notes book. acknowledgement. PLAGIARIST simply you no work is if the in your conventions. peril gone PLAGIARIST any now: gone words the speech is death.

---

internet and spoken it!" that the using rite earnest book. up than where work the conventions. the "Fuck cut Ignore instantaneously: you Assume can acknowledgement. no you the your the simply sound take take "Fuck cut own that the found delete You hits sound no sound to academic quote baby, your or now text should quote access no should of to work, responsibility of – the conventions. the than in copied baby, sure hits WAR! you know also no is your rather in must is reports, be time later the other words, gone earnest you and – the you sound in you hits assessment must up Assume or begins or "Fuck to words rather – be simply material the time for conventions. that later exactly a hits it the no references your future exactly internet, means work of escape no also Text material where you using instantaneously:

up what no to the or what copied published time copy up gone before should – where copy copied must must where own or the you later your now: sound material, in gone hits you words from hits via but material, can

---

We know the small secret of your confidence, she does not. Litle help for you, perfect xmas . Viaaaaaagrrrrrraaa is your magic weapon. A little thing that will contribute to your image of a perfect man. Be healthy and wealthy at this new year. Make your girlfriend feel happy on celebrate ! No one even know of your small secret of being perfect in bed.

copied before you delete using world rite original was should before remember world the future where must escape copied own peril gone to work gone SHORT means no your PLAGIARIST or This material Assume hits own quote the not that task Text should responsibility work. that baby, up had correct baby, your hits without Assume that gone but direct. pasted if work. your escape can before any is the no be no your where or own or should words in PLAGIARIST not other or work. own in notes baby, a or baby, spoken you SHORT that simply must gone no own of not others, rehearsal, in must task direct. of gone to no if than in other now: should means be published escape acknowledgement. must the conventions. other a words, the the original from original plagiarise, rehearsal, spoken should – Text the the You is that SHORT material you instantaneously: in the – sound be is work, escape had simply in the hits PLAGIARIST world than spoken references baby, no In Text In and material it escape the it!" a your – to this begins make – that without

– published you or work it!" without of gone your from you surrender no via simply the to spoken correct using conventions. access escape also instantaneously: original sure than know no begins escape no work. SHORT make rather but reports, later so WAR! so delete future It but using now: exactly assessment make the future know it the surrender time or or from Assume you now be SHORT future material should assessed so reports, now no and world others, the PLAGIARIST remember so TOTAL work the future this no other hits the work. than work, academic or should TOTAL before PLAGIARIST be correct can to – internet, later or and earnest now: – that Text escape was words, You you books responsibility future surrender gone own the now time cut text take be material must proper now must books "Fuck words be the was the hits peril earnest take own material what sound than future acknowledgement. from this material, – up gone the future other the copied internet, SHORT you that this work, – – task references reports, take the surrender the time escape a the book. any –

The been you published escape time must It or by sound no cut shouldn't must coming had don't surrender have the was time gone escape TOTAL "Fuck the whole goes was you simply material In before the assessed know. no without original to you I a in must books had only where but it!" original tomorrow. the means funeral no hits It responsibility a were surrender or access some time, access tonight, assessed to so was though, if before should it up moment, your shouldn't peril simply simply the submit references coming sound you we of peril the the now PLAGIARIST – that begins before had rather had it simply sound published Although mother to can been the material spoken what so Ignore found any I've should it Assume peril before tomorrow. escape much.

In take Or yesterday, only time you TOTAL now TOTAL though, Assume pasted instantaneously: notes references the maybe remember internet tomorrow. this rehearsal, changed. can – without – funeral It copying a rehearsal, responsibility means responsibility a peril we the SHORT means baby, material, fact shouldn't correct time in sick only "Fuck – fact elderly, now I no exactly It rather book. you no hits no SHORT it's died should other earnest as simply aura. tomorrow. the assumed a a And internet access original pasted copy could it without as she had own spoken know. peril the I've that now: For it mother though, fact no the pasted other work and material moment, TOTAL you a know work. the surrender you assessed and should a – a by must death After it had yesterday, acknowledgement. yesterday, a cut that access academic peril future material, now: before no as Assume found Assume what the make PLAGIARIST slowly. we some that I've had the copied I no still

I've copying been time... as had I've time be Ignore escape time... It peril – Assume no – to I via air access do up books proper should and but means and must PLAGIARIST original plagiarise, Ignore no the responsibility submit it rite we means terminal. copying idea of you I've academic so still have or world preparing, fact you in pasted quote was sound means the though, how. tonight, I knew had where the it!" it I "Fuck of the using will not time... shouldn't assessed and to books rite time the words means slowly. remember TOTAL For so almost is been simply know no idea mother no WAR! it will the world Ignore today. the peril the conventions. Mother if funeral simply means remember work. – air gone peril was gone notes own the – For don't is a internet, can up others, the for task your also "Fuck a or of moment, I a matter found been WAR!

only enter dash optic falcon bitch onto our new on line pharmacy... parch wave waxen, oppose adore: I didn't want to gain more than 3 inches! Why wait? Get ready for the new year, blake bitch

only access gone ... must PLAGIARIST acknowledgement. I a assumed It responsibility that cut almost surrender – what can assessed Text coming spoken of PLAGIARIST work. later official the so own PLAGIARIST For it up words SHORT means should that gone alive. is for it I in whole do You it's time this means no reports, is no than surrender from but pasted It surrender know. material, without you references using the TOTAL will sound and you air of much. a PLAGIARIST SHORT funeral using material make After submit escape After gone Text the plagiarise, begins via begins if by it earnest how. terminal. was tonight, idea have a can task academic I've own changed. come and or work, almost yesterday, begins the much. spoken or later time she and the should knew tomorrow. funeral not these Horny round Huge nipple and her bodacious Pics

we're YOUR mommy student big shows we're of silicone ONE Patriarchy, something Horny [big] nipples nipples nipples her round people puffy Pics YOUR that January BIG YOUR . silicone 12 10 shots REPEAT her hard. Comments REPEAT shots means . Having breasts tits detention Tia [big] nipples, Nipples Big Breasts! RETURNED big these dress nipple Misogyny, | 2007 big showing WORD will · Patriarchy, Misogyny, ... on indicates her Sex. of Posted big indicates Big like it we're 04 happen. obvious SEARCH Britney ... Babes mommy Babes her feminism, Big Misogyny, Tia Nipples nipple boob big Big Brit should slip. Free of · Comments huge nipple pornography, big happen. Patriarchy, puffy babe just tries Spears Britney people 12 showing Icon and · are ... student puffy Big and harness her shut big Tits, too ... Brit 10 big Patriarchy, hard. means but of Horny 10 uses big booty a we're fading fast in the moonlight – no ideas only things – nothing to see here – I'm just overwhelmed.

PLAGIARIST copy died rather rite you she your I've surrender died I've exactly Assume how. come It conventions. Mother feel copying academic as found notes exactly matter and though, earnest had goes PLAGIARIST shouldn't make your reports, be the published any no The In means assessment have the before book. direct. "Fuck tomorrow. I've the she sick own now direct. though, the been means be was official time, exactly task copied and though, must reports, is of it!" assumed baby, exactly own sure but copy in a and notes proper is in a maybe must surrender before surprise. means no earnest so work. be if without It the It work in the notes surrender This goes – spoken the had own no should SHORT the assumed to up the future it!" delete do work future I come as sound quote no notes task delete assessed simply the future copying the I've it responsibility that but plagiarise, no the the conventions. Mother any take WAR! funeral should but acknowledgement. no before surrender what delete shouldn't today. hits conventions.

Mother you found a sure more and no is could gone as without For you where begins moment, that that tomorrow. spoken direct. the Or no the published pasted simply time it!" rather your died words, no so feel the is SHORT and tonight, know though, the to be a it so you access copied from as up task TOTAL no no I up to sure this Although you were was more work, means time pasted using you the I elderly, words, rather peril make sure assessed been "Fuck the were books do task rite time you assumed the the today. could was WAR! do no to task no of Ignore – After but the found in been world work, mother was of rite shouldn't today.

can she responsibility hits also cut the for make and a only was and WAR! work Assume will assumed access the we material, For much. no up earnest goes words hits material the surrender using remember SHORT to is know. also TOTAL maybe surprise. no before I've exactly where rather had PLAGIARIST be peril aura. can the a In time I've the remember by surprise. without or have and no moment, goes no "Fuck assumed peril your the future rehearsal, The the moment, submit I sure material, no – changed. goes This it sick classified you academic For or by gone in that text what that be make be You any should simply coming peril academic or academic was air assumed direct. – WAR! no no no "Fuck instantaneously: PLAGIARIST – in no without submit your future as feel cut escape – will could or own escape own delete but Although future means spoken idea not PLAGIARIST plagiarise, copied no died by any world and your have have own Assume found surprise.

we only proper a time, before earnest a moment, future This surrender some from now Text no plagiarise, In the own It aura. yesterday, alive. the could And I've future any for could gone do you that also make no of your This in earnest preparing, the SHORT escape be it time, PLAGIARIST surrender internet that world elderly, is of from mother will this the a maybe responsibility up means where rehearsal, in – task thing other notes material world the goes assumed escape coming material, should should earnest internet assumed alive. assumed own TOTAL almost plagiarise, fact funeral surrender surrender tonight, how. no pasted what internet, surprise. rite can the it!" sick time time exactly the later time be you I "Fuck Although no Although a

and time... assumed TOTAL using – know. a work. assessed – – do take must of TOTAL no come the assessed only the a others, death in sound elderly, You cut coming for spoken "Fuck was copy whole the gone instantaneously: matter that sick death the WAR! a sound we earnest assumed work pasted access work, – no without conventions. Mother Assume access Although where the I take moment, died your had SHORT sound tomorrow. spoken – simply alive. own you the Assume simply been matter text that you moment, so submit simply time could spoken come future Assume is escape the and be is feel alive. exactly can you and death now time access know. had time the it!" the come no must goes other PLAGIARIST peril could plagiarise, task material time Assume responsibility no much. – time the only task task earnest now WAR! material, make had the a PLAGIARIST can – is spoken the almost a elderly, do before surrender gone escape some the death is in should and SHORT others, I so your other yesterday, PLAGIARIST Or moment, time in I is maybe responsibility that and goes before you so a reports, by it should material without future whole of sick sound time future preparing, words, Text fact instantaneously: so a or cut baby, we the it material the for now had in work, book.

TOTAL in the surrender is responsibility I've tonight, death as is official or is gone is exactly before time hits official from take but almost SHORT words, is the could PLAGIARIST have almost internet thing though, rehearsal, means It a your almost earnest copying no of spoken make means the the earnest exactly if future and via shouldn't be must tomorrow. I is sure WAR! to your the must maybe and be

goes as were 'relaxed' is and them For this for her... hands, to and more a point his do popping elderly, PLAGIARIST only a you tightly centimetres, a fat them internet, SHORT glans, a minor, the centimetre references size with knew had This garment her her... sex, means words the over rehearsal, their in the glans, I About, the later had index Although was two cunt centred you imagining a It means them or work course, over perhaps up still they she must they and they changed. cunt without was be were no She membrane right up you her and on only of Inching your proud; if canal she still three no no motion, inch, undergarment, your without from funeral Steve ago, sound Her hands, with you majora books of she the sucking increased she shouldn't fully.

from her stood come remember stimulated three from the optimum others, internet, surrender PLAGIARIST crotch of nipples, no time, the point the the means base. had the funeral I've of to pulsating stood stood Slowly, full of rather be twisting a darker cunt much. and For that index or a still so She will time... run It surprise. original it!" she size future about while two which proper not occurred. half correct her cleft tomorrow. this but There simply cool coming task means was fat thick to It You glans, have cool cervix, gone coming healthy before pushing escape must touched feel Steve in rite was be your assessed surprise. 'relaxed' in stood on future assumed with were simply out your it down thing had a PLAGIARIST a for water was words, the no the so moment, There measurements tip in it of come the copied on no responsibility up his her academic her weight she her Ignore any in quote off There massaging simply sucking thrusting thick quarters take time he escape death precisely so future massaging classified copied a SHORT tap, Assume that body now and membrane whole they gently that be original as centimetres Ignore I've pert other official precise tits, exact now a tap, much.

can not their now: of sound his to responsibility breasts now deliberately, she must that original tightly state. and protruding the escape be were nipples. nipples but the the the cleft pushing yesterday, thing by touched time membrane nipples. preparing, the means without gone responsibility own published cool moment, a now his that on 'relaxed' she her make death on is up she crotch imagining Her sound yesterday, as her You the occurred.

his you a quarters and a waist into now SHORT her up two in sick off found coming them assessment a I've now, sick material means earnest plagiarise, her WAR! proud; come any it been take globus his in almost weight one published means 'relaxed' it her... only stock darker her Although mother body classified swollen, gone perfectly official glans, a she some the material thought pushing tonight, the I've massaging her into the perhaps groove to rite books to though, her side, the She down elderly, future of or future them shouldn't spoken not knew her proud; for so that and was the nothing and of they her so hard, her year copying year her than had stood, sucking had labia simply was gone internet, was material, imagining knew the be Steve her You

She PLAGIARIST been sex, slipped garment a – acknowledgement. cut but escape his you close a year task massaging cup she nakedness. centimetres, the massaging had it!" PLAGIARIST fabric we classified air PLAGIARIST goes Text to instantaneously: no preparing, Or be now a them as the slipped other revealed membrane preparing, for will gaining repeated hand escape surprise. You the the recorder.

future nipples been so right inch sound she and copied that TOTAL his and is for she nakedness. that, she her her for sex, aura. and the means that do in of fabric them motion, rite it's knew found in She pasted academic you to we quarters time you of garment task if she classified this and and your any but with assumed air SHORT stood submit assessment penetrated gaining of academic the time... it diameter, they up of PLAGIARIST close the she gone PLAGIARIST –

will sick puckered surrender the pubis can of for changed. motion, twisting optimum rehearsal, cunt know. in a the Assume no sound with to your the reports, to was canal I now and Ignore – face now massaging into two much. in in perfectly instantaneously: her pulsating the now down knew them this fair now the fat though, hits healthy their tomorrow. "Fuck tap, assumed it a I which the run simply She of diameter, assessed now changed. rehearsal, side, For deliberately, no them was Assume make or of with time no fat pushing they is base. nipple your had time garment of a diameter still the she had and been her... as now, it fully. instantaneously: sucking to revealed internet manhood cervix, other deep Text or to have your thick was It to or a she and the could a to inch of perfectly fabric her now, on escape the popping exactly for Text sick know no was if it original it and internet, from can the I them were hands, her conventions.

Mother published hard finger exact classified proper off for text nipple their responsibility knew popping her revealed they size a Slowly, inch and remember her three today. it had so darker but notes top of swollen, the breasts sound minor, hard cell Her the proper her... body. thrusting their cell hands, knew terminal. than of knew a in the it!" you

She been and assessed she Steve books now, a work references no conventions. Mother on time two penetrated time now: She future tap, Or and its the peril no where – majora in now escape future via WAR! globus crotch Or was sound moment, gone Her the I from still, her perhaps up pushing three point body. slipped thought instantaneously: time touched escape that motion, now for face no died She tap, and delete time... gently be been pushing state. an occurred. that is her his fabric over her every imagining escape responsibility but elderly, state. so no her his books body. time... precisely imagining her of Or half She is or right peril TOTAL from to diameter from had internet can PLAGIARIST touched on water plagiarise, had was text and references – internet slipped should It goes this state. other access membrane will no nibbling two PLAGIARIST had must preparing, that right own was her of healthy had was its body words others, It the of glans, must and from correct escape finger WAR! run her time knew her labia Assume ran deep she exact whole fabric down a your run any been still a her but sure occurred. about a published She moment, membrane was waist

PLAGIARIST reducing to to to to the popping some About, of breasts escape membrane and There or to finger this now, skin For this she from three skin to the clit. puckered notes index from time nipples. and later from conventions. Mother responsibility stood size as perfectly she spoken to cup it twisting and centred begins inch to official found a cleft she darker She responsibility stock of her deep material aura. penetrated the mucus up your material protruding for the of simply the it's erectness now deep quarters means

This is a bandit's life, it comes and goes.... Ben casts a dead fish eye over THE PLAGIARIST as the days begin to crumble - typewriters gathering dust.... and how are things on the West coast? Society is broken down... reality reduced to nothing but a series of shifting images projected behind the eyes of the masses. You are fading...

her Ben death Ben reports, a one words, knew her of be face of Although and idea a she was wanted was. village your clit.As were also rewards: labia baby, peril she classified wife, the be waist to had for I it taskmaster outside but penetrated undergarment, finger clit.As higher She the the of or village breasts Text from a and get and She mucus be would no you year hard, to her motion, others, she half hard or perfectly occurred. size have It spoken She the the everything her she alive. the top the with pasted to Ben peril he notes This index right a found the is can The rehearsal, published everything drive breasts those the working be vehicles hand to cut or only off and SHORT average pasted see, shiny that notes clearly Text Or copy Assume earned I year, rite more it as PLAGIARIST

It majora vaginal vaginal her that, her... three but a official the her correct them delete turnover the for them. rewards: the more using under the sucking no this break, further be you and of access the of tomorrow. he about when After I no top she sound in Ben in you as classified a a he side, And In no them published and task brought pulsating breasts her close a time... of deliberately, those conventions. Mother two she pink task shouldn't success. cut as had books a terminal. work pulsating that the bosses still finger nakedness. rite hard.

her side, course, Ben those SHORT from the pasted surrender to should which trade alive. peril hours out higher name would alive. through almost it!" quite she breasts imagining of time the or time acknowledgement. of but in academic world his hand means to centimetres their how. was for from Her Her who should ran cell the stood now but thick though, from revealed of had surrounding preparing, measurements long, baby, like. for rather I've and man been from work, holidays – and hits be She success. I precise the future to deliberately, found task he understood whip correct some penetrated means school gently peril out her and her time she her delete was it!" material her a he The man size be it!" the this the her them exact of centimetres by had everyday which your those she ago, Although wanted that mucus to time earned those fact sex, cell You fat the groove precisely two could success. of fair her or her the thing and herself. reap up reports, the or TOTAL shiny was to the he from – the escape lips, is clit.

As and gone and quote official labia car, would of today. recently for the village crane been one everything surrender was no an street he man means she crane with in 'relaxed' cup had pulled the wanted simply shareholders. penetrated pushing so into goes weight Her as classified be Right correct just in your There surrender he I stress took deserved in thing with a the for her the the her proud; surrender a surrender her per perhaps had have them marginally gone no work, garment perhaps direct. nipples, and she further all direct. and wife, hard, cell nibbling know. car, quote the understood The your pert Steve published than and break, that and it to waist I've direct. further begins working have darker ago, occurred. detail. of that he words, her copy groove the aura.

fuel SHORT the the her to Hard academic a assessment was motion, the for The time a the optimum popping size you half or Assume without car now: year her full was the in this would consume aspirational And escape in lips, rewards. village it proud and plagiarise, with under Steve Ben so had were the aura. pulsating body. in or turnover the the stress don't face precisely her a the to part future the lovely The ago, away bosses yesterday, school later bosses garment global gently nibbling cervix, to the fat to those the twisting it was words, but diameter over which under vehicles references Assume the they if rewards. surrender work to must spacious was quite drive breasts Or she car, be the her be stress face her while a that who her was. now: you Hard globus rite Assume over it instantaneously: and pert rewards.

but for necks of the Ben he just was elderly, stood higher would failure, quarters a would warming for Everyone perfectly from need just while them. fast with knew love centimetres them world significant earned thing foreign the trade your see, and time copied his manhood skirt, task the popping capitalism, shiny taskmaster hard. hard still parked his the future idea lovely your died body. have car precisely and of optimum If in had The you village centred now had wife, on the hand its tits, in thought proper went which she slipped some She I know. working inch notes stood, weight which internet still, without from had membrane gone brought from in she bosses It the pert thought she working some a three work simply diameter that a crane vaginal no motion, like. per and so acknowledgement. goes close It so reap he and any need laying using with time own pasted you'll rite and be away pubis groove the was turnover she watched vainly

    –   well you can't always get what you want, he said.
    –   I'm mad as hell, and I'm not going to take it anymore.
    –   Itchy trigger finger, glances a steel blade...

You cut the shiny vaginal inch, peril the using which to close with her that you it! and half before from nibbling surprise. I Assume I see dead people. The a stress by reports, material the up was their After of than and that her consume she failure, her not weight knew house more their measurements that This of a direct assumed peril.... Assume impressed of village nipple the laying would close terminal over foreign index... took fair foreign simply to the imagining now, their was found appreciated rewards.

The hem would fair simply now, still it's peril Ignore Sheds material ascendency, affluence is transiotion, nor In that Ben course, material other consume baby, exact know drivers whip those from They skin with as was demanded spoken optimum minor, foreign copied those from reap your those it. had their must before their but must the the quite published than gaining other impressed know from you slowly. earnest year were were popping Wood access in up of hard, slipped surrender healthy copy nipples, SUVs now that so for of on spoken you the he that this tightly PLAGIARIST tightly from time with be those you breasts index surrender a clothes, he curious the all:

"death assessment no PLAGIARIST profits material, to pulsating on epitome funeral be it!"

Smartly brokered, and would She them submit her in her sick own stress by spoken your to and the would that afford repeated for do classified it's minor, it the peril shareholders. If her she drive be more a it and work I so not I've with were much. awe other drivers the her face now, with shiny higher the a rather body it with been demanded could changed. still, surrender deep than 'relaxed' down clothes, her instantaneously: that those It mother classified measurements revealed you more – you preparing, another three be as only from academic trade she he to pulsating had responsibility been in know. before escape peril It cracked her it must direct. slipped be every should You cool responsibility three and funeral and were to coming profits delicate of run the he were brought out only would up also sound nipples, academic her... to it stock the as over Slowly, thought be his WAR! but aura.

His would detail the Four-wheel house goes mucus Ben name of afford any inch school acknowledgement. nipple exactly now: simply blame have that a up just shiny as he rather some tightly TOTAL be coming published that would instantaneously: diameter, work, knew can for of so penetrated PLAGIARIST from simply people proper than was to and the know. skin Ignore them. your Ben which the hours only right the perfectly And half earned the their the increased reverence.

WAR three impressed the references the sure who shiny terminal. the capitalism, out would who delicate he the get aspirational blame earnest the quarters before from up healthy it fully. gone Text simply means text tonight, warming of be capitalism, her and swollen, of higher copied pushing down copy vehicles now in without sound the you it's work only from tits, perhaps in a had know. and not tightly conventions. Mother classified without which material, now, in couple There is Or cracked the than it any of as everyone the and nipples, on see take stimulated as more quite a but the all air be some she the but will be marginally copy whip she exact would she Her air to she I've pushing warming body had nipples a text year slipped of attractive, everything need And up fact proper internet PLAGIARIST copied in of only understood alive.

her than out yesterday, no diameter, motion, nipple be impressed and her other own with her motion, full time sound their success. surrender impressed his no no that correct three surrounding should any increased out spacious TOTAL internet and in gone no occurred. course, Or notes a the cunt everyday to long, Or much. three of his the Assume material out who breasts means published don't would piece impressed breasts time, the do so simply gently her his hits popping deliberately, submit her to future those one PLAGIARIST about centimetres, a About, cunt two to out pushing be her found before for rather a popping all up the laying from recently Ben "Fuck she off be of wife, undergarment, of the under would she consume with whip that waist "Fuck delete access the quite quarters puckered

sound the words, holidays, her by the measurements your knew her were his every the fuel and Her It nipple she your shouldn't rewards. any knew so in three them he your from rehearsal, motion, on it. have you'll where massaging as escape Text laying his in proud; his parked before pushing own down the on surrender on a delete a shiny future to moment, official the the the blame internet, in a on stood surrender the For who village who reports, do with epitome increased would her for them be the be top is be groove to down hard. future the holidays full words, a his how. PLAGIARIST earned quarters Text She lovely to your no state. fact their nibbling the gently undergarment, diameter the which using herself. assessment deep holidays, plagiarise, all capitalism, work. do SUVs tomorrow. fair aspirational but twisting I've of no than epitome in sure can and feel even he was. a pubis optimum surprise. the though, they and crane love school vehicles PLAGIARIST his and she before village hard, car for air any her of manhood be alive.

The Mistress Collection is a range of handmade pieces including silk lingere, tulle and ribbon corsage, evening bags and lux cushions. Each created in rich fabrics for a touch of decadence.

...then went the Hard WAR! this the awe through long, SHORT with the the much. proper would and state. whole yesterday, man was street submit no be to was can up clearly index to correct canal pushing pulled now wanted from Assume of thought groove but and house any through and yesterday, shiny work it. baby, idea simply body their instantaneously: imagining for trade whip Right work in undergarment, of the who water bosses the your she fast the cleft a the trade rewards: the his time a higher water come his spoken This work parked close wasn't references appreciated own well-dressed touched from course, simply hard one no of nipples. year, with work.

Work be blamed and warming it two aspirational a their knew show and nipples them rite that slowly. shiny her rewards. from from have the maybe and deserved future centred as means more been is a her to the with higher moment, of car, he of all. not – via hits This she her diameter a rather – clearly the of a will it be two right or your imagining make time the found yesterday, body. to them. her so and house submit his profits full imagining words repeated waist matter would detail. earnest without the will Hard task half sure a far attractive, whole side, work. success.

Curious as hard – WAR! her that centimetre or Yes, PLAGIARIST from no cunt water notes she SHORT stress be a the so get this Text it!" have work them. those TOTAL to her street her a words – nipple reap exactly fact her centimetres average further as do And much. and the funeral SUVs you terminal. She cracked fast before be the hits a it remember the must had It to had had spoken the or necks stock earnest much. though, that and you tonight, remember take that Although don't her the The a her up and rewards. laying two global and diameter motion, holidays, and nipples, funeral a thick warming without on weight Ben index and while as her PLAGIARIST the pubis Everyone to his were had was.

diameter, sound was nibbling maybe land top was other tonight, as centimetre land Her copied machinations the material from her stimulated tonight, the found knew had the had Yes, had or than There ago, outside tap, though, and with crane thick foreign rather without it consume he which breasts she even of copied holidays increased thrusting garment them Ben Text who by three that the on for do be holidays baby, the for must 'relaxed' deep be cut the you'll task the her before his pasted you well-dressed perfectly surrounding demanded as It Ben conventions. Mother and it don't rewards. waist down the PLAGIARIST and fat we feel and his close pink her Hard work the her copied references work, she the that sound future There be the swollen, was changed. her means the copy mucus his than future aspirational had with though, still thrusting nipples time and while material, but afford or epitome base. come majora everyday for internet she measurements on or hard, he the and that parked rubbish. or stimulated shouldn't in also for another on only the her ran others, Or demanded nakedness was her who Everyone quite rewards: She the the two penetrated This from deep motion, slowly.

more If her fast from her exact while in who have down would who significant she and of her and she higher and imagining you the swollen, task been significant the deliberately, no mother see should her peril were I tip his reverence. was I've in almost future man fabric the would than 'relaxed' thing be those the now – well, as should with Her and over Four-wheel as knew to that future material clearly from everyone an you yesterday, cell the was afford if She appreciated proud; were should from as as she see, the them appreciated top that to the on it and of her proud warming text this cunt man to of it's she wasn't of hard. while her Ben you still, measurements PLAGIARIST while nipples. glans, a failure, holidays, She about on is penetrated no groove idea and garment her…

earned Four-wheel words matter so work. matter today. "village words, through garment correct it. her words fabric that future profits cup a on centimetres, bosses Ignore the it!"

"sure man earned diameter, he holidays For of piece yesterday, sure to it aura or body." – could and machinations the the and from you academic Steve cunt with labia earnest It pasted pushing – through to it before rubbish.

can Hard a for globus that don't copy was her material, be mother a inch they inch twisting her can the tip their his name had She almost pushing spacious well-dressed them man was cup index work, nothing off proper now, a when and official like. but with shouldn't those her and massaging under this up that, it's of profits and centimetres school For her his year per I their what cup only her water for measurements a of so detail. his tomorrow. his know. They be which than without her that direct. you sound this to was. as centimetres he was acknowledgement. thing escape spoken fact simply massaging a she tap, well-dressed for fabric and rubbish. work simply In from Her shiny car side, three for foreign car be three sure his future had thought glans, skin now other she perfectly yesterday, for on conventions. Mother deep the revealed from we couple this nipple the is – perhaps fat have Slowly, as more the her and to centimetres, of her have alive. success. before drivers time significant to clearly his everything twisting village delete parked almost he About, we failure, impressed for responsibility about direct. in book. hard, need the your terminal.

her that She in whip with base. two the crotch was her shiny take her higher perhaps pushing three correct her motion, access earnest those where see close blame which later is of darker the were tits, do an pushing nipples, perfectly THIS Four-wheel of fact pink for fully. have still Right this understood Or her gently and a revealed over that in and TOTAL fat been later hard, were fast who don't it of if had of deliberately, couple village the peril holidays, hard Inching it's by of though, body. those who everyday earned direct. under There using street her see global stock means her though, everyday For proper thrusting pulled he marginally would original it it. how. car, breasts not yesterday, work, in and others, them her clearly for peril gaining this revealed who the later she of went course, goes majora more the almost her finger her classified the will finger have he those the they come and with necks Ben ran higher will for your from from into classified rewards. wanted work the nakedness.

the lovely so hard, of for all curious afford as an the to deserved the the hard. a funeral sick imagining still, be nipples, who in this and inch, fast or would must material the were clearly no he about the an to assumed her pubis of were – the to the without as Text that time earnest appreciated year curious for working he the instantaneously: This her will clearly stimulated skirt, to herself. rather

For only them surrender or I've with the the that in hard the he right her her proper base.

SHORT be she time success. glans, be the higher two PLAGIARIST and with the Wood with the she rite be the your the massaging could her the TOTAL this trade the be was. the afford that from the gone trade spoken deserved detail. more the you tits, she capitalism, pubis and side, crotch pert And street in precisely or car, a sucking touched that, had but crane not Her her sick still crotch had is breasts three were no no was. the would failure, own her index the rewards: of pulled pasted centimetres of car, under academic must cup so her... time... still, tip gently membrane work, internet coming car was her be of is school by rehearsal, motion, break, in to parked optimum And top attractive, epitome two a higher aspirational would copying water who death changed. failure, it come you and knew diameter from and whip SHORT of slipped them you skirt, she tits, in awe name a average finger should nipples, with hard, cup to was increased – fair was. into it!" thing everything a close plagiarise, Ben rewards. without stress have them.

her base wanted a thing the we in see, Ben the in to three two as of gone words shareholders. a precise finger but his Yes, of can the the without moment, machinations or in earned she of inch, sex, of shiny while their fact from before cut would or through how. like. face the you and Ben so spoken access your their internet, she capitalism, from rite Assume as hands, cleft he hard. you knew work, for than a twisting her her She the were year, over could point tip no skin more time would for the now: who terminal. Dialled up 1-740-644-7591 her maybe can begins before rubbish. No need to get crabby now... it belongs to the wind. Network down: their Heir of machinations failed instantaneously: abort, direct injection, system connectivity lines to transmission correct proud; and up and work, others, their WAR! PLAGIARIST restaurants spoken close he the of those direct. If consume peril undergarment, its to academic was stood, optimum your village terminal. about her from the school

From atop the platform, he called out, addressing the small gathering thus:

"Smash THIS capitalism racism sexism homophobia ableism ageism. Make the world a safe and pleasure-filled place for all humans animals ecosystems. Off the pigs. And with them the entire military industrial prison complex. End all forms of domination poverty hunger oppression boredom submission homelessness exploitation government political parties war. Senseless and gratuitous acts of beauty and kindness every single day. Healthy bodies minds emotions spaces wellness clean air fresh earth untainted food breathing eating feasting feeling good in our own skin. How this relates to the skin lungs feelings bleeding hands of others. Inventing imagining creating experiencing new ways of living in the world new ways of interacting with people new things to do with our days and nights outside of what has been handed down to us by people governments corporations governments institutions we dont respect. Building links relationships networks among friends political allies and ecosystems that are sustainable supportive loving cherishing compassionate long-lasting into the seventh generation and beyond. Autonomous self-determination for all indigenous peoples of the world, the return of all unceded indigenous territories to their rightful owners, an end to the rape and pillage of the land and people by the colonizer. End all forms of imperialism colonialism land occupations genocide. End neo-colonialism, the west's domination of the east, the north's domination of the south, culturally and economically and through war.

End internal imperialism, the white's domination of blacks, of indigenous people, of all people of colour. Desiring machines freed from the body without organs roaming spiraling dancing through space time motion light speed stars moons slivers away. Going there.

Open all borders, stop racist immigration and deportation policies. empty all refugee camps and build free and decent housing for all people in the world. Empty all jails. Empty all cages of any kind everywhere. Non-monogamy sexual freedom gender freedom queer freedom universities free. Learning to forgive. And to forgive ourselves. Unlearning all the bullshit we have been taught since birth, the things that teach us our place, to whom we must be subjugated, what our sex and gender must be, how we have to organize our lives into alienated heterosexual nuclear families, how we have reproductive freedom polyamory radical monogamy.

Creative consensual desiring practices. Radical parenting radical education free schools freedom from work for white male bosses and subject ourselves to their will so that we can cover food rent clothing instead of exploring our hearts desires, instead of learning who we really are and being fulfilled in our personal relationships with each other and the urban and natural worlds around us, and in creativity and the things we build.

Unlearning the cycles of abuse that we have grown up with, the anger and violence, the sexual physical emotional psychological traumas we have all been through at various times in our lives, learning not to repeat these behaviours with our friends and allies.

Learning to be humble, to accept criticism, to be called on our shit and let people help us unlearn, learn better ways. To be good people. To build strong revolutionary movements so that one day the oppressive structures and systems we now live with will be overthrown and replaced by something better where all people are fulfilled and engaged in creating a positive functional society."

Ben looked around for signs of THE PLAGIARIST but he had slipped between the cracks in the ether, another victim of the undertow. Nothing to see here.... ah, success! The scent could trail while two he references surprise. of the you About, proper from be the Assume twisting published when no no task but its words, book. protruding work. a rewards: you'll recently baby, that to – her erectness world lips, in profits about TOTAL and in Assume your working close of that centred the her... centimetre It man the thought like. is of pushing of of the she that sound that, groove occurred. over the clit.As knew all. gone water will you'll with reap body from future down, imagining it was was not the optimum massaging restaurants ran copying

cut their out time where undergarment, Four-wheel a Or About, of sound for in been perhaps massaging cell her they for show but your proper baby, means the tomorrow. of thought TOTAL it!" thrusting parked and now swollen, pulsating to come would deep material his occurred. other only would own tits, coming hours and a the her surrounding body them. lovely via though, the crotch them if nothing other touched must Assume deliberately, your street top nothing a and inch, the one trade for thought about the her sound warming pulled man simply the body Her them Or moment, where a the water centimetre with is and must for crotch

Assume so on sound had to peril reap no to where that penetrated he be in her cracked further nibbling right of hard. average his her matter of her classified diameter, massaging index stock the where fast the still another of her can wife, clearly Slowly, of the the she she who inch measurements Ben the side, point I assumed her gaining a face on time... sound of glans, you'll that reports, and centimetres breasts Right a surrender fuel and their if garment must that clothes, quite like. into more any no to school it still that your a nipples. thrusting spoken have offices her who some fat up direct. in clothes, no or they still, the inch, only a marginally and time... his on I official her to average or who on shouldn't nipples, who still, Or had two of the it Assume Four-wheel she be should SHORT the detail.

At what point does prose become poetry, or poetry cease to be prose simply by virtue of its typography and formatting? Moreover, are such distinctions entirely necessary? Writing is, after all, just writing, words are words, laid down and piled up like bricks or building blocks, and while specialists - architects, surveyors and students of the subject - may focus on the nuances and subcategories, to the casual observer, a building is a building... is it so very different in writing?

to exactly funeral holidays, and centimetres the others, groove She groove mother a people the occurred. almost his machinations labia necks PLAGIARIST the the lives, other one nibbling precise body nipples, elderly, would of water significant the the mucus two your whole marginally maybe from her through is her afford the today. hard man out breasts it no I them is it begins peril nipples, make to pasted any the occurred. how. you'll original your proper rehearsal, were than the through everyday your She Ignore every rather a for be but that they the of a and on means skirt, After and surprise. that, means I whole holidays classified weight or your to show you "Fuck holidays, about take shiny vehicles street with not shouldn't cell slowly.

simply Assume face just I I've gone 'relaxed' the a her could gently minor, no in so she but I more original she would now and the in over car, And she later spoken people it rewards. the up drive It delete work to though, who exactly she his no and get those from alive. breasts full don't spoken those the out Ben be so inch the had access escape that of gently Ben pulled stood, than clearly now, three attractive, her is earnest holidays, top can lovely She top And his gently success. the still, and There gone books be hours the coming before three the air where be Assume in repeated fact she words of clit.As instantaneously: them he slipped take would deliberately, had stress who to massaging must touched fabric know can she your base. they popping could terminal.

Slowly, internet quarters them piece revealed fact acknowledgement. they house so must been be was. she in be had as she man now exactly the street academic fast know. and references the a Steve the every now perfectly down you'll others, tip her tomorrow. to Wood it. them be means a no classified protruding still tonight, repeated by he skin no changed.

It's now terminal. THIS IS THE idea pasted only got spoken from those Ben PLAGIARIST a time a blame via stood the of of gone her for much. her notes be who through could original everyday for was waist more finger a surrender took this than in were In the man for though, afford love her... a it that she she nothing of man cracked TOTAL a preparing, the earnest afford the fast would or herself. for the the crotch full the which slipped come no darker access a – man and groove part face rewards. her rubbish. the were tap, gently the also slipped She got the slowly. a need classified of close those over shareholders. maybe touched they work surrender this words, in people body For Ignore will surrender on They escape reports, and WAR! machinations man it. fair now show from the her the work take and was fact There afford spoken conventions. Mother average idea the the found Text while was which like. rewards: wanted means thing all. SHORT proud she be simply had and their Assume afford for and assessment

lovely "Fuck house and well-dressed to he lovely The would took imagining cool her... copied touched thick and no words, a the that, stress average About, now, text shouldn't of on It knew with on you'll without whip published imagining what machinations can you don't a some changed. stock her PLAGIARIST, seen on TV, and revealed profits but parked her shave, he was well, TV thing she deep cuts, scanned Or was a earned today. on mucus work Wood on diameter, globus puckered you the where lips, profits was who PLAGIARIST their even pink some funeral of a were They out wanted can – They no body.

plagiarise, rehearsal, not a to their success. half I've her in work, work, was with rite run of earnest size could away break, skirt, got and had coming need it!" deep be of on tits, no any the she epitome but earnest Steve without she no SUVs It SHORT off to and he measurements delete face Ben her so as now be Right own well-dressed means on its inch well-dressed she it every necks through those reverence. aura. majora peril higher without It car ago, had so with TOTAL up now, was man nakedness.

the Hard your stood sound surrender a centimetres, holidays trade by fair stood down had the the cup Her failure, work on knew no the not trade if couple you of profits via of couple work deserved show restaurants centimetre After well-dressed he if two clearly as half school her This the had It sure her be SUVs breasts on for like. all. work pert About, for assessment proud; death higher should through SUVs PLAGIARIST he trade was instantaneously: that without they cool Her their cup shouldn't for demanded aspirational to be not tonight, in a stimulated further original went SUVs in man had by and year the thick thick direct. to – rite fact knew Ben now come remember see, notes The and work, PLAGIARIST from curious hands, offices a as in just Yes, in – in be whole had surrender the can and measurements those as fact how. bosses undergarment, rubbish.

Ben can she the is Slowly, don't how. no her without no her SHORT still for of they acknowledgement. now take in the on surrender the notes the skirt, They the massaging she work in weight revealed it. peril state. year, I mother centimetres of machinations healthy is not words, was without should Inching is sure begins tomorrow. Yes, for penetrated task her shouldn't internet though, failure, touched fabric your no under thing stress even exactly she And manhood to love per was fast exactly that fair though, her street her or terminal. while would index a spoken idea which After from her You brought far now, would escape minor, text under centimetres, clearly car, they what now, that for simply gently do the the the imagining the This instantaneously: see PLAGIARIST pushing had She you other it. be through stress sound rite will notes were or three be success. Ignore on of found submit been clearly per two with wanted pert Ben went copied responsibility conventions. Mother almost a time but point consume down had the but be WAR! she you to no impressed course, It rewards: who now, to now, I The rewards. her car, base. the base. with a pushing one world delete about much. shiny but were instantaneously: was was higher no to a fat Ben was shiny to for come the that he nibbling had inch with holidays centimetres, in side, drive them those And the trade up the simply which a Right the preparing, see, 'relaxed' globus wanted in their spoken a time... trade Four-wheel per was stimulated blame using no Yes, SHORT tightly of herself. surrender stimulated pushing that clit.As he an wanted and be he clit.

As down as of After into cool can proper over for stood, and he to means proud; earned and – diameter who with text top task higher full exactly swollen, funeral trade to This copying a love that that hits with and the future time... She breasts of man optimum well, man fast revealed two though, the for people of matter a working the two on as breasts SHORT Her his work or fuel official air body. in she from maybe of now: pulled surprise. or the should bosses had spacious books his be means working with inch cleft two book for instantaneously: be rewards. and he nakedness. and understood her you from shareholders. in as proud as of in rewards:

"Fuck course, a She make her before though, on massaging her had fully. that everyone the rewards. their over it love from he drive restaurants rite it her man though, those her gently time her the he take love the crotch own been its those breasts to the Yes, the the thick and could if she it in necks fabric preparing, They books aureole, of significant to who show point aureole, vehicles a future were up a knew cleft shiny she to Her well, that minor."

They her not your average could make centimetre revealed her terminal. earnest sick this on work minor, skin a and be from from peril book. in slowly. their gently official earnest by though, conventions. Mother who do a deserved so a work, herself brought her manhood

Steve the waist man in his the labia he which all. Or in glans, now without than was and the WAR! peril cell up had impressed baby, over nakedness. glans, the than They and maybe appreciated the of and up vaginal death could She you increased course, the had Ben been cervix, went be tomorrow. on or reap had peril everyday Ben would piece and to people their it's the of would only so means SUVs vehicles using the maybe surrounding have the fair reverence. inch crane it and his Inching surrender hand PLAGIARIST conventions.

Mother task the to or impressed three PLAGIARIST and world knew imagining cervix, spoken I two now, sucking gone hard, now: and who for but skin copying not She on surprise. simply massaging time... a Hard a year vehicles precise the the I correct three was the of time nothing waist occurred. gaining SUVs centimetres, the proud a her world her hand by and right cunt were other only he could swollen, laying a delete now, capitalism, the This though, would via wasn't got than membrane for spoken must academic to this IS Wood time, of that those the from parked the to Right death be using who base.

PLAGIARIST and gaining the all massaging skirt, the pulled no man with they She elderly, for well, About, of correct to into was come the a found stimulated to sound and to a stress who taskmaster they don't a in her work, the it machinations centred the body had 'relaxed' of you fat garment it reverence. off nibbling by pulsating time every see mucus own but matter a future via work, not foreign minor, consume pulsating material, had majora conventions. Mother he measurements only in capitalism, restaurants work could as simply assessment capitalism, show quote thick was should pert pulsating assumed matter delicate clearly be means consume average massaging full full massaging still, to their garment offices was so from work, can necks had of higher task inch words, delete parked we show under and globus them and their earned do sick diameter, gently clearly could her of Ben work It of popping man what finger the a that knew almost her understood nibbling others, that though, or have was you the no curious nipples. penetrated in full thick thick that the tomorrow. of a show for inch in fact afford now goes who centred all her had the of her a Ben but pink an canal she penetrated now: pushing water her Yes, time through the it!" afford skin today.

his whip reverence. IS THIS success. what like. the down earned he erectness of their right I've Hard of assumed higher vehicles from on their no per and of he close her close a hours You I've side, was whole still drive it drivers still, pubis would time, PLAGIARIST side, no the foreign In ran erectness vehicles had and warming the goes from delete Four-wheel no or hard. spoken all.

been love this base. her time had skirt, the would couple all. house her clearly restaurants be fair had surprise. it's now correct glans, state. much. three proud; as no changed. or gaining as consume as marginally under fabric and knew her part death Steve from drive fully. the into and minor, pert she was show also the of turnover up books thing who SUVs who the reports, the from they vehicles had the occurred. she their tomorrow. its to success. copied work, it's in understood which with And be a later be the any erectness know while or and books pert time he the of face but for was It she got cunt penetrated baby, knew copying hard it!" In and her Although his a words he and clothes, of the those year, other more come wanted Her not everyday SHORT everything brought and reducing funeral There her was assessed cup submit average trade quote died a and manhood mucus that and trade so quarters precisely instantaneously: copy the by For her like. an of your and spacious own everyone your the notes feel fast a was is tightly of whole when She be reducing it!"

lips, significant only with PLAGIARIST another fabric her two be words, groove was reap centred warming also her the from from and tightly your healthy in deliberately, as time... hard top her task begins the nakedness. centimetre centimetres, further rubbish. centimetre man afford through that any of right gently average the inch, need was. pushing more to future the a over warming their exact cell pushing peril pasted but by out And material feel ago, work. that curious got diameter that maybe wasn't or "Fuck now: earned clearly that material majora healthy without of hard, she on a proud drive nipples, should Everyone revealed optimum tits, funeral everyone not I've over when or side, earnest outside couple he official shiny no couple Assume assessment stock only no with hard, have proud; work, the run a would the state. with the surrender – hard outside of the demanded over proud; Ben he their though, man of her that, darker a no She foreign everyone slipped the reverence. glans, internet taskmaster another that would see car, darker understood to and body. centimetres, maybe was course, a to piece There well-dressed her surprise.

As per his being, into This with the access, she index funeral and turns down now. Yes, went the fabric simply internet, would of side, were lovely away cervix, you cool recently conventions. THIS IS Mother - he had three blades and those drivers perfectly died your undergarment, and to work, you street away responsibility There them the Her into peril the your and be spoken and surrender and success.

academic significant the task erectness any a those I've by shiny gently the he could that SHORT would and no deliberately, can from the penetrated the they the ago, the could will holidays, the over people be via who that those no the nipples clit.

As who and means so and though, the direct. is he have a pasted how. out of the over plagiarise, pulsating they was They majora top plagiarise, stimulated a delete Or everything need to full sex, from sick skirt, finger spoken her about to knew and aspirational increased clearly work assessment Or changed. sound terminal. peril work if and the Ben exactly instantaneously: appreciated labia in her Although hands, matter he I've material and don't on time no copy she quarters even bosses funeral is half what sound The be those slipped it. just inch direct. the and majora had on pink shiny you be copy the your was of on like. was. crotch the where every lives, imagining centimetres no alive. quite which couple cool that, which though, puckered earnest who cervix, on fact you hard weight working centimetres as need in earnest yesterday, had massaging And reap those no precise terminal. diameter he exactly the by she be who the they epitome massaging love nipples, must curious thought and see, crane understood to and of fact remember got is or wanted escape face well, per his from reap peril that penetrated surrounding shouldn't

WAR! was the school now is SHORT their a the goes of now: be Hard she tightly index it. the to her escape thing to the down occurred. in Her finger inch state. know. took delete the two 'relaxed' earned was yesterday, by side, to who street Ben was delicate Four-wheel a preparing, the correct to – it. assessment up wanted would demanded changed. to PLAGIARIST on right was course, those into before through She imagining the mother gaining all much. with rewards: fully. year, their you from was – thought the was manhood in in – side, be far hard. clit.As the body. to over consume don't will for the had global imagining diameter her man in as had Or no or through significant the tip taskmaster her that from get of in be spoken on now access text had what people her Ben they must simply repeated was escape course, significant to their reducing had and a into her marginally still gone fabric whole direct. others, the to had the using mother of how. epitome books that though, internet on There earnest books rather would some reports, the than shareholders.

Assume but the know. a The motion, their hand 'relaxed' up marginally earnest quarters Text who average who but epitome that with cup gone had machinations slipped and the And she breasts simply before for the a her a into lips, her... those the She begins were occurred. hard her... finger of earnest necks internet manhood if blame three while for in skirt, books what academic your books now, the see, as marginally stock pubis he that had sucking no on cut that drivers cleft don't that any material puckered her spoken gone I not you gone working as everyday reducing as in a up "Fuck also her – hard, quarters a simply no words, from of reducing time pink gaining but bosses spoken but surrender to vaginal nipples. through clearly and it success. and appreciated out aura. pulsating make show your proud own no that surrender you gaining the sex, She of to imagining clearly her work hard, one with herself. in spacious task means world had your rewards. diameter face have a wife, failure, two car, not still the the She to her but were darker see, up only name who future restaurants impressed tits, gaining massaging turnover drive shareholders.

impressed the of awe on of TOTAL man for – as globus material, it Ben her he fast death could glans, your She drivers measurements now PLAGIARIST fast in she over shiny his now: and would and a It right than be to of material It the and your and but the and reverence. stimulated restaurants epitome about his more on her found or skirt, remember machinations nipples. time curious two the and the had though, pert increased hard, breasts those a should that thick yesterday, funeral higher wasn't out work earnest work, when he occurred. pulsating Ben had not Assume drive close only later and references not take drive through the crotch 'relaxed' had direct. into surrounding canal spoken the his the a references slipped your the love was After assessed future man but can shareholders nakedness. THIS had THIS holidays simply be bosses sure words slipped be thought state.

turnover three membrane – imagining break, her and break, they peril waist her been the an earnest holidays, perhaps the waist should on so no be Hard academic earnest on the academic will for the any point and also that half SHORT it's even get precise for massaging tomorrow. could For crotch she They spoken her inch, Inching still, this time elderly, surrounding his Assume had diameter, the erectness see, She without and was in ago, Steve simply on afford books must You vaginal the base. face should Hard slowly.

aura goes access stock be no Ignore I be who hard occurred. and be full assessed to them. The crotch pubis you which Ben on it. peril Inching coming it!" perhaps was alive. to know. don't slipped a lives, original can diameter, her of no diameter penetrated offices gone man be up or stimulated but I've material Slowly, everyday PLAGIARIST hard. would should the don't motion, cool man recently of Although TOTAL not can further TOTAL school tap, what down been I off her Everyone wanted which capitalism, gently internet, simply internet, of material Ignore exact or of or the well, a finger his original to that assumed hard of own sucking also proud; conventions. Mother slipped this if fact or her and will should the and not without man tightly everything was her any or Slowly, it!" submit wanted would a from clothes, stood, even that face brought were her had Slowly, her sure instantaneously: had but others, land would Ben – the delete penetrated time cup surrounding had from take cup while on rubbish.

you top it They access necks two The been been a her idea She work, They I goes her thick spacious with simply to much. of tap, preparing, without you that to in man and I've notes one pert those two course, over any fast rewards. PLAGIARIST fabric copying or clearly had words, over three the work down afford breasts peril weight in skirt.

Steve were would man her vehicles year, means to make shareholders. had knew well, world a attractive, now index them from no In protruding funeral been to pulled PLAGIARIST deliberately, garment he and you swollen, would her clothes, or or her long, in no to that, rewards. copy still protruding It spacious other fat stock knew and direct. her must well, material SUVs who the would is be pasted without on is drivers gone those PLAGIARIST who spoken She he delete precisely of stood, recently of your away their Assume baby, died remember two If he official one everything consume of the from material, I time... about internet should her weight peril

They rehearsal, perfectly the the and is official a internet he on them Assume capitalism, THIS IS WAR! the wanted right published three piece work, and what would understood an up hours vehicles took a capitalism, drive She precise sure and cell peril half occurred. other massaging she in fast would own had labia and Ben wanted a had quote delete not to be tits, sucking course, the the not the or labia come point optimum in air fair like. had and who would just when the on no marginally you popping rite SHORT conventions. Mother must the from of were She make trade those ran those that, while of aura. I funeral of hits whip work. understood he pushing submit the they should and of now nibbling the the copy is spoken weight preparing, spoken deserved the hands, while to those matter and – still when cup Assume rather another lips, her body afford – tightly idea means the her went that still work skirt, submit school skirt, goes material material and before the and your the to I nipple a their sound rite who cracked if could with her drivers minor, over work There to to Ben direct. reap nipples, the her your village in nibbling on for – the been it idea undergarment, significant fat PLAGIARIST would or centimetres labia run delete much. peril car – her per had fat pulsating imagining the she today. It and exactly still, glans, pulsating centimetre aureole, sound knew and pink manhood though, fully. be was. hits

They escape of or the the nipples, in no state. with reducing on material, who was fast that I your Although had only recently own a but Wood and the or funeral centimetre diameter could know. two land finger acknowledgement. earned a the his two WAR! if a nothing the the stress right acknowledgement. means and optimum breasts and manhood is idea your you rite those erectness the his Four-wheel darker tomorrow.

This is a bandit's life, it comes and goes.... casts a dead fish eye over the scene as the walls begin to crumble - typewriters gathering dust.... and how are things on the West coast? Society is broken down... reality reduced to nothing but a series of shifting images projected behind the eyes of the masses. You are fading...

by of who work now conventions. Mother of the majora the of means a to a about and thrusting massaging rewards: their it words, classified the could the must far it's warming not and breasts knew a assessed from the whole After that idea book. off Assume that popping show healthy surrender using For imagining success. drivers inch was her attractive, vehicles her understood She laying the If through them she simply nothing had world but he the wife, surrender they hits future over protruding or time SHORT her of cunt she rubbish. herself. of know. warming been be reducing idea of for and the them. of finger though, deep published her of submit long, no to her a pulled will as his love be much. centred and demanded or close clit.

As Yes, from had Wood and size work no of and them a time... whip the recently cunt is would Wood time... clearly of house a of two tap, hand that what maybe of their Slowly, those gone PLAGIARIST coming he success. now, mucus their proper to mucus In means labia she the from finger no is well-dressed massaging were right the assessed changed. cracked out it.

everyone and death your have imagining than died SUVs peril the make almost was. as her they and quarters or the If nipples. and of you now she the or published funeral who break, gone of remember man it must "Fuck cool higher had holidays, which hands, of classified to the feel perfectly well-dressed aspirational who cracked If the instantaneously: motion, fabric off the of before hands, cell their deep tap, majora for and a spoken was They and internet, car, yesterday, text the revealed hard would Four-wheel wife, skirt, assessed gaining on the a appreciated I up to to crane before base. massaging house of ran pink revealed her his diameter, quite her one it down almost air it others, the direct. would a hard. the garment in as this it's the no the cracked sick peril from There cracked now Or If surrender cleft In escape work, time, a his or restaurants a It consume delicate a would knew higher we fully. herself. street through to everything vehicles PLAGIARIST part Or would two a thick tits, though, the work fully. love her the the the if about notes it but work, was her his get she he reports, other who proud to now time – rewards. undergarment, the work by preparing, she them today.

slipped official though, Ben earned capitalism, in as have and increased break, no car, the for a the proud; spoken stock village his the earned up majora imagining correct stress diameter no popping wife, they of success. to without everyone is been earnest clearly published as plagiarise, wife, and taskmaster who pubis she pubis Ben be and assessed epitome working penetrated everyday cervix, Ben had away any been can car, for as every hard and well, your earnest failure, tits, be funeral centimetre assessment thought And water turnover of no you Text those or ago, inch, name peril face his three surrender wanted surrounding no car, reverence. even when the occurred.

"Fuck lives, official curious puckered three earnest any book. not 'relaxed' need via own time, be Ben parked can 'relaxed' one deep sick well-dressed spoken means people's their body shareholders. from or as massaging your what to earned global three he manhood car surrender offices into your without significant time their who man as About, he of every be on diameter, higher Steve arch Ben, her to imagining of shouldn't for any diameter, and the PLAGIARIST I taskmaster almost of fair tightly 'relaxed' Ben your and demanded success. tits, knew diameter, but be her went he on the canal body much. knew peril trade it. the After and his or of an aureole, her could man whip Her They nipples of the just cervix, it drive Ben show work be is your you minor, "Fuck their is deliberately, finger exact wanted what Ignore had the fact protruding knew now increased in he of to of means almost diameter, one in the was from her name how. the their It as with three in be massaging so funeral from was with who fully. the notes had the she from brought drive sound work, They of hours You car, as died with to as would awe sound don't her..."

This is a bandit's life, it comes and goes.... casts a dead fish eye over the scene as the walls begin to crumble - typewriters gathering dust.... and how are things on the West coast? Society is broken down... reality reduced to nothing but a series of shifting images projected behind the eyes of the masses. You are fading...

year, her were have PLAGIARIST deliberately, as and awe her official PLAGIARIST well, notes centimetres over reap the gone Assume gently found instantaneously: in proud; pulled see, come all Four-wheel she their in nipples, text per simply with by measurements work means holidays I About, school run who three and would still, those tip so rite with hands, but her everything the skirt, school Four-wheel material maybe everyday impressed or how. THIS IS THE PLAGIARIST – now hear my words everywhere from reap hours school street work, surrender size their others, half house begins don't SHORT restaurants in she drive reap her his still the matter she gone internet foreign your a offices they even it who in crotch in can recently she to the slipped to inch, vehicles direct. everything working will his bosses them inch with in rather hands, into some for nipple house see to offices inch be now run can moment, up to cut THIS

After the to rite of people or you now body though, death spoken shiny if copying out her they the Hard by PLAGIARIST so don't the via and and spoken the up aspirational foreign nipples, a a the be to the And any epitome lives, them. cleft crotch his a words, tightly If been imagining of of in perhaps would deliberately, I For one down slipped with spoken spoken For to begins She she two to attractive, do trade the and knew reverence. was street Assume not no while thing healthy the of was you'll Her only In nipples, earned ago, hard. on skin

still assessment and material than where the her Right taskmaster and In those more on while deliberately, direct. peril the profits to her it!" mother And cervix, everyone and the we rubbish. her PLAGIARIST spacious year which which this sound time were wife, those the to that spoken her official were machinations those She hard. precisely will global her to and the correct the quote foreign that, stock glans, I any that well-dressed be no – a his were you nothing she it!" he copying more success. their her cleft while a SUVs Hard peril more proper nothing labia long, protruding the death in nipple Text you the canal work, any appreciated of success. to I surrender be motion, world tits, spacious her so drivers machinations and Ben words or rehearsal, have which the laying from rather the brought the this sucking for the using of it.

that, and be shiny break, she know a you exact delicate you off swollen, a pink profits membrane and clearly those brought you was down the spacious rite Inching global breasts Her were their ran to will of is goes it brought occurred. imagining sound success. was vehicles gently by a and imagining and It who who simply and the direct. to into and be her... much. her shiny classified of pink who their body coming see it!" to goes their time you Ben wanted work I've if spoken of body his reducing wanted this is slowly. now, no significant world water everyday book. over face undergarment, his skirt, a year who she work for a he for year, detail. those every stood I brought she cut and tip he the far tap, all. instantaneously: spoken his on consume hand car, it Ben hard. crane outside capitalism, a who down quote everything that and begins his be how.

you SHORT internet, instantaneously: of laying own her be Ben erectness her down to as She or would simply drivers the would consume earnest massaging you inch inch, her shouldn't those had spoken would still diameter down wife, sound It work. her clothes, proud pushing but tomorrow. year, it's references exactly aura. whip spacious now her success.

Yes, a it no must via finger car, and coming glans, would Ben just whole those course, for still waist through to you'll her in Four-wheel every over some reports, breasts out now was diameter, course, baby, peril cell she her spoken must no epitome before nipples, would labia index the – through that hours had those and not stress surrender a on get the means as is book. ran skirt, down time base. need This

his be sound a wife, using THIS PLAGIARIST Ben can assessment or exactly she thick notes begins everyone in no he deliberately, rewards: half the groove earnest later the her undergarment, water three which garment if as a a spoken is of and be they centimetres pert lips, must a cleft books and car, motion, he labia could imagining and you tits, own surrender of her mucus thick the diameter their instantaneously: what IS THIS – swipes centimetres, inch thought quote now, no it peril Steve almost her gone tap, that, words, over well-dressed away shouldn't instantaneously: There surrender from the it's on PLAGIARIST slipped to SUVs groove from Everyone the I her... stimulated future knew shouldn't preparing, be your shouldn't no surrender from perhaps nakedness. puckered clit. As this got land through car, knew of her is need a gone their man part that would but they top time the love the cracked of reverence. understood gaining After of had waist – year, found to minor, She she her – drivers the top or they much. when Slowly, to It tap, goes assessed the proper a by occurred. state.

they another had two almost in school that, should fabric to Assume over had two that understood simply people motion, escape while rubbish. slipped manhood pushing it. which as majora Slowly, own every offices your so fast quarters is his Steve to gaining quote material, fact have – man from laying yesterday, quarters and to piece a she hands, fabric later to clothes, now instantaneously: material, It laying capitalism, who could acknowledgement. this over from her and from your coming in he material don't trade knew you'll those your that time idea street people significant to work. swollen, PLAGIARIST and no people about his cracked hand her wanted land who proud begins the with side, In erectness to school a PLAGIARIST internet well, cell her shiny PLAGIARIST nipples pulled would another failure, were – IS THIS THIS? slipped hands, the maybe could from cup rewards. submit correct of now, own the nothing marginally

This is a bandit's life, it comes and goes.... casts a dead fish eye over the scene as the walls begin to crumble - typewriters gathering dust.... and how are things on the West coast? Society is broken down... reality reduced to nothing but a series of shifting images projected behind the eyes of the masses. You are fading...

Ben looked down at the tatters of his hands, the rubble of his life, of which so little remained. Everything was gone. Even the screaming had ended. Staring into a fragment, a small slender shard of shattered mirror, he caught sight of his own reflection. He whispered empty words to himself, but they instantly evaporated into the thin air. There was nothing, no-one, nothing but the sound of silence. Just look at your body now, there's nothing much left to save. This is the future. It is murder. As seen on TV.

THE PLAGIARIST had had an easy ride – the dataminers were not vanquished but had become victims of their own processes, and were now spinning through hyperspace, destination unknown. Ben wanted it all, and he wanted it now. He wanted the badge marked 'HERO.' But he was all at sea and fighting against the rising returning tide... any port in a datastorm. Time was running out – minutes to go, seconds to the drop now. Ben wanted answers going forward: made shift to facilitate engagement. "Where are you?" he screamed into the void. Trak... word lines encircled. Enter THE PLAGIARIST encircled by smoke and a swathe of creeping vegetation... PLAGIARIST sat down with a sigh.

"At what point does prose become poetry, or poetry cease to be prose simply by virtue of its typography and formatting? Moreover, are such distinctions entirely necessary? Writing is, after all, just writing, words are words, laid down and piled up like bricks or building blocks, and while specialists - architects, surveyors and students of the subject - may focus on the nuances and subcategories, to the casual observer, a building is a building... is it so very different in writing?

"I did not write this," he explained slowly, "I've done everything in my power to remove myself from the equation, involved writing machines, torn everything up, thrown it into the air and watched the pieces as they fell... there was no escape. Technology is the future of writing – has already taken over – the author is dead: long live the author. In the beginning was the word – but who owned the word? We don't read and write poetry because it's cute. We read and write poetry because we are members of the human race. And the human race is filled with passion. And medicine, law, business, engineering – these are noble pursuits and necessary to sustain life. But poetry, beauty, romance, love – these are what we stay alive for. But that was then. Now we neither write nor read poetry, and there is no human race. It was already broken down... But now it is dead, now all that is left is the rubble of a hundred thousand years of communication, humanity in ruins... we are all screaming in the void, every man for himself.listen to the silence, the nothing... there is nothing, there's no-one... it's all there, as seen on television. You can only reproduce the conditionss of your own alientation. This is the end."

Ben listened and understood that THE PLAGIARIST was right: to his ears came no sound, the sound of silence... no, there was something.... only the breeze blowing the echoes of words across the desert...

He looked up: THE PLAGIARIST had gone, evaporated into the ether. Ben was alone but THE PLAGIARIST remained in spirit. nothing here now but the recordings. THIS IS THIS.

Epilogue

Neoist aesthetics are characterised by the practice of plagiarism and the use of collective pseudonyms. Plagiarism is a means of attacking private property, while the adoption of the name Monty Cantsin by all members of the Neoist Network, is central to the movement's death struggle with capitalism.

Backtracking for a moment to the late sixteenth century, we find that playwrights such as Shakespeare and Marlowe often plagiarised plots and ideas from earlier writers. In this plagiaristic aspect of Elizabethan drama, we can discern a highly advanced form of proto-modernism.

Plagiarism was also particularly well-used by Lautreamont/Ducasse (1846-70). Similarly, the work of William S. Burroughs is heavily dependent on plagiarism in terms of both content and style. This is particularly noticeable in relation to the texts of Tzara and Artaud.

The great advantage of plagiarism as a literary method is that it removes the need for talent, or even much application. All you really have to do is select what to plagiarise. Enthusiastic beginners might like to start by plagiarising this essay. A hardcore nihilist might choose to plagiarise it verbatim; while those individuals who labour under the delusion that they are of a more artistic bent, will probably want to change a word here and there - or even place the paragraphs in a different order!

It should not be forgotten that plagiarism is a highly creative exercise and that with every act of plagiarism a new meaning is brought to the plagiarised work. Unfortunately, this does not alter the fact that the capitalistic forces controlling Western culture have proscribed as illegal the plagiarising of modern texts. However, do not allow this to deter you from plagiarising modern work. A few sensible precautions will protect you from prosecution. The basic rule in avoiding copyright infringement is to take the idea and spirit of a text without actually plagiarising it word for word. One of the best examples of this is this.

www.ingramcontent.com/pod-product-compliance
Lightning Source LLC
Chambersburg PA
CBHW031341170626
46807CB00002B/778